BLOOM & DARK

A BURNINGSOUL NOVEL

BLOOM & DARK
A BURNINGSOUL NOVEL

REGINA WATTS

PAINTED BLIND
PUBLISHING
LITERARY ALCHEMY

PAINTED BLIND
PUBLISHING
LITERARY ALCHEMY

Burningsoul Saga Book I: Bloom & Dark
© 2021 Regina Watts

Text: Regina Watts
Typesetting: M. F. Sullivan
Cover Painting: Vanette Kosman

http://www.hrhdegenetrix.com
http://www.paintedblindpublishing.com
publicity@paintedblindpublishing.com

With great thanks
to the Marquis de Sade
and Gene Wolfe,
and with special appreciation
for Richard Wagner.

1

IN THE DEN
OF THE SPIRIT-THIEVES

IT'S HARD TO call the removal of my breastplate a mistake. Doing so saved me from the acidic blood of the spirit-thief who had just fallen beneath Strife's enchanted blade.

Yet when the Scepter of Weltyr stood so near my grasp, and those that had called themselves my allies now pointed spear, axe and crossbow straight at me, I could not help but think that stripping off my corroding armor was the greatest error of my life.

"Have you three been ensorcelled?" My alarmed cry was my only defense. I was too amazed by the abrupt turn of the trio to think of brandishing my broadsword as I might against a foe.

"Ensorcelled!" Branwen's fine pink lips, kissed so many times in the darkness of the camp against my better judgment, peeled back from her perfect teeth in a mocking laugh far too cruel for her delicate elfin features. She steadied the aim of her crossbow on me, and this doubling down—this conscious dedication to shooting her bolt right through my heart—confirmed that this was no jest.

A lock of golden hair fell across her narrowed blue eyes and even then I felt the compulsive urge to brush it from her face; to tuck it back behind that long and delicate ear.

"Yes," she continued, "ensorcelled, perhaps—by Oppenhir, god of money."

"And death," I reminded her, taking no satisfaction in the tension of her mouth or the further narrowing of her eyes.

Grimalkin, (who had, of all my companions, been the most unpleasant from the start of our journey at the behest of the Temple of Weltyr), said from within the wild red depths of his beard woven with the runes of his dwarf clan, "That's enough, paladin. Look, you're wounded—keep wasting time and it'll be your wounds that kill you. No guilt for us."

His face placid as always, yet in that moment as firm as it had been when we were strangers, one-eyed Hildolfr said in that fatherly tone, "Rorke...be reasonable."

I couldn't look him in his remaining steel eye. Instead I focused on the black patch that replaced its missing twin.

"The three of you have gone mad. The Scepter belongs to the Temple: to Weltyr, Himself. If you dare misuse its power, as have these unfortunates"—I gestured with my sword amid the tentacled corpses littering the sacrilegious site where we stood—"then, like these unfortunates, all three of you will be doomed to die."

"We'll all be dying eventually anyway," Grimalkin said, his take on the common tongue closer to a bark than the usual tones men used to address one another. "Might as well die rich, fat, and well-laid."

"You don't have to fight us, Rorke." Though his spear was unwavering in his grip, Hildolfr maintained a steady stare into me until, by some gravity, I was forced to meet that powerful eye. "You could come with us. Claim our private client's reward for the Scepter; split the price four ways."

While Branwen and Grimalkin shared a noise of disgust, Hildolfr gestured toward them with his lance's tip. "At this price, a four-way split is still far more than the Temple would have forced us to settle on. Twenty-thousand gold pieces total, five thousand apiece? That's still enough, well-invested, to ensure a happy retirement."

"Speak for yourself, human," said Branwen to my terrible pain, her pretty face absent of all the charm that had won me while contorted in a greedy scowl. "We elves live longer than dwarves and men combined—a retirement for you is a happy vacation for us, little more than that. I'd be just as glad if our friend here stuck to his ethics and refused the split."

My head swam with not just confusion, but pain. Before its removal, the armor had burned through and permitted my chest to be superficially seared with the blood of the decapitated priest whose head had leaked a hole into the floor.

For the first time since I was a boy, my sword trembled in my hand.

"I won't let you take it," I told them. "Surely if it's a larger reward you're after, the Temple—"

"Weltyr's worshipers couldn't afford a quarter of what this client promises," answered Hildolfr plainly.

"Who? Who would dare sneak beneath the nose of a god, let alone that very Creator who watches it each day from dawn till dusk?"

"It doesn't matter," answered the old man, now eying not my face but the burn across my chest. "Come on, Rorke. Let us at least heal you and go our separate ways without complaint. There's no reason we can't still be friends."

"Traitors to man and God alike—I'll have no 'allies' such as your lot ever again, Weltyr willing."

"Suit yourself," said Branwen, finger tightening on the trigger of her crossbow.

Only by the grace of Weltyr did I dodge that bolt. Branwen, accustomed to fighting from a distance—and doing so against those who would not live to see her fight again—did not realize her tell: namely, that just before her finger tightened to command her crossbow, her shoulders hunched against the anticipated force of the projectile.

By this I managed to duck the whistling shot and then, in the subsequent flurry of motion, a swing of Grimalkin's axe—but Hildolfr, his lance effortlessly piercing my ribs, was responsible the blow that fell me.

My breath hitched. The sting as my lung ruptured was like nothing I had felt or would care to feel again: I struggled thereafter against the urge to breathe and looked in mute shock into Hildolfr's eye. It gazed back, unashamed as it was unhappy.

"I really am sorry, Rorke," he assured me, sliding the spear's tip from my ribs.

Limp-mouthed and quite uncomprehending of my own pain, I looked down at the blood flowing from my side. I touched it, examined Weltyr's spilled ink upon my dirty hand, then looked again between the faces of my companions. They had brought me along only to find the Scepter—only because a paladin or cleric of Weltyr could sense the nearness of the holy relic and guide them to its location. Now they were done with me, and revealed that all this time I had been to them less than nothing.

Weakly, I made one last swing of my sword. Grimalkin's axe sent it clattering from my hand. I followed it to the ground, groaning, crushed beneath the weight of my injuries. Thank Weltyr, I did not fall in the acid blood of the dead occultists.

"Just go to sleep," Hildolfr told me, his voice soft, his lips beneath his short gray beard taut in displeasure. "Just go to sleep, Rorke. It's much easier when you're asleep."

My failing vision and rapid blood loss left me next to no choice.

AN UNEXPECTED RESCUE

ONLY WELTYR KNOWS how long I lay in that temple, left for dead. Not long, I must imagine. I did not hear my companions leave: I only know that, when I opened my eyes, they and the scepter were already gone. Crippled by pain and the nearness of death, I could not move to even touch the nearby handle of my sword. Misery sat upon my chest.

So, Weltyr—it was Your will that Your loyal servant should die alone? Should die, not nobly upon the battlefield, but from the injuries bequeathed to him by avaricious traitors to Your very Name?

How ashamed I am now to remember those bitter thoughts of mine! But dark-souled Oppenhir's approach rots the fruits of even the proudest, highest tree. Indeed, I was convinced the footsteps I soon heard were those of that pale-faced god to whom Weltyr assigned the cruelest duties of the cosmos. I shut my eyes again, praying that sleep might once more find me and I might not know that moment when his bony hand plucked me from my body.

Instead, a woman's voice rang with gay laughter through the obsidian hall. "Oh, Indra! You were right, how silly I was to doubt you!"

"I'm *always* right," answered another woman, her musical tone terse with customary exasperation. "I can't help that no one listens to me."

"Look at all this! Why, the tithes are all still in their box. Haha!" A rattle reached my ears, a thunderous rain of copper and silver coins as the contents of the tipped box spilled down the side of whatever bag received their plunder. "Some adventurers they were…didn't even take the loot!"

"Why, look, Odile—they did take something. The altar is desecrated, see?"

"Hail Roserpine! They took that blasted scepter with them, did they? Good! Perhaps the spirit-thieves will leave on the same ship they came in on—if there are any left, that is. Oh, joy! Just wait until the Materna hears about— What's this?"

A gasp, high and delighted, accompanied footsteps so soft I barely heard them beat their fast approach. Soon, though I was too weary to open my eyes, soft hair tickled my cheek. The woman called Odile, in bending over me, revealed I still had the capacity for some physical sensation that was not pain, and in that moment I was already grateful.

"Oh." This gasp was lower than the first. With a tone of abject pleasure, Odile cried, "Why, he's a terrifically handsome one!"

"He is, isn't he?"

Indra's voice had joined Odile's. My dark eyelids darkened further as her shadow fell across my face and blotted out the slowly dying candles of the temple. "A shame he's dead."

"So sad," agreed Odile, whose voice was more brash than her delicate companion's. "May Roserpine guide him to a happy rebirth...I hate to think of one so handsome lost instead to Oppenhir's oblivion."

Their steps began to trail away again, their chatter changing subject to the matter of the tapestry hanging upon the nearby wall ("Surely we could move that for at least five gold pieces—wait, what is that, Moronian silk? Oh, no, five *times* five gold—") while panic stirred in my wounded breast. Though my whole body burned with fever from my suffering and my head ached like my chest and lung and side, I willed my lips to part. By Weltyr's kindness, my vocal chords eased out one simple word.

"Help."

Their chatter stopped immediately. "Why"—Odile gasped—"he *is* alive! And there's you, Indra, always right..."

"As though you're one to talk," muttered Indra, nonetheless following her companion back to me. "Can you hear us, soldier? Are you still in there?"

"Please," I managed through desperation to add, having strength after that for hardly so much as a breath.

"He's still in there, all right. Stand aside, Indra—let's see..."

A delicate finger peeled back the tatters of my tunic while a hiss rose from Odile's lips. "Oh! Queen of Chaos, what a terrific burn that is."

"That's not all—look, he's bleeding!"

"He is...just how is it you've managed to stay alive?

Poor pitiful human."

A sinking feeling tugged at me. I had not considered that, as we were in the Nightlands beneath the earth of Ramshead, my rescuers were not likely to be human. This was not normally a problem so far as I was concerned… but the non-human entities one found in the Nightlands were notoriously unfriendly toward all who dwelled aboveground. Even so, I had little choice but hope Nightlanders had the capacity for good nature just as did my friends and neighbors from the surface…and after this cruelty from my traitorous companions, I so despaired that I had already begun to wonder if we who walked beneath the sun were not the more abysmal set of people.

"Here, man," said Odile beneath the pop of a bottle's cork, "I've a healing draft here if you'd like it—"

Indra, in high worried tones: "Odile! But—"

Odile continued for her, addressing me. "It's twenty gold pieces a bottle—that's right, as much as we could hope to fetch from that tapestry once we get negotiated down. We'd be wasting money if we just let you get up and walk away, so you'd better be prepared to cooperate with us."

"He might *hurt* us, Odile."

"That's true, he might. Move that sword well away from him, Indra…we'll sell it, too. And him."

Her voice rang clearer as she turned back to me. Shrewd Odile sloshed the contents of the bottle, saying as she did, "Hear that? That's sweet life in my bottle, human. Roserpine's song flowing through all the world, caught in this sacred fluid. You can have it back again, for a price—promise yourself to our ownership, swear it on your very honor, and I'll let you have a second chance to feel and hear and see."

"But what if he lies, Odile? What if he has no honor?"

"See that tattoo, the starburst on his neck? That's the Crest of Weltyr—he's a cleric of some kind, I'd wager. Well, man?" Another slosh of fluid. "You're already a slave to your god. What difference is it for you to be a slave to the two of us?"

I could not afford to think twice, to delay—nor could I speak. With a slight jerk of my head, I made an attempt at a nod, then let my skull twitch back into its resting place.

"A wise man," said Odile admiringly. "Not too proud. I like that…perhaps in the end you'll prove to be a bargain."

A soft hand as chilled as the stones on which I lay caressed my chin and drew open my lips. Soon the glass bottle pressed there and, beneath her guidance, a thin stream of burning fluid flowed from the vessel's neck. I gasped at once, choking on the elixir from the first swallow its fiery flavor provoked; no doubt that inhalation made the healing of my lungs that much faster. Soon, though I hacked and coughed my way through this choking, I did so without any more pain than a man might have after a faint cold.

In a matter of seconds I was well enough to push the bottle away and lift one hand toward the chest that heaved with my hacking. The cork bolted shut the bottle and Odile said with pleasure, "Well! He only took half. Yes, a bargain already…"

"Poor man! Listen to him choke."

"It's a difficult thing to be alive…the body's natural inclination is always toward its death, and it bitterly protests the least delay."

I had managed to sit up throughout the hacking, and though my eyes had opened I saw only my own lower

1

half. When, wiping my mouth with a hand covered in my own dried blood, I lifted my eyes toward my saviors, I tried not to visibly balk.

Durrow. I should have known it by the talk of Roserpine. Instead I was astonished to find two pairs of eyes, one lavender and one pale white, each without pupil or iris but nonetheless bright with anticipation. Each gazed back at me like gems inset in two perfect charcoal faces. I'd heard it said dark elves were black-skinned; but to my eyes their flesh contained a richness that held notes of blue, almost purple.

And never had I heard it said that they were so alarmingly beautiful.

"There's our happy slave," enthused pale-eyed Odile, placing her bottle back into the pack she handed to Indra. "All better now, and ready to please his new mistresses."

"He really *is* very handsome," said Indra, admiring me through lavender eyes half-hidden beneath a flow of soft white hair she frequently pushed from her delicate face. "Why, all the market will fight over him."

"If I resist the urge to keep him for myself…come on, priest, what's your name?"

"I—"

My mind, burning with death and sensual beauty, struggled to straighten itself. Somehow I managed to produce the automatic sounds, "Rorke. Rorke Burningsoul. I'm a paladin."

"A warrior-priest then," gracefully corrected Odile, staying me with a hand upon that same healed chest I'd touched without pain during my coughing fit. I glanced down at her slender fingers splayed against my chest and marveled at the contrast of her flesh to mine. "Stay still a few moments yet, warrior-priest Burningsoul… the superficial wounds heal faster than the internal ones.

Breathe deep, lie back…tell us, did you do this to the spirit-thieves?"

"By and large," I said, grunting not just with discomfort to lie back down but also with displeasure to remember my betrayers and the lost Scepter. "Ah—my companions and I were sent here by the Temple of Weltyr to liberate His Holy Scepter from the bowels of this infernal cauldron of the black arts."

"And they left you here to die of your injuries after the battle?"

"Not quite…they got a better offer."

Exchanging a knowing glance, the durrow women studied me again. Gentle Indra pushed back her hair to take her turn to speak. Most of the white locks loose from her thick braid were successfully hung behind her long, high ear. I ignored painful memories of Branwen's sweetly-delivered lies as Indra asked me, "You mean to say *they* did this to you? Your companions?"

"The spear wound, at any rate…"

My hand lifted to rest upon my eyes and I groaned in heart-pain, saying, "Would that you had left me to die! What a disgrace I am—how can I serve Weltyr when I've failed Him like this? May Oppenhir's fires cleave the ground and snatch them down to Urde's very core for what they've done!"

Odile studied me, her face illegible. "Who were these companions of yours, slave?"

Striving to ignore the appellation until I could find a way around my new vow, (Weltyr, after all, would surely understand that an oath made in duress was not a valid agreement between any two spirits, whether human, durrow or any other), I described my trio of companions.

The dark elves listened carefully until, at last, Odile assured me, "Well, they're long gone by now. We saw no trace of them…only a dead spirit-thief that made us think we'd ought to do the neighborly thing and come knocking at their usually so well-guarded temple."

"You must be a mighty warrior to have claimed so many of their lives," Indra marveled, far more genuinely intrigued than her companion ever could have been.

"Only by Weltyr's grace," I answered, "and only at the cost of my own life."

"Not quite. Why, your Weltyr *would* have seen you dead, had not Roserpine intervened and guided us here."

"Hail the Dark Queen," said Indra, to which Odile blasphemously answered, "Praise to the Face of the Darkness."

Weltyr, forgive me! I ought to have tried to discourage their errant ways then and there, but I was too weak and too much in their debt to criticize their pagan religion. Eschewing my duties as paladin in those moments seems now the first step down a dangerous path—but there are times when, in truth, danger is the very will of the Bright God. There is strength in danger. Sometimes, there are even gifts.

After considering me for another few seconds, then rising to her feet, Odile said to her companion with a hefty sigh, "I don't think he'll be fully healed before the bloom. We should camp here a dark—doesn't seem like anybody will be back anytime soon, anyway…assuming there are any escaped spirit-thieves left living in this brood."

I glanced between them. "The bloom?"

"You haven't spent much time in the Nightlands, have you, human? The fungi here bloom once a cycle and take to glowing…we spend our waking hours in the rhythm of the bloom and take to bed when it's faded."

"Aha! Like dawn. It's dawn you mean."

"It's bloom I mean," corrected the woman sternly, sliding her rucksack from her shoulder and digging about for flint she soon extricated. "If you're to serve a durrow mistress here in the Nightlands, you'd do well to learn our ways. Count your lucky stars we speak the common tongue in this region…there are durrow farther east whose language you couldn't even hear with those piddly little ears of yours."

Then, with a flashing grin and a glance down at my lap, she tossed her bag away and said, striding to light the altar's flame, "Let's hope they're the only small thing about you."

Sex was the last thing on my mind in such a distressing moment, yet the effects of the potion were invigorating in more ways than one. Perhaps it moved the blood about in the name of healing, or perhaps some other cause was buried deep in the ingredients—or perhaps it was simply awakening from near-death to find myself alive in the presence of two trim, exquisite women. Whatever the reason, my manhood ached beneath the fabric of my tunic, at once harder than it had ever been among the enchantments of Branwen's false words.

Indra happened to glance toward my lap while her friend stoked the fire in the brazier upon the altar. The evidently gentler durrow's dark face darkened further beneath the rich innocence of her blushing—she glanced quickly away, stuttering, "You must be hungry, Burningsoul! When did you last eat?"

Soon enough I had strength enough to sit up and even join them by the fire crackling patiently in the silver altar bowl. The women provided me with hardtack and jerky of a kind I'd never tasted, and though it was certainly of no aboveground game or cattle, it was in that moment the most delicious meat that had ever passed my lips.

I scarfed down all they gave me while recounting for their curiosity a few stories about my companions, who were so dead to me that I related them like figures of some distant past. The wounds they had dealt my mind as well as my body were so great that I wished only to forget all three, and telling empty stories such as the first time Branwen seduced me or the fistfight Grimalkin and I got into while shipwrecked upon the Northern Shore was, in so many ways, an effort to drain myself of any remaining feelings I might have had for them.

"And what of this Hildolfr," asked Odile when I seemed through, "this one-eyed man?"

"His is the betrayal that most surprised me…I had taken to regarding him as a kind of long-lost father. A mistake never to be made again, certainly."

"You're an orphan," observed Indra with interest. Odile flicked a pebble at her gentler friend.

"Of course he's an orphan. All paladins of Weltyr are, male and female alike. They're raised to take up the task of fighting in the god's name because no one with a family would dare throw their lives away—not with such single-minded brutality as called for by Weltyr."

"Brutality! I and my brethren only do what's necessary for the Bright God."

Odile snorted. "You certainly convince yourselves of that, anyway."

Hoping I might find a gentle inroad to making her see metaphysical reason, I probed, "How is it that you know so much about the servants of Weltyr?"

Odile's sharp white eyes darted across my face, or seemed to—it was difficult to tell without pupils marking a point of focus. "I was born in a village many leagues from El'ryh. It was a happy colony, well-situated near the surface, and so we were spoiled for fish and game from

6

aboveground. The Knights of Weltyr didn't like that. Too many of us coming and going with too much freedom. They took action to prevent what they thought was a raid in planning—they slaughtered every last member of my colony.

"I survived only by Roserpine's generosity. Her darkness cloaked me when the bloom faded and I managed to escape the slaughter in search of a safer home. Finally some merchants found me and brought me to Roserpine's Palace in El'ryh. Ever since then, I have been keenly interested in Weltyr and the ways of His servants…it is frightful to me to think that a god is capable of such cruelty."

I always grew terribly uncomfortable when such indictments of Weltyr's servants were made in my presence. The need to defend the Bright God had a way of clashing with my drive to show compassionate understanding to all sentient beings, which was foremost among the vows I took while accepting my sword and my duties. Instead, to my later embarrassment, I tried to suggest that, "Where I'm from, our people regard Roserpine as a fearful goddess in her own right."

"But if you believe your god is all-powerful and mine is nothing beside Him, surely it would make no sense for Roserpine to be more fearful than Weltyr. His ire has drowned whole villages, hidden the sun from the sky, brought plagues upon the face of the world—Roserpine, meanwhile, feels nothing but love for even the most wretched creatures. Spiders and snakes and night-beetles: she loves them all as much as she loves us."

Fiery Odile lifted her head to take a swig of the wineskin she gripped in one fist, her shoulder-length white locks tumbling past her ears with the motion. The tension of her slender throat hypnotized me until she took a breath and thrust the wine at me, saying, "Perhaps she only seems fearful to you because you know your kind have done all they can to earn her wrath. So far as I can see, our only crime is failing to bear the stare of your All-Father's burning sunlight."

"Is slavery not a crime?"

Odile laughed at that, glancing over at Indra. Indra herself produced a light giggle of semi-embarrassment as she admitted, "Perhaps, when a slave is mistreated… but I'd wager a great many slaves in the Nightlands are far happier than they ever were while walking beneath the sun."

"How could that possibly be! Liberty is the greatest gift Weltyr ever gave mankind. The free will to do as one pleases—in taking that away, what's left?"

"Great pleasure," answered Odile, watching with approval as her friend took a small sip from the wineskin, then put the rest aside. Her eyes settled upon me, her lips crimson against her dark flesh as they contorted in a sensual smile.

"Our slaves are put to many uses, Burningsoul… some of which not even a strong-willed man such as you might find objectionable." The sterner elf glanced quickly toward my lap, then went on to ask, "How are you feeling after that potion?"

"Fine—better than fine. Strong as an ox."

"That's very good…but not quite what I meant." Her smile widened and seemed as though to glitter as she asked, "Is that prick of yours still hard under there?"

Somehow, I had been expecting any kind of question but that! I sputtered, all elegance of rhetoric flying from my mind—the women laughed together at my meaningless noises. Odile shook her head and remarked, "How shy! What else should we expect from a man raised

8

around the Temple of Weltyr, though…it's a wonder this Branwen girl managed to get anywhere with you. Go on, slave—stand up."

Odile's tone shifted at her command, her smile fading somewhat and sliding into a hardened expression of lust. "Take off your clothes. We should try the wares before we sell them off…who knows? Maybe we'll want to keep you for ourselves."

With a glance between them that revealed shy Indra waited as expectantly as her friend, I tried quickly to come up with some argument as to why I should not. After all—in agreeing to this first demand, however pleasurable the results might be, I was opening myself up to the pattern of a true slave. There were those who were slaves through circumstance—through war or ill-starred birth—and then there were those who were slaves in their hearts. Slaves who submitted their free will, their dreams, their ambitions. I would never be such a slave to any earthbound man or woman: my soul was long-since delivered into the righteous hands of Weltyr.

But my cock? Well…the body does have a mind of its own. "I'm not so certain you ladies would be able to handle my appetite," I assured them both. While they exchanged a grin I advised, "Most refined women find an insatiable man to be somewhat unbecoming."

"Quit delaying and strip," said Odile with an imperious wave of her hand. "Unless you've taken a vow of celibacy, in which case we'll find work for you as a packmule or field hand. But I think you would much prefer the sorts of tasks I have in mind."

With a briefer glance at wildly blushing Indra, who ran her fingers along the edge of her tunic and over the soft divot of her collarbone, I found only anticipation in my heart.

Unable to see immediate harm in it, I stood to obey. "I've taken no such stultifying vows, as Branwen could tell you...some men vow to be mute or eschew women or beat themselves once a day every day, but I have only vowed to enact justice in the name of my God."

While I removed my belt, I met the unrelenting gaze of the lithe durrow who watched most intensely. Without looking away, Odile reached back for the wineskin and took a swig. I bent to remove my boots and obeyed her when she urged, "Slower."

Indra leaned over and whispered something in Odile's long ear, which twitched but a catlike degree. Odile laughed and nudged her fellow traveler. "What are we, girls? You needn't *whisper*, Indra! He's a slave."

"But it's just—" Indra turned her lightly hued eyes toward me before lowering them, her dusky lips contorting with her bashful inability to say more.

"My friend here says you have a cute ass," said the crasser durrow, laughing at Indra's embarrassed sputtering to hear her address me such a way. "And I don't disagree...you'll have to forgive her shyness. She's a virgin, see."

I slid my tunic over my head and tried not to look too pleased by the sound of Indra's astonished gasp. "And you're not."

"I should wait and let you find out..."

Grinning devilishly, Odile swigged from the skin one last time before setting it aside. She crooked a finger for me.

"Come here, slave. Let's play a game. Your gaze is too intimidating for poor Indra to stand. You won't be frightened if I blindfold you, will you? Or will it soothe you, as darkness is said to soothe aboveground birds and horses."

I thought on this for a few seconds—they had, after all, revived me, and I had no cause to mistrust them. All the same I said, "Just let me close my eyes. I'll feel more comfortable…especially not knowing what you're up to."

"Very well. Then sit down, you great worried beast. I won't have you fidgeting and pawing at the earth for as nervous as you are."

After settling upon the cloak arranged beneath our makeshift encampment and ignoring Indra's ache-inducing glances everywhere but my stirred cock, I shut my eyes as Odile bade me.

"Very good," she said, the air from the hand she waved before my face like a cool wind upon my brow. "Now"—I felt her rise beside me and listened to something jingle—"let's see how observant you are. Indra, now's your chance to try a man…go on, take off your clothes, your gear."

"Oh, Odile, I don't know—"

"How shy you are! Come on, I'll help you…"

My head swam at the sound of two beautiful lips mingling in a wet kiss, this vision hidden from my starving gaze. The women apparently wiggled out of their clothes while fondling and petting one another. From the sounds of the moaning, Indra was not very virginal—but, as I would soon find, lovemaking between two durrow friends was different from lovemaking between true lovers, and more different still from durrow interactions with men.

At the time, though, these nuances were lost to me, and though I yearned to open my eyes and sneak a glance of the proceedings I instead left them shut. In this darkness, I basked in the mystery of how a woman could be so shy with me yet so forthcoming with her female lover.

"All right," said Odile at last, separating herself from their kissing with a breathless laugh of husky delight. "All

11

right…now, sharp-eyed paladin, it's your job to guess whose kiss this is."

There was delay—then, much as on my waking, soft hair tickled my face and was followed this time by still softer lips. I tilted my head back, willing my eyes to stay shut, sighing low into the wine-flavored taste of the tongue that trailed demandingly past my lips.

"This must be Odile," I said as my visitor slipped away with a laugh on my correct choice.

"A lucky guess!"

"Nothing of the sort…you were too forceful to be a woman who's never lain with a man. And, anyway, you tasted too strongly of wine for it to be fair Indra. Would you like a kiss, Indra? I'll be very gentle, on my honor."

At the nervous hitch of breath somewhere to my left, Odile laughed. "Go on, Indra! Don't be so skittish…go on, there you are."

The younger durrow had knelt beside me, an act that even in the darkness behind my eyelids thrilled me from the top of my skull to the tip of my cock. With another muted sound of her breath being held, Indra leaned into me and pressed her mouth to mine. That cool and delicate cavern yielded itself to me, so unlike that of her dynamic and exploratory friend.

Blindly reaching up to catch her delicate face in my hands, I savored her gasp into my mouth and dared instruct her on the burning passion of a man. Her wet mouth and the charming organ twitching shyly within left my cock all the harder, its unrelieved ache after the application of the potion doubling on contact with the elves. Gradually her delicate hand trailed over my heart, but as my grip upon the back of her neck slowly pursued the line of her spine, Odile said, "Ah-ah," and a third dainty hand caught my wrist.

"Don't spoil the rest of the game, warrior-priest… come here, Indra." While the smaller elf peeled out of my incomplete embrace amid a short, shy sort of giggle, Odile informed me with a smile in her voice, "Now you have to guess which body is which. Keep those eyes shut…"

The women laughed and the sound of bare feet dancing upon the stones thrilled me. In my mind's eye I could visualize them twirling hand-in-hand, but soon enough I lost confidence that I knew which side each was on.

When they separated, one pair of feet tapped across the floor to me. Whichever elf had first approached me knelt deftly by my side. With hands alone, I caressed the soft skin provided. First an arm, then a slender hand, then a soft thigh; as my palm trailed up that thigh and over the offered plane of a stomach, I tried to picture both women in my mind.

Odile's bosom had been a fair bit more sizable than that of delicate Indra, and it had been these luscious orbs I expected to encounter in my blind journey—yet, much to my surprise, my hand managed to cup an entire breast from the soft swell at the base to the nipple hardened with eager anticipation.

I laughed gently at Indra's unmistakable gasp on our contact. "Why, Indra! How brave you are to go first…I was certain it would be Odile."

"She pushed me," admitted Indra with a light laugh. "And, anyway…well, I wanted to go."

"He's too good at this game," insisted Odile. "You must be cheating, Burningsoul."

"I swear on Weltyr's light my eyes have been closed all this time."

"Weltyr's light doesn't reach these caverns," answered the more curt of the two elves while kneeling at my right.

13

"Only Roserpine's eyes see what we do here."

Now was not the time to correct her and assure her that wheresoever mortals saw, Weltyr's eyes also dwelled. Instead I sighed into the graze of her hand over my thigh and across the protuberance throbbing in my lap.

"May I open my eyes now," I said, turning toward the sterner durrow.

"Oh…if you must. So long as you promise not to frighten Indra with your gaze and make her shy again."

Smiling, I at last looked upon them. The breath froze in my lungs. Rest assured, Branwen had been beautiful before her inner ugliness spoiled her exquisite looks. All elves I had seen were joys to behold, and the druid was no exception. But somehow, never having seen a durrow with my own two eyes, I had not expected them to be even more exquisite than that.

Free of clothes, Indra and Odile were a pair of obsidian statues, the sheen of their healthy flesh almost amethyst with that same blue-purple tint I had noticed in the firelight before. Fair Indra's tight frame was already dimpled with goosebumps from my many caresses, but bold Odile's warrior body most drew my eye in that moment—and not just due to the fact that it was she who tickled her soft fingers up and down the shaft of my throbbing manhood.

"Have you ever pleased a durrow, slave? No? Well… you'll find we can be generous mistresses. For instance, this is the perfect opportunity for me to educate sweet Indra here—and rest assured, you'll benefit greatly from my teaching."

"I suspect I will." My stomach tightened with the same lust that ached my cock as her hand shifted from teasing to grip me properly. "Please, use me as your aide. I'm happy to oblige."

14

"What a good slave," remarked Indra, who gasped to see my prick twitch in Odile's hand. While the more untrained of the two durrow reached a tentative fingertip to caress the head of my penis, she enthused, "Why, Odile, it twitches like a snake!"

"More like a mouse caught in the maw of one…that's all the more evidence that he's well-disposed to being a slave, you see. The more eager a man is to serve a woman, the harder this organ becomes. Oh, I love a big, hard dick! Especially when it's attached to a big, hard man. Watch how easy it is to agitate into an even more impressive state…hold my hair back, human."

How happy I was to obey in that moment! Yes: some men were slaves in their hearts, and I was not one of them by any means…but when the superficial trappings of slavery earned such sweet rewards, I was willing to pretend I was suited to the task. While I marveled at the smooth white locks I drew back from Odile's foxy face, the elf lowered herself to lie upon her stomach and bent her head over the crown of my glory. I gasped from the first penetration of my passion past her sumptuous lips. As her wet tongue swirled into expert motion around my throbbing head, Indra made a small noise of slight scandal.

"How *easily* you do such things, Odile…and eagerly. Why, it's such a frightening looking thing! I don't know how you can stand to."

The more muscular of the two durrow lifted her head and encouragingly told her companion, "Oh, it's a great pleasure to suck a cock! Go on, come down here with me and give it a try…if you don't want to suck it, you can kiss it like this."

She demonstrated with a few lingering kisses, then the application of a tongue so red that the mere sight of it trailing up and down my length made me all the harder. "See? It's nothing to be afraid of…"

Biting her lip with an uncertain glance up to my face, Indra pushed her own hair, now free of its braid, back over her smooth shoulder and bent to emulate her friend. Soon two pairs of lips, two wet tongues, two suckling warm mouths worked me over while I throbbed in ecstasy.

By Weltyr, perhaps I really had died for good… perhaps this was my reward for a lifetime of devoted service to my true master. Who could really care whether they were dead or alive when serviced by two beautiful women?

While, with one hand, I held back Indra's hair to assist the more untrained of my mistresses, I allowed my other hand to slide from Odile's locks and down the slope of her back. Soon that wandering hand settled against the thick flesh of the backside that had drawn my eyes since she lay herself down to go to work: the durrow moaned low, arching into my touch.

"So our warrior-priest appreciates alternative routes of bliss," quipped Odile, lifting her head from the dagger she now permitted her friend to sharpen alone. "Well, perhaps if we keep you long enough you'll have a chance to try me…but I think I'd rather have you in my cunt, and Roserpine knows poor Indra's long overdue for her first fucking. Here, priest, relax. Serve us as a toy and reap the rewards of helping. Come closer, Indra, here—kiss me, oh, your pretty mouth, how you pout!"

"I'm frightened! You'd ought to show me how to do it first, Odile…I have no practice."

While my prick throbbed with pleasure upon hearing the more innocent of the two elves begging for her sister in faith to embolden her by example, Odile chuckled to coat her mouth in lurid kisses.

16

I resisted the urge to satisfy my own desire for a stroke or two, sure the women would use such a movement as an excuse to reprimand me—and, at any rate, Odile was quick enough to take me in-hand again for a few achingly slow tugs.

"Very well, Indra...I'll show you how to ride. Just watch me carefully. See how the head is shaped?" Her fingertip trailed around my glans. I shuddered as she went on, "It's perfect for penetration...once you've used a prick once or twice, you'll find it very easy to affix yourself atop one."

"I'm afraid I'll put it in wrong and hurt myself."

"Don't be...such a fear is common for young virgins like yourself, but wholly unnecessary, I assure you. Especially if you take time to prepare...Roserpine knows how wet you get for me, after all. Here, feel—"

Catching the younger durrow's hand, the more worldly of the two guided these dark digits and soon enough gasped with approving pleasure as Indra tickled her labia. More used to this form of pleasure than anything to do with a man, Indra familiarly caressed the shimmering folds and meanwhile Odile softly moaned.

"Oh...yes, Indra, just like that. Just follow your fingers to the source of my pleasure, plunge in—ah, by the Queen of Darkness, there's a good girl."

While Odile moaned to be finger-fucked by her innocent friend, she humored me with a few strokes of my sorely aching cock and went on without looking at me.

"When you've a prick in-hand, just follow the same trek your fingers did just now—back to the source of the waterfall. Then ease the tool against yourself very gently, and when you can feel it press just into you, lower yourself upon it as far as't pleases."

"You make it sound so simple," remarked gentle Indra while withdrawing her fingers and casting another, more uncertain look to my length. "As though it were nothing."

"Oh, it's not *nothing*…it's one of the greatest pleasures in the world, after all. Roserpine carefully molded this device so as to please herself, and us in turn…it's a natural fit, one into the other, like the hand into the glove."

At last, much to my relief, Odile straddled my hips and pumped my member toward her shimmering apex. She knelt astride me in the reverse so I had a throbbingly beautiful view of the shining round flesh of her ass, which I sensed was some reward for obeying her. These dark elves did make the notion of slavery easy, I had to admit! Though I wished I could have seen more as she demonstratively spread her lips with one hand, hovering ever-closer to me.

"Now watch, sister, and see how easy it is to take even a cock as large and finely-crafted as this great tool."

After far too long of teasing, (so far as my frayed nerves were concerned, anyway), Odile pressed me to her dusky lower lips, then past. I lost my self-control and groaned at the flood of her passion, overwhelming to both of us as, degree by degree, her body swallowed mine. The darkness of her exquisite durrow flesh contrasted sharply with my passion-reddened cock and only added to my desire—not near so much, however, as did the echo of her throaty moan through the sacrilegious temple, or the eyes of Indra upon the unfolding scene.

"Oh, sweet man! Praise Roserpine, what a slave our mistress has made for us! Oh—"

Having filled herself completely and thrilling me with a burst of pleasure from a hard bump against her wet walls, the dark elf braced herself upright against my thigh and quickly found a rhythm she enjoyed.

"Ah—you shouldn't have let me go first, Indra, I might just ride him all dark—Roserpine, oh my goddess, he's terrific—"

Now frightened Indra's lavender eyes shone with cheerful desire and even curved with her mystified smile. "Why, you do make it look very fun…oh, it excites me to watch you…"

Indra's delicate fingers ran over her pert little breasts while Odile extended her arms and drew her in. "Touch my body, warrior-priest," the riding durrow commanded while embracing her friend. "Touch me while I touch sweet Indra! Leave nothing on your mistress unexplored."

No need to tell me twice! Thanking Weltyr for the gift of this waking fever-dream, I filled my greedy hands with the thick flesh of Odile's thighs and trailed up the slope of her lovely back—but ah, the globes of that shapely ass were what most drew my gaze, and soon enough, my grip. My fingers sank into the wonderful flesh that bounced and slapped upon my abdomen while she pleasured herself upon me, my manhood throbbing in her chambers a mere toy for her pleasure.

Indra, meanwhile, moaned beneath her kisses, and each exchange of pink tongues between these sumptuous mouths only increased the agony with which I was wracked. I sought to relieve it with the occasional buck of my hips up into the durrow's valley, my jaw clenched as I gripped her backside to push her down against me all the harder. Odile moaned, glancing at me over her shoulder while her fingers trailed down to fondle Indra's drenched cleft.

"Be careful, warrior-priest…I enjoy a man who will fuck me in return, but not all durrow are as pleased. Be mindful when we reach our city that you know how to follow a woman's direction."

Yes, yes, of course, whatever she said. The truth was in that instant she might have told me to please her while standing on my head and I would have been willing to at least attempt it if I knew the act would make her wetter. Already she was dripping, and I saw that pretty Indra too was similarly inflamed; with a pair of fingers, Odile rapidly manipulated her into a state of frenzied panting and sweet, girlish whines that soon enough burst into a sharp, high cry.

"Oh! Oh, Odile, sweet Roserpine, oh, how could any man be good as these fingers—"

Chuckling, her lips peeling back from bright white teeth in a dark and beautiful smile, Odile gathered Indra's gasping face in her hands for a lingering kiss. "You'll see in just a moment, ah, I'm very close, myself…oh! This paladin is the finest slave I've had, the biggest cock by far—yes, yes, I love the way he fills me up. And you love it, too, slave—don't you?"

"What man could resist a woman so eager? By Weltyr, I feel attended on by angels—"

The wicked girls exchanged an even wickeder spate of laughter and Odile redoubled her efforts at pleasure. As I throbbed in her confines, she swore again and murmured, "So, so hard! Oh, you'll love it, Indra," before commanding of her petite friend, "Get down and put that tongue to work."

As though she were as much a slave as I was destined to be, Indra hurried to obey, flinging herself upon her belly between my legs to lavish affection upon Odile's clitoris. Now and then her bold tongue dashed across what of my shaft was visible. Each time I groaned to encourage her. Soon her pretty hand caressed my balls and sooner still Odile's hard slaps down upon my cock increased in speed to a point of no return. The embrace of her body around me tightening to a sublime tension, Odile gasped and then, once more bracing herself—now against Indra's white-haired head—screamed with the ecstasy of her release.

Her cunt clenched rapidly around me while she pounded herself through her climax, that sopping chamber begging for my seed. I withheld my own bliss, anticipating the pleasure sure to come with Indra's virgin body.

With the slowing of her climax, so too did Odile's motions gradually come to a halt. She shuddered, gasped, moaned a little more as she dismounted; my cock sprang out of her and received one last burst of pleasure as a drop of glistening honey dripped out upon its head. I groaned, watching her draw her friend up to her knees and similarly position her—this time, facing me.

Though another anxious expression crossed Indra's dainty features, soon she grew determined and looked down at me where I lay prone between her legs. Odile was a luscious woman, thick with sensual curves and many wonderful handles a man could grab whether he was riding or being ridden; Indra's body was tighter, smaller, but no less beautiful and still benefiting from a few pleasant-to-touch soft curves. I rested my hand encouragingly upon her thigh, and this seemed to please her. She sighed softly, her next inhalation catching in her throat as Odile gripped my cock and angled it up toward this untrod territory.

"Now, don't be afraid…it'll hurt at first, but I'd wager you're wet enough that, very soon, it won't matter. I'll guide your hips, here. Feel how hard he is?"

While I softly sighed to feel the caress of Indra's smooth, shining labia, Indra herself nodded and stared down at me.

"Oh"—she gasped as, with her other hand, Odile gently urged her down to allow the head of my cock to barely penetrate this unused palace—"oh! How wide it is! How can it fit?"

"Like this," answered Odile, laughing cruelly at Indra's shriek when she pushed the younger durrow down upon my shaft unmercifully.

The groan that tore from me to push through Indra's defenses by no will but that of a third party left me breathless. A pleasure more immense than even that given by wily Odile flooded all my senses and, though she was obviously ached by the cruel prank, Indra's own noise of shock and pain soon faded into moans of bliss.

"Oh! Odile—ah, Odile, you're right! He's so big!"

"Isn't he? Ah, what a pleasure he is…if we couldn't fetch so much for him on market, I'd be tempted to keep him for our private use. There, see!"

With a look of approval and lascivious pleasure, Odile released her friend's hips and smiled to find Indra was more than capable of adopting a steady rocking pace on her own. "What a good girl you are…you've got it perfectly! Such a fast learner."

"You make it easy to follow your example, Odile…oh! Oh—good Roserpine—"

Indra's eyelids fluttered upon her lavender orbs while she worked herself upon me, still at a pace more unsteady and with strokes not quite so thorough as those of Odile's. Nonetheless, each short lift and quick plunge she made left me seeing stars. I dared allow an audacious hand to trail up her thigh and fit upon her abdomen, and thank Weltyr, she was fond enough to let me.

The elf was so tight I might have sworn I felt myself inside her and, better still, when my thumb lowered to toy against the clit within the dark folds of her nether lips, her body tightened even more. It were as though she wished to squeeze my manhood clean off, and I'd have let her have it in the fugue of ecstasy she gave.

Meanwhile, moaning, running her hands over her thick breasts and reaching down to massage herself between those luscious thighs, Odile leaned up to kiss her friend upon the gasping mouth. Then, to my astonishment, the devious elf leaned down to lay a kiss on mine. I groaned at the taste of the two women mingling in one, my tongue sparking with bursts of pleasure each time Odile's wet organ lashed across my own. My thumb worked Indra's clit and Indra pumped herself up and down; my right hand soon commenced to assist Odile with her drenched mound; and, not very long later, all three of us reached our respective climaxes.

First Indra, overwhelmed with the newness of this ecstasy and the caresses from both myself and her friend, exploded into cries of bliss that signaled the onslaught of pleading clenches. Seeing this, Odile moaned sharply and, while kissing her, gasped and cried her dear friend's name.

Her channel shut tight around my fingers and I slowed but did not stop my work, easing her through the same ecstasy that very soon claimed me. I groaned, thrusting up into pretty Indra's belly and seeing stars to spill my seed inside the valley of this virgin durrow.

"By Roserpine—oh, Queen of Darkness—" Gasping out of their kiss, then laughing to see how stunned by pleasure I was, the educated drow turned to her innocent sister. "Has he cum? Get off him, let me see it, ah, I want to see your first load dripping out of you, Indra—"

All but pushing her friend from my lap, Odile moaned with delight and spread Indra's lower lips. In a frenzy of lust even after two orgasms, this wicked woman dove upon her friend's exposed anatomy and began at once to avidly lick and suck her little bundle of nerves. While Indra twitched, thrashing amid the overwhelming onslaught, Odile lifted her head and groaned in pleasure. She spread her friend's dark labia and turned to make certain I watched the thick pool of semen that oozed from Indra's newly defiled pussy. The contrast of the bright white cum against the elf's dark flesh somehow emphasized my conquest—if the marking of mistress by a slave could dare be called such a thing—and left me nearly ready for a second round.

"What a fine job you've done, warrior-priest! Good thing you didn't take that vow of chastity...the world would be much poorer for it, the two of us included!"

3

THE CITY OF EL'RYH

BEING THE SLAVE to a pair of durrow mistresses
wasn't all fun and games, of course. The duties of pleasing
them accomplished, I slept soundly through the night—
the dark, as it was called in those Nightlands where all
things were night at all times—and was awoken by a
shaking pair of hands to find Odile's smiling face above
mine.

"Good bloom, warrior-priest! Hope you slept well…
it's quite a walk to El'ryh."

Quite a walk was one thing. Quite a walk while laden
down with tapestries, golden goblets, silver braziers, and
everything else that was not nailed down…now that was
quite another. By the standards of most men my body
is well-trained, hewn for battle in the service of my
Lord—but the haul of wealth the women bade me carry

tested even my fortitude. While sweat poured down my brow beneath the burden weighing upon my back, my mistresses laughed in casual conversation together ahead of me.

In truth, the stress was such that I saw little of where we were going—only that the glistening cavern walls, illuminated at first mostly by an orange lamp that Odile gripped, were steadily overtaken with a strange series of white and green phosphorescence. My traitorous former companions and I had observed the phenomenon but now, understanding it to be the cognate of the dawn, it filled me with a twinge of hope that the worst of this was over.

"Are your eyes not so sensitive that this bloom is light enough for you," I asked of Odile, observing that she still kept the glass-enclosed lamp burning in her hand.

"To be sure, Paladin—but this is a special lantern." Odile gestured to it with her free hand. While I examined it as best I could before having to regain my grip upon the stolen trove of treasures, the elf went on, "Its light can be turned on or off with the twist of this switch, and in all my years I've never seen a thing Nightland creatures hate more. Misshapen—You are aware of those, aren't you, human? Our perverted cousins, cursed with the bodies of spiders and the feral minds of animals—especially avoid it at all cost. I bought it from a friend who said she took it off the body of an adventurer."

"Then I'd venture a guess his light didn't do him much good."

"Oh, it did, but it was she who felled him." While I could do little more than produce a noise of plain displeasure, both durrow laughed. The elder one went on, "Come now! As though that sword of yours hasn't killed plenty of men!"

26

"None who were sleeping, or otherwise minding their own business."

"Don't feel too awfully for him...she said he was a servant of Oppenhir, here for who knows what depraved art."

While I tried to decide whether I should be relieved or unnerved to think that even durrow were ill-disposed toward Oppenhir and his pale servants, Indra now took her turn to ask questions. She turned to study the sword I had insisted I keep on my person, thus adding to my load but proving comfort to my mind. "What's the name of your sword, Paladin?"

"Strife," I answered.

Odile laughed to overhear us. "Some name! Who wants to carry Strife around on their hip? Here I thought most of your kind named their blades things like Peace-Bringer or Oath-Keeper."

"Not at all...many of the legendary forebears we were taught about in the Temple of Weltyr carried blades with names like "Needful" or "The End." To bear a weapon such as Strife is a great and solemn duty—an honor that reminds us it is no small thing to kill a man. Certainly not as much as it would seem to you."

Odile snorted. "Men are animals just the same as any other—women, too, though that opinion is less popular where I come from."

"We begin our lives as animals, yes, and these are animal bodies...but Weltyr imbues us with the sound and vision of consciousness, rather than that of mere creatures. After all—were I but an animal, or a creature like a misshapen or a spirit-thief, then your light would send me fleeing just the same as them. It'd send you fleeing, too, were you but an animal, Odile."

With a noise like the annoyed suck of a tooth and a

27

muted scoff, Odile said, "Go on, pack mule, pick up your pace. You're slowing us down."

That may have been so, but the journey was long and, after a certain point, treacherous enough that I couldn't help but think it would not have mattered how slowly I went: one way or another, the task would have taken us the better part of the day, especially once we reached the city itself. Somehow, the vastness of El'ryh did not strike me as a possibility in all the times I'd heard of it. While I understood it to be the Nightland equivalent of Skythorn, the sprawling city where I was raised and trained, I somehow could not comprehend its size until I saw it for myself.

As was the way with cities, however, we gradually met other travelers coming from it. The women greeted a female, this traveling on her own and geared for some subterfuge; soon we also crossed paths with another group of women, a chattering trio.

At one point, in a narrow cavern, the elves drew me aside and we all waited to permit the passage of a tremendous black carriage being drawn by an enormous tarantula—this vehicle was being driven not by another elf but by a human man who regarded me with a sense of cold exhaustion before turning his eyes away and urging the spider on a bit faster.

"Are durrow much in the custom of keeping male slaves, for pleasure or otherwise?"

Indra answered for me. "Of course…it is Roserpine's will."

"But what do your husbands think of this practice? Sure they must take exception."

While Odile laughed, Indra looked at me with an expression of puzzlement. "Husbands," she repeated. "Our animal trainers?"

"He doesn't mean animal husbandry, Odile, although he'd might as well. It's a practice aboveground...humans believe women untrained in the sword can't take care of themselves as well as a man untrained in the sword. Husbands are proscribed to care for these women."

Scoffing, I assured them, "That's not so—the bond of marriage arises out of love. It is a symbol of Weltyr's love for the souls of mortals. What do you call it her—helpmates? Companions? Either way, matrimony's not the slave-bond you would make it seem."

Odile laughed and shook her head. "We have no such structure here. Durrow come together and part as friends or enemies like the changing of the seasons. We live hundreds of years, human...can you imagine five hundred, six hundred years spent looking at the same face every bloom, every dark? And in the case Roserpine has meted out but a little life to us, when we're to die in battle or of ailment, is that not all the more reason to fill the time with as many lovers as we can? Durrow do not feel 'love,'" she insisted, noting some sign artfully drawn in silver painted upon the tunnel wall.

I glanced up in time to see a list of required documentation for aboveground merchants bold enough to bear their wares here to the Nightland capital.

Odile, now shutting off her lantern and leaving my pitiful human eyes to adjust to the low light of the natural bloom, went on to say, "We feel fondness for our friends and even sometimes for our slaves, but our hearts are hardened against deep feeling—love as you mean it. Attachment to this tangible reality severs our connection to Roserpine and only ensures that our passage into her arms will be painful."

"But surely you long for tenderness. Surely even durrow wish to have someone they know they can trust."

29

"I trust Indra," answered Odile, "and that's enough for me. Mind the top of the gate here, human...don't lose your burden before we're to the market."

At the threshold of a gate I struggled to see beyond the sagging of the tapestry over my shoulder, I could at least note a few details. First, the broad cavern leading to this particular entrance of the city was, nearer to El'ryh, hand-carved with designs as elaborate and beautiful as any I have ever seen.

Once as a boy I was shown a dagger, its handle hand carved from the horns of plain-kings. Even though such an object implied the death of as great and sacred a being as those gigantic creatures were, I remember being wholly taken by the intricacy of the artistic carving of that ivory handle.

The flowers and vines arranged down its length brought to mind some kind of netting, a mesh of bone; it was exquisite, and the decorations announcing entry to the underground capital brought it to mind in an instant.

Next I noticed, to my surprise, that the city guards were female. Powerful women whose heights were a match for mine—truly these were giantesses among the delicate dark elves. They looked far more capable of battle than even Odile and grinned beneath the cages of their visor to see me.

"What a find, sister," remarked the one to the right, the only one I could see completely owing to the obstacle of the tapestry. "How much did you have to trade for that one?"

"Only a little healing potion...good to see you..."

With a wave, Odile crossed into the broad platform that overlooked the city and gave weary travelers a chance both to gather themselves and to enjoy the view of El'ryh. She yawned and stretched as though her journey were

30

already up just on her entry. "Oh, home! What a sight for sore eyes."

"Look, Burningsoul!" Indra nudged me, smiling, and I grimaced while trying not to drop my burden. "Isn't our city beautiful?"

Though I lifted my head at her direction to humor her, I have to admit now that I was wholly unprepared to say El'ryh was, in fact, truly beautiful. Indeed, 'beautiful' was not the word to describe it—extraordinary, breathtaking. These would be more accurate descriptors and still not quite enough.

The underground city was, in every way, an incredible rival for Skythorn—even to the spire carved out of a central column towering from the distant bottom of the city to the glowing ceiling. The top of this cavern was painted so thickly in the phosphorescence of the bloom that now I understood far better the parallels between it and the light of Weltyr. Even my human eyes could see readily beneath this amount of light, this somewhat eerie glow that loaned the entire city a faint blue tinge.

This, also, could have been the blue fire of the wisp torches that served as permanent lights throughout the city, tall upon their mounts so as to guide the way down long spiraling pathways carved from the walls. These paths were wide enough for perhaps fifteen to twenty people to walk side by side together; on the day of my arrival foot traffic was very light, but I could easily see how during hunting seasons and times of holiday or trade the path might become crowded and the gate, backed up with lines of people attempting to get in or out.

And that was just my initial impression. I was so taken aback that I barely saw the lesser spires scattered around the city, rising up its countless stories. Each terminated at a height shorter than that of the central column but nonetheless proved to be quite impressive. All these, like the perimeter of the cavern, were packed with doors. Gradually I realized that though, with the onset of time, many handmade structures had filled the available space at the bottom of the cavern (almost invisible from where I stood for the sheer distance), these doors carved into the walls were surely many things—homes, shops, inns, taverns. All the amenities of life.

I marveled, quite astonished by the vision, and wondered at the amount of time the initial settlers must have spent carving their domiciles. I supposed they did have much time on their hands, being elves. The entire effect made me feel as though I had stepped into a swirling hive of bees, and the deeper the eye followed the path of the highway down the cavern, the busier the activity grew. I could then only imagine just how packed its markets would prove when finally we were upon the cavern floor.

"Well," said Odile with a sigh and another stretch after a few seconds to appreciate the view, "come on, let's go, don't delay...the sooner we get down to the market, the sooner you can get that weight off your shoulders."

Thank Weltyr the road to the city was so broad—but it certainly could have been shorter. Had the ramp been carved any more narrowly I might have woven so much owing to exhaustion that I'd have tumbled to my death. Luckily, with Indra to my right to helpfully guide me and Odile before me to, if nothing else, serve as a point of focus, I managed to keep my swaying down to a minimum...though the dizzying heights and seemingly endless curve of the highway did not make it easy.

We were on this new road, traveling from the height of the city to its depths, for at least the passage of an hour. Surely it was more, but by this time I was in a sort of fugue state and had no more energy for counting the minutes than I did for talking.

While the durrow chattered among themselves I dodged passersby, focused on keeping the goods I hauled balanced, and did not realize until we were at the base of the spiraling path that Indra had every reason to be confused by my question about husbands.

I did not realize until glancing across the sea of moving bodies that all durrow were female.

This revelation was something of a shock and, at the time, I thought I was surely incorrect—surely the crowd simply blotted out my view of the delicate male elves among their female compatriots. But, no: as we dove into the throng, Indra behind me and Odile ahead of me, I found myself more shocked.

Every durrow that we passed was, at least in body, feminine.

"You don't *have* men," I remarked at last to Odile, who laughed at me. Not cruelly, but rather as a woman might at a naïve child.

"Oh, we *have* them…men like you, men we've stolen or lured from the surface. But you're right…durrow are not born as men."

Indra nodded. "The misshapen are said to come from a sorceress's efforts to create a male durrow."

"Instead she managed to create a whole species of abominations! But I'll give it to her…she did produce males."

Doing strange arithmetic in my head, I inquired, "But—reproduction—"

With another laugh together, both women looked at me with fondness. Odile at last advised, "Warrior-priest—if all we required were slaves to labor and build for us, our magicians just as easily could create homunculi, or resurrect skeletons, or call up familiar helper-spirits for that."

Though it astonished me that I had never heard of such a thing before, now I understand why those aboveground kept this secret of the durrow closely guarded. On hearing about an exotic race of exquisite elves who were entirely female and wished to enslave men for purposes of insemination, what young man wouldn't risk life and limb to deliver himself into the belly of the Nightlands? Many would lose their lives and many more would find, as I already had, that the general duties of a slave did not really compensate for the so-called privileges afforded one.

Yet, there would still be those fools who would try, as a young man overflowing with fool's bravado joins armies or counter-intelligence groups. Violence is not a life that one should choose unless it is thrust upon one, as Hildolfr once remarked to me. The same was most certainly true of servitude. But whatever a man's circumstance, it was Weltyr's will that he should make the best of it.

And I must admit, taken aback as I was by the constant flow of exquisite women passing me while we made our way through the busy market crowds, I could easily see how what I intended to be a short period of servitude before some grand escape might be weighted to my benefit.

For now, it was anything but enjoyable. In the heart of the market we went from stall to stall and the women pawned the wares I had carried from the raided temple one artisan at a time. Praise Weltyr, they stopped first at a textile merchant who, to my greatest relief, accepted the tapestry that had proved the most onerous of my burdens. Next came a goldsmith who worked out of one of the freestanding structures packed into the "pit" of El'ryh, as that lowest level of the elfin city was called. This slender wadjita, a snake-woman, turned the gold brazier over in her scaled claws. The yellow light of her eyes faded as they narrowed in assessment.

"I'll melt it down for forty percent," she announced at last, yielding a noise of displeasure not just from the durrow but from me, who hauled the blasted thing all this way.

"Forty percent!" Odile repeated the figure, visibly appalled, then demanded, "I could take this up to Sigur on Fourthlevel and he'd ask for nothing more than twenty."

"All while skimming off the top...ask him to melt down a candlestick and he'll hardly yield enough gold for a ring. Forty percent," repeated the snake-woman, setting the brazier down on the counter between us again. "And I can have it for you by tomorrow's bloom."

Exchanging an annoyed look with Indra, Odile insisted, "Just because you haven't any legs doesn't mean you get to charge us ours."

"If you're going to start hurling insults then I suppose I'll take zero percent, because I won't do it."

While Odile curled her lip at the wadjita, Indra piped up.

"Maybe we could make a trade? Our slave here won't be needing his sword any longer—"

"Strife?" Appalled, I lay a protective hand upon the pommel of the blade. "You can no more take a paladin's sword than you can take his manhood."

"We do that here too sometimes," advised Odile. "But only in cases of extreme disobedience or violence against one's mistress...anyway, Indra, he's right. He'll have to give up that sword at some point, but it could fetch much more than the reasonably charged smelting of this brazier. Although..."

After tapping her pointed chin with a thoughtful look at me, Odile again addressed the proud wadjita. "Since he all but suggested it himself, what would you say to using our slave for a few hours instead of charging such exorbitant prices?"

Though I balked a little, when I looked more closely at the snake-woman who was then peering back at me I had to admit she was quite lovely. Her sharp, shrewd features were accented by the glittering colors of her green and gold scales, and as far as exoticism went, one couldn't get more exotic than a cold-blooded woman. Odile went on, "Indra and I can both attest to his value in these matters—can't we, Indra?"

"Oh yes," agreed the durrow, able to stow away the bashfulness of the day prior when talking business with another woman, "his prowess is quite admirable."

Still assessing me with those reptilian eyes, the smith asked, "And what says the slave of this? Not all men are comfortable in a wadjita's cold embrace."

There was something quite beautiful about her frigid features and the high, proud brow revealed by her swept-back black hair. Never having known a wadjita before, I have to admit I was rather intrigued. At last, spreading my free hand, I suggested, "So long as I am permitted by my mistresses to keep my sword, I would consider it no great sacrifice to have to lie with a sensual and lovely woman such as yourself."

With a laugh of surprise, the wadjita arched her thin brow at my mistresses. "He is a charmer, isn't he? Well… perhaps twenty percent."

"Ten," corrected Odile, seeing her inroad, "plus however long you like with the warrior-priest."

With an annoyed look and a drum of her slender fingertips upon the counter, the wadjita answered, "Fifteen,"

36

and Odile rolled her eyes. At least, I thought she did…it was hard to tell with these women who lacked in pupils.

"Twelve," the firmer durrow tried one last time, yielding a scoff from the smith.

"The only difference between ten and twelve is an insult. Fifteen and the pleasure of your man here when you come and pick up the gold, or you can take it up to Fourthlevel and pay twenty."

"Fine! Fine…I suppose it's not unreasonable." Still sighing, Odile yielded her handshake and pushed the brazier across the counter to the wadjita. "We'll be back tomorrow to pick it up. You can have your time with the man then."

"Very good, very good…looking forward to it." With a sly, crooked sort of smile toward me, the wadjita took up the brazier and disappeared through the curtain separating her storefront from the living and working quarters in the back.

What a strange feeling! The women casually pawning off my services as though I were but an object left me somewhat staggered—it was certainly a clear introduction to my new, hopefully temporary way of life, but even then, reality did not fully set in until I met Valeria.

One hour passed; then another. Slowly, stall by stall, the burden of the spoils was lifted from my shoulders. I was grateful that, though more than a few merchants studied Strife with avarice lighting their features, my saviors permitted me to keep the blade for now. Odile, I sensed, understood as a consequence of her study of Weltyr that the sword was the physical manifestation of my oath to serve my god, and that to have it stripped from me would be a source of great dishonor.

I was soon to find, however, that not all were so respectful.

After my burden was entirely lifted and I was free to look around, Odile split the spoils between herself and Indra.

The latter suggested we eat before heading to the palace. Soon, while we sat on a bench at the edge of a somewhat quieter quarter of what seemed to be homes, I managed to ask the purpose of the visit to the palace.

"All new slaves require vetting and the assignment of some value before they can be traded on the market," explained Indra through bites of the small but meaty lizard that had been skewered through and roasted above a wisp flame grill. "The Materna, Valeria, will have to give us permission before we can even begin to think about trading you off."

"It's really very odd," I confessed, "to be treated as mere chattel."

"But that's what you are," reminded Odile. "At least, what you are now. Try not to be too prideful...if you find yourself here, it must be your Weltyr's will to see you take a lesson in humility. After all—on the surface, human women are traded from family to bridegroom for the price of a steed and some copper. Consider yourself blessed that you'll be worth gold."

I wished to protest, but Indra went on with a charming pout. "I do wish we could keep him, Odile."

"Then we'll have to feed him! What a hassle. Better that he be auctioned off to some rich woman who can add him to a busy household and see to his maintenance. You might have to accept, though, warrior-priest,"— the shrewd, white-eyed durrow glanced at me—"that not every mistress will be as accepting of your cultural traditions, nor your need to hold onto that blade of yours. Your purchaser might demand you give it up. Even the auction house might."

With a grim glance down at Strife in its sheath, I asked, "Is there no way that Strife and I may both be brought into a home? Surely women of the Nightlands wealthy enough to purchase a slave would have cause to seek protection."

"It's true our city is a dangerous one, as many cities are...but one of the greatest dangers of all comes from our own unruly slaves. More than one mistress has had her throat cut in her sleep owing only to the bitterness of her captive. But..." Humming, arms folded, Odile studied my face.

"You are a man of honor," she admitted. "If you were not, you would have fought us last dark or this bloom— or tried to dispatch us while we slept, as I just described. While I have no way to influence with any certainty who will choose to purchase you, I can at least advocate for your noble qualities and advise that you would make a better watchman than, say, a footman or laborer."

"Thank you," I told her, truly meaning it, a hint of relief blossoming in my heart. "You both have been extraordinarily kind to me since coming upon me in the den of spirit-thieves. I am grateful to Weltyr that you were guided to find me, rather than a more cruel and unrelenting member of your kind."

"And there are a great many of those," warned Odile. "Perhaps you would count me among them if you were not quite so well-disposed yourself...or so handsome."

Though I chuckled at that somewhat, Odile didn't. She simply resumed stripping glossy white meat from the bones of the lizard she consumed.

Yes—I understood very well that courtesy begot courtesy, and that a slave of the Nightlands did not often win his freedom by struggling against his shackles.

"Is it possible," I dared ask, attempting not to sound

39

as interested or scheming as I truly was, "for a slave to buy or otherwise earn his liberty here in the Nightlands?"

"Slaves are not permitted to keep their own coins, and those that do are liable to have a hand cut off for thieving from their mistress. That said…yes, certain mistresses have been known to release slaves of whom they are fond. Usually lovers who choose to remain with those mistresses. However, this is a rare occurrence. Perhaps one out of every five hundred slaves that pass through El'ryh are gifted with a mistress kind enough to consider such a boon. Even then, warrior-priest, you would not be equal to us in the eyes of Roserpine or the laws of the Nightlands. If you were ever caught without proof of your freedom it would be possible for you to find yourself re-enslaved."

"Are freedmen permitted to return to the surface, if they choose?"

"Yes, if they choose. But most, after so many years in the dark, choose to remain. As I said…if your mistress frees you out of affection, it would be a most ignoble crime of the spirit to reject that gesture and abandon her."

Perhaps she had a point. Weltyr may have understood that my initial vow, made under duress, was not an oath to which my soul was truly bound…but who knew how even one full year of slavery could change a man's heart? Especially if his mistress were particularly alluring, dangerously lovable. I would have to find a way to escape this city and my bonds as soon as I possibly could—every day I waited put me at greater risk of spending the rest of my days there, not a servant of Weltyr but a servant to any woman holding my deed.

"All right," announced Odile, standing, dusting off her hands, tossing the skewer into the nearby bin, "let's go to the Palace and hear what your appraisal is."

Then, chuckling, she looked me over once and added, "Good think you don't seem shy."

"What's that supposed to mean?"

The women, looking at each other and exchanging a high laugh, didn't answer.

4

VALERIA,
MATERNA OF ROSERPINE

THE PALACE OF Roserpine was, I discovered, that great central column that formed the heart of the cavernous city. It was the hub of all the traffic and by far the most visited landmark in all of El'ryh, with eight grand entrances around its vast circumference and scores of guards stationed at each of these broad doors.

At our chosen entrance, Odile and Indra barely paused once they explained they were there to have me appraised—I gathered Odile had brought more than a few slaves through the Palace in her lifetime, which was surely at least twice my own. It was so difficult to tell with elves: even ancient ones seemed fair as human maidens.

Even with Odile's casual word, however, I was stopped by a gilded lance.

Neither of the armored guards flanking the entrance so much as looked at me while the one to the right told my chaperones, "Unregistered slaves must surrender all weapons at the door. Owners may pick them up later."

Falling back on the heel of my boot with one hand now braced upon Strife's pommel, I looked between my impromptu mistresses. Odile, looking displeased, argued, "His greatest skill is that of combat! How can he demonstrate such a thing without his sword?"

"If his combat is worth any price at all, he'll be able to demonstrate his prowess in it unarmed should he be asked to. Pick it up once you've a price for him and you three are back outside the Palace."

Turning her gaze back upon me with a sigh, Odile put her hands on her hips. "You'll make this easy on us, won't you, warrior-priest? We'll get your sword back later, no problem. By Roserpine's infinite eyes do I swear it."

"Keep it in the scabbard," I told them grudgingly, unstrapping the sign of my oath and passing it over. Fancying that the sigil on my neck itched with the separation, I lay a reflexive hand upon it until spritely Indra sidled against me and ran her fingers through my hair.

"It's seldom we meet with such obedience in a new slave! I really think we should keep him, Odile—we haven't had to beat him yet, not once!"

"My mother taught me to beware slaves who are too obedient from the start," answered the speaking guard to our right, lifting her lance away and permitting my entry while her colleague accepted Strife. "Always said they were up to something."

I could not help but avert my eyes, if only to look toward Odile as she led us both into the shockingly bright marble halls of Roserpine's palace.

Despite the irritating and hopefully temporary loss of strife, my gaze was almost immediately soothed. What a sea of loveliness awaited my shocked eyes when we passed the gates! Everywhere I looked there loitered the most exquisite women: chatting, laughing, brusquely passing back and forth on business. I could barely spare a second to admire the marble walls or the gold-inlaid crimson rugs that spewed like tongues down the lengths of the corridors. Every pillar was carved with artfully envisioned legends, every ceiling decorated in rich frescoes that put those artworks of their aboveground cousins to shame.

Yet everywhere I looked, I found myself blind to such splendid decorations. I saw only those beauties whose mothers' mothers and their great-grandmothers once had these very works commissioned. So moved was I by this abundance of gentle features and feminine bodies that it surely showed on my face, for Indra and Odile laughed at me as they had when first we entered El'ryh's marketplace and I realized the nature of this feminine species.

"Look at him, Odile!"

"Already forgotten about his sword, by the sight of him." With a chuckle and a knowing glance toward my hips, Odile crooked a finger and said, "Well, warrior-priest, come along and be obedient. Soon enough we'll find you a mistress who doesn't mind your gawking."

On, then, my temporary owners led me through the halls of the Palace of Roserpine. In truth, these passageways and staircases and many, many doors were arranged in routes so convoluted that, had I not been distracted by the abundance of gorgeous elves around every turn, I still would have found it outrageously difficult to keep track of our path. It was a good thing I was not to stay there,

I thought to myself at the time. Had I been confined to the heart of the Palace, where at last we once more found ourselves barred by a pair of armed and armored durrow, escaping the tower would be such a grand order that escaping the city itself might thereafter seem almost a simple thing.

Other durrow with other recently captured men—most, I noted, in manacles, with one or two hooded in the fashion of hunting hawks—waited in line ahead of us for their turn at appraisal. Roughly every five to ten minutes, such a pair (or, more often, group, for it seemed durrow often worked in duo as did Indra and Odile) emerged from the smaller set of doors to the left of the vast hall, and the next in line would be permitted in through the main entry.

After meeting the fiery glance of a young man perhaps five years my junior—who, seeing my unmanacled hands, let his lip curl in disgust as though I were a traitor of the whole human race owing to my cooperation—I had my attention snagged by Odile.

"You have been very decent for us so far, warrior-priest, so I don't think I need to ask you to pay total respect to the Materna…but whatever manners you have shown us, you must be ten times as obedient and respectful to her."

"Important, is she?"

"There's no more important woman in the *world*," insisted bright-eyed Indra, whose growing anticipation of our audience with this Materna had, up until that moment, been attributed in my mind to my imagination. But it seemed I was not misreading her: her gentle eyes seemed to glow with the starlight of excitement, her hand earnestly clasping my arm. "The Materna is the very manifestation of Roserpine on Urde—she is our guide, our great mother."

"And she's the one who approves slaves for sale and sets starting prices for auction," said Odile in a tone far less awestruck, "so if you behave well and show her there's little training you require, we can fetch a pretty penny for you just as soon as you hit the auction house."

Though I thought to myself that it was a damn good thing for their wallets that I was putting on a show of such obedience, on seeing the next group exit a few minutes later I wondered if that luck didn't go both ways. Not all mistresses were kind: I watched a dwarf get a bolt from an electrical wand right in the back, and, grimacing, had to stop myself from crying out in protest against his treatment.

Had Strife still been upon my hip I might well stepped up to defend him—but then the guards turned to us and said, "You can go in now," and Odile gripped me by the arm to lead me in.

The audience chambers of the Materna were yet more extraordinary than the halls through which I'd been guided, yet somehow I saw even less of these black and white marble walls or the enchanted ceiling that, to my later surprise, I would find depicted the passage of the stars from my home aboveground.

Somehow, upon stepping through the doors and making our long way up the purple carpet to the Throne of Roserpine, my stubborn mind saw nothing but the Materna of the Nightlands: Valeria. There is something to the haughty beauty of an arrogant woman—a woman who not only knows she is beautiful but thrives on knowing that beauty and on demonstrating its superiority over other, lesser forms of loveliness—that has, I must admit, always appealed to me.

There is a difference between this and confidence: Branwen's air of wild self-possession, for instance, was different from the tranquil beauty of a certain kind-hearted nun at the Temple of Weltyr. Such a meek woman humbly accepted the burden of her charm but regarded it, always, as a generous gift (or sometimes curse) from God and therefore had a way of also bringing out the beauty in others around her.

But never had I seen a woman for whom beauty was utterly alienating. Valeria was truly that, and seemed in her heart to be as alien as the tentacled spirit-thieves. Even without pupils, her violet eyes seemed unfocused into space somewhere off to the right of her, as though she were listening to the voices of spirits that were not there.

I swore these luminescent orbs glowed like the great jewel upon her finger, a thick indigo gem surrounded by small stones black as Oppenhir's void. It rested at the edge of a jaw that, though delicate as the rest of her features, seemed firm and finely cut as the marble around her: two other slim fingers fit to her cheek to emphasize the delicate glory of her bone structure, the slight bored pout of her luscious lips. Through streams of bright white hair poked the tips of two elegant elf ears while, crawling betwixt her sumptuous breasts and embracing her waist, a glittering snake made as though to hide itself within those ivory locks.

I was so stunned by the sight of her that, though the durrow who had brought me were quick to kneel, my own genuflection was delayed. Odile's tough little fist in the back of my knee brought me quite literally back to earth, though I could not bow my head as they had—and when the Materna deigned to turn her focus toward me, I was glad I had not looked away, for I was permitted to see the moment when her bored eyes widened in the shock of a woman waking up.

"Presenting Odile Darkstar and Indra of the Nocturna Clan," announced the vizier, a tall and slender durrow whose hard features and short hair gave her a distinctly male air. While checking a looking glass that, owing to its magical properties, automatically updated its information based on whatever had been observed by the guards at the base of the tower, the vizier waved a free hand and explained, "Here for registration and appraisal."

Her sharp eyes having fought back her strange expression of surprise, the Materna leaned forward in her seat. "The slave is unbound," she observed, looking me over.

Odile kept her head lowered, her right fist over her heart. "Yes, Your Worship. He has proven the picture of obedience from the time we came upon him amid the bodies of the spirit-thieves."

The vizier's head lifted sharply from her looking glass, now seeing me for the first time. As the Materna studied me all the more closely, her right-hand woman asked, "Say again?"

"Yes, sister," enthused Indra, daring to steal a blushing glance of the Materna before directly addressing the vizier. "This paladin of Weltyr single-handedly emptied the spirit-thief den that has plagued our southern-bound travelers for nigh on a decade."

"Well," I began, meaning only to admit that my companions had been equally important in the defeat of the unholy spirit-thieves. Odile elbowed me sharply and, realizing how much such a claim must have increased my price, I fell silent for the sake of my mistresses.

"I dreamt of that den just last dark," marveled the Materna, who leaned forward in her seat with that be-gemmed hand poised against her neck. "Perhaps someday I'll learn to take Roserpine's dreams for sooth."

"How could one man kill all the spirt-thieves of that den?" Looking almost appalled—perhaps sure I was lying—the vizier lowered her looking glass and studied me closely she could stand to. "One of their number is mighty enough to annihilate most any human."

"And he was on the cusp of death when we found him," answered Odile unhesitatingly, looking not at the vizier she answered but at the Materna. "Oppenhir hung but a hair's breadth above his head before we arrived and gave him a few sips of elixir."

Now the Materna did speak up, her keen eyes never leaving me. "And what was a paladin of Weltyr doing down here in the darkness, in a pit of spirit-thieves?"

I realized now that I was being addressed directly. After a quick glance at Odile, I explained myself. "I was awarded with a mission on behalf of my god, who tasked me in the retrieval of a valuable relic. A holy scepter."

"And did you retrieve this relic?"

Head lowered, jaw tensed with frustration, I was nonetheless forced to admit, "The precious object slipped through my grasp when my traveling companions betrayed me. They permitted me to find and cull the spirit-thieves so they might claim the scepter with ease, then sell it off to the highest bidder as though it were little more than a dusty artifact or overpriced art object."

"You speak very eloquently for a warrior. Are you sure you're not a spy?"

"I speak as I was taught to speak by my teachers in the Temple of Weltyr. Paladins are not your average fighters, Your Excellency. My friend—ah, that is, my mistress here"—Odile glanced sidelong at me but soon corrected her gaze to the Materna—"calls me 'warrior-priest,' which is closer to the truth."

"And what are you really called? Among men, and the

women who no doubt scream your name at night?"

Taken aback, able to utter little more than a slight laugh for more than a second, at last I managed, "Rorke Burningsoul, Materna."

"Burningsoul," she repeated, her fingertips trailing unconsciously beneath the gold-inlaid halter of her gown. At last, blinking herself from a stupor, the glorious leader of Roserpine's army glanced between the durrow flanking me. "He certainly seems obedient enough. Have you seen him in action on the field?"

"Not in fighting, Your Worship," answered Odile with the ghost of a smirk.

"Undress for us, human." The Materna settled back in her seat, drawing the hem of her gown up a few inches to aid in the crossing of finely built legs. "We would see how you are shaped beneath that bloodstained tatter of a tunic before we decided on price."

"You heard her," said Odile for effect, though I was already in the process of removing my belt.

The truth is that any manner of military life quickly strips the shyness from a man, but it was surprisingly easy to be bold before all those watching women—servants and nobles of the royal court who studied me with glittering eyes, each of them inferior to agonizing Valeria only by comparison.

Some men would have had cause to be embarrassed to disrobe before such an audience, perhaps, but my physique was as much a point of pride for me as were my fighting skills. And, at any rate...the Materna was like a painting of Anroa, the love-goddess Weltyr crafted for Himself from the mingling of starlight with the darkness of the sky.

My heart was seized by the thrill of her unflinching gaze, and though all the durrow in the room were just as

51

bold as she, I was not half so moved by their attention as I was by hers.

First the tunic, then the trousers, then all the rest of the scraps of fabric I wore fell at my feet. A few pleased murmurs rose up from the durrow around, and as the vizier stiffly reminded her mistress, "This is a thief who has stolen the precious artifacts already alienated from us by the spirit-thieves, Your Grace," the Materna lifted her hand to bid silence.

The holy woman's eyes slid over my body and I could not mitigate the natural effect her scrutiny had upon my anatomy. I stared on into the heart of the closely-gazing woman, who then—to the surprise of the room, my comrades, and most of all me—sat back in her throne and announced to my mistresses after only a second more of contemplation, "You will give him to me."

With a sputter of displeasure and a look over at Indra, Odile dared say from her kneeling position, "But…Materna, Your Worship, we gave him some very expensive elixir to bring him back, and—"

"I will reimburse the cost for you."

"I was hoping to consider it an *investment*, Your Grace."

"Are you saying that I should pay you, Darkstar?" Odile's lips clamped shut and the high priestess went on, "Need I remind you that whatever goods you brought out of that den of spirit-thieves belong, by rights, to Roserpine? How many times, after all, have the spirit-thieves killed and emptied the coffers of hapless durrow merchants, simple travelers? I have no doubt you spent the morning pawning off any number of treasures that should have been brought here for assessment along with this new slave of yours."

"Well," stuttered Odile, "well—"

"Still you argue!"

"It's only—we promised his services to someone in the market. I would prefer not to break my word. Your Grace."

"Then you had ought not to make an oath that isn't guaranteed. Offering the services of unregistered slaves is a foolish mistake. Their appraisal might reveal them to be spies, sickly—worse, impotent, or celibate."

"We can assure you he is not celibate," answered Odile, the words a grumble under her breath.

"Then you have already been well-rewarded for your acquisition, taking an opportunity as you have to try the goods. Consider yourself lucky I am not inclined to punish you today, either for theft of precious artifacts or for consorting with an unregistered slave."

At last, with an irritated glance to me, Odile bit her lip and ducked her head, silencing herself.

The Materna folded her hands before her waist. "You're wiser than you act, Darkstar, I'll give you credit enough for that. Take the slave to be marked and have him delivered to my chambers."

Now it was my turn to speak above my station, given the approach of a few guards who did not seem inclined to give me a chance to dress again.

"Wait," I said, earning an arched brow from more than a few durrow but a look from the Materna that was anything but surprised. "My sword—Strife. It was checked at the door of the Palace. Surely you can no more take my blade from me than my arm, my heart."

"We take the arms and hearts of slaves quite often," warned the Materna, incidentally echoing the warning Odile had earlier for another part of my anatomy. "Do not tempt me to show you."

"If I cannot be in possession of Strife, you had might

as well end my life. The sword is my bond between myself and Lord Weltyr—surely you, Materna, appreciate the importance of these embodied gestures from the divine. You are a priestess of Roserpine; you know the gods are not kind to those who break their vows, even if forced by circumstance."

For a flash, the dark lids of her eyes fluttered down at the ring gleaming upon her finger. Then, with a sigh, she waved that same bejeweled hand. "Very well. Someone get the sword to my chambers, as well, with the usual locks and charms."

The vizier looked almost panicked by this and stepped forward, only at the last second remembering her station and leaving the near touch of the priestess's arm incomplete. "But Materna—"

"Not even the most powerful of Weltyr's paladins could slice a hair from the top of my head, Trystera—not when his sword has been charmed to leave his mistress unmolested. At any rate…if he is to serve me as a private guard, he will need a weapon of some kind or another. What will he do without one? Wrestle my would-be assassins to the ground and crush them to death with his bulk when he dies of whatever poison bolt or dagger they've been forced to expend on him? My word is final."

Then, like a mechanical device of dwarfish engineering switching off as quickly as it switched on, the Materna once more settled back into her seat with a last wave of her hand. "Darkstar, Nocturna, you are both dismissed. The next time you scavenge an emptied den of our enemies, remember this lesson."

The women exchanged a look—Odile annoyed, Indra sorrowful—and rose unsteadily to their feet. "We thank you for your audience, Your Grace," answered Odile, who was indeed far wiser than she pretended to be. With one last darting look into me, she turned away and led Indra off in the direction of the exit doors. While they departed, the guards already on their ways to me each took an arm and proceeded to drag me along.

Amazing that women a full head shorter than I was could still prove so strong. "What about my clothes?"

My question yielded a snort from one. "Don't flatter yourself, slave. If we cared to, even the lowest-born durrow woman could command all the unattended slaves in the capital to strip off their clothes. No one here is interested in you."

Almost no one, anyway. The Materna's interest had been clear enough, which was perhaps the only reason my chaperones saw fit to speak to me at all. I did not push my luck with them and decided it was best to stay quiet, much as obedience and respect had so far served me in avoiding the more brutal fates of slaves.

Not all aspects of a slave's harsh entry into the world of El'ryh were spared me, however. For some reason I had thought I would be taken directly to the Materna's chambers: instead I was brought into some strange box of engineering I assumed to be dwarven based on the tiles arrayed on its front wall. Each bore a numeric character and the chaperone who had spoken to me was also the same that touched one of these tiles. At the tap of her finger, the box in which we stood gave a jolt; then, amid the grinding of gears, the box steadily dropped us down the floors of the palace.

After a few seconds of this marvel of invention, the silver doors that had shut us in slid open again. I was guided out into a hallway bereft of windows but plentiful in doors. My pair of guides dragged me down the left, and by the step the hallway was ever more suffused by the oppressive heat of what I knew by instinct to be a forge.

Sure enough, the silent guard threw open the last door of the hall and I was amazed to find a wide array of enslaved men working within. A few—new, I sensed, and untrustworthy—had been quite literally chained to their stations and crafted their swords or spearheads with looks of bitter disdain for the task, as if willing these devices to turn upon the mistresses who would someday wield them.

A durrow overseer, whip in-hand, kept close eye on the workers (or at least pretended she had been for the benefit of her arriving comrades) while a berich dwarf forge-master—either the only free male I had yet to see, or simply a very high-ranking slave—strode up and down the ranks to inspect the work of the captive smiths.

"We've got a new one here," announced one of my guides, pushing me toward the berich who, as they had promised, spared not a second glance at my nude state. I had the sense that the gray dwarf saw more than his share of new registrations, though he did look surprised when the guard continued to him, "He's to bear the Materna's crest, so you'd better dig that iron out from wherever it's rusting."

"Rusting is right." The berich chuckled, stroking his wild white beard and studying my expression. "It's been ages since the Materna took on a slave of her own. Looks like this one's already owned, too."

His dark gaze hovered around the sigil of Weltyr upon my neck before he turned away, studying the irons arranged along the wall opposite. Each, I gathered, was the crest of a durrow house; whether it only accounted for those servants of Roserpine ranked highly enough to dwell in the Palace, or of every noble family in El'ryh, I could not say. I only know that my body tensed as the dwarf picked the iron from the farthest peg along the wall and, sure enough, blew dust off its surface before strolling to heat it in the fire.

Somehow, my situation had not been real to me until that moment. I glanced reflexively toward the door and suggested, "Surely, obedient as I've been, such a thing is unnecessary."

"Oh," said the berich dwarf, "it's necessary...trust me. You don't want to be caught in the city without a brand of one kind or another. Better to have one and get it over with than go without and get a whipping and re-sale the first time you set foot in public to fetch your mistress's lunch."

My throat tightened to see the progressive reddening of the metal, red as the swords being shaped all around me. A few of the more adapted—that is to say, crueler—slaves smirked, but most kept their eyes on their work, fully accustomed to blotting out the screams of new arrivals.

It was not the pain I feared quite so much as the thought of being marked for anyone or anything but Weltyr. Surely, as with the oath, my Lord would understand that I had no say in the matter, and would applaud the dignity I showed throughout the course of my ordeal—yet I could not help but recall my brief conversation with the Materna about the gods' treatments of oath-breakers, whether consenting or no.

The berich dwarf turned with the iron in his hand, and my animal instincts overruled my prior decision to win privilege by obedience. With a kick in the knee of one durrow, I wrenched my grip from the other and scanned the room for an available weapon. Options were plentiful in that hot smithy, but I was not quick enough—or rather, the elves were quicker.

While the one whose knee had bent beneath my kick

recovered, her sister-in-arms, cursing, drew a bullwhip from her belt.

In a practiced motion its singular tongue licked the air, then swept across my back. I swore, myself, but did not stop my effort to retrieve the flail mounted upon the wall nearby. Soon that cruel whip wound itself around my throat and squeezed like the python that slithered about the Materna's shoulders. I gagged, caught in its grip, and had no choice but turn in an effort to yank it from its wielder's hand.

Alas, this was not to be. Her partner, having recovered, caught me by the wrist and swept my feet from under me. When I went down she followed, her slight elfin frame nonetheless packed with muscles and more than adequately equipped to subdue even the most powerful male warriors. I caught myself with one hand upon the hard stone floor while she maintained her grip of the other and climbed astride me as though I were a horse. Playing my part, I bucked and twisted and attempted with all my might to free myself of either her powerful thighs or the lash strangling around my neck. All to no avail.

Meanwhile, the berich watched.

"I understand how it is you're feeling at this very moment. We all do." I detected, from the corner of my eye and the rhythms of the clanging of iron on anvils, that few if any of the laboring slaves had stopped to watch my humiliation. My ability to see any of this was vanquished when the durrow upon my back pushed my head down to the ground and bent my hand into the crevice of my spine. I would have hissed with the pain of it had I air enough to do so, but darkness swiftly encroached from all sides of my vision. The berich stood over me, a dwarf towering over a human, yet one too old and beaten-down by his own servitude to enjoy it.

"You're just making it harder for yourself, though. Come on, lad…stay still, this'll only hurt a moment. It'll be over and you'll be up right quick."

Had I been able to produce any sounds, the hiss of pain to have my arm so manipulated would have quickly devolved into a kind of snarl. The hot iron of the brand seared into the flesh upon my shoulder, its pressure enough that it seemed my whole upper arm burst into flames. Sweat sprang upon my head and to save the pain of the iron bouncing around as a consequence of struggle I instead fell still, teeth clenched, head swimming with the deprivation of both blood and oxygen.

"There you are," said the berich, lifting the brand away. "Not so bad."

"Whatever happened to your obedience?" The durrow on my back jeered and, releasing the pressure against my head, unwound the whip from around my neck. I gasped for air when I could and once more struggled, succeeding in bucking her from her mount upon me. As she cried out and barely caught herself while fallng to the floor, her companion looked on her with obvious derision for her weakness.

"Get yourself up, come on." I wasn't sure if she spoke to me or her companion while winding her whip back up to sling upon her hip again. Bending down and catching me by the forearm, she dragged me upright and told her embarrassed partner, "Let's get him to the Materna's quarters and be done with him before he gets any other ideas in his head."

Though I glanced back toward the berich on my way out of the smithy, he had already turned to replace the iron upon its mounted peg.

5

A SLAVE'S LOT

MY SHOULDER THROBBED all the way to the Materna's chambers. Thankfully, it was not long before we reached them. We once again took those doors of dwarven engineering and now, as it shifted up in an altogether less alarming sensation, the guard who seemed to do the brunt of the speaking told me, "You'll have your sword soon enough, but don't feel too clever. By the time you have it, it'll have been branded just like you—marked with a sigil to keep it from being turned against not just your mistress but any durrow."

"Am I not meant to protect my mistress? What if some would-be assassin were a durrow just like yourselves?"

"No woman of our ilk would be so foolish," answered the other guard. "Roserpine would have her head on a platter."

"And so would the whole city. The Materna is much too valuable and admired to be assailed."

I glanced between them, unwilling to prove supplicant in manner, treating them as casually as I treated Odile and Indra. "I've heard it said the durrow are insidious schemers, each with infinite designs for wealth and power."

"And humans aren't?" The senior guard shook her head and, at the opening of the doors, led me into a bright, wisp lantern-lit hall where more guards milled about and looked upon us now with curiosity.

"Humans are such chauvinist beings…this one's for the Materna," said the guard, pushing me toward the door at the end of the reception hall lightly furnished with sofas and a few merry purple exotic plants to further brighten the décor. "One of you may wish to keep an eye on him until she retires to her apartments for the dark."

"As you command," answered the guard who caught me up by the unmarred shoulder without sparing the least glance down at my unclothed state. "Come on, slave. We've been given word of your arrival…let's make it easy."

The door at the hall's end was opened for us and the guard led me into the chambers beyond.

My first thought, oddly, was of the Temple of Weltyr. Indeed, a great nostalgia washed over me to step into the Materna's chambers that first time, for I was reminded at once of the rectory where the Light God's priests lived and entertained visitors. I never saw much of those chambers, but the impression made by their bright, airy windows and exquisite antique furnishings never left. They felt almost a kind of blueprint for the chambers of the Materna, whose front sitting room with its lounges and low round chairs bore the same brightness even if it did not possess the same, somewhat ascetic sense of old-fashioned furniture.

"These are your mistress's quarters," the durrow who had led me in told me while I looked around in awe. Following my gaze to the window overlooking the dark city of El'ryh, she went on to say, "It is situated in one of the highest floors of the Palace. Attempting to climb your way down is extremely ill-advised."

"I wouldn't dream of it," I said absently. If she heard me, she did not acknowledge me and went on with a certain degree of automation.

"You will serve as the Materna's personal attendant. Much will be expected of you. If we decide that we can trust you, you will be responsible for bringing her meals and running errands for her. That is only if we decide we can trust you, and if Her Holiness deigns to utilize you for more tasks than the caretaking of her person. Until such time as she informs you otherwise, you are to regard everyone you meet—even other slaves—as your superiors. Disobedience will be met with harsh measures, and any effort to damage the property or person of a durrow is considered a capital offense. Again, this includes slaves. Is that clear to you, human?"

"Very clear," I answered, tearing my gaze from the striking view of the city and glancing, as I turned my head, down the nearby hall and into the interior of my mistress's bed chambers. These were largely blocked from view by a folding screen expanded between the doorway and a broad bed wide enough to fit five people, let alone two. "What about matters such as my own food? Bathing? Where do I sleep?"

"Your mistress will decide all of that."

Here was to hoping she would be generous. From the look in Valeria's eyes when we met, she was not necessarily poised to be cruel. I held onto hope that I had read her properly. My shoulder still burning slightly from the new-laid brand, I only further thought to inquire, "All this casual talk of assassins—is this a common occurrence for the Materna? I was under the impression that she is untouchably holy."

"She is…but you should know, holy man, that there are many in this world who have no respect for the divine, and even less respect for the fleshly beings that consort therewith. We have had recurrent problems as of late with spirit-thieves, and even a few individuals employed by them, routinely disrupting the peace of our tower and our city as a whole."

I laughed lightly. Upon the sharpening of her features, I assured her, "That won't be a problem anymore—I slew them in their nearby den before I was brought here."

Though the guard seemed poised to respond—maybe even ready to express admiration for the act—we were interrupted by the opening of the chamber door.

"Arrogance is not a survival tactic that serves in the Nightlands," said the Materna, cutting a surprising-ly delicate figure in the doorway where she stood. "Do not think, just because you have annihilated a brood of spirit-thieves, that more are not aware and ready to seek revenge."

The guard had dropped to her knee swiftly on the Materna's entrance—but, much as I delayed when given formal audience with her, now I was frozen by her beauty much as by the wrapped sword cradled in her arms. She may as well have held my very heart.

"Strife," I said, as unconsciously and eagerly as I might name a friend from whom I'd been separated.

To my surprise, the Materna slightly smiled.

"You may go, Fiora. I will instruct my slave myself…

my needs are very particular."

"As you wish, Your Holiness."

Bowing once more as she straightened up, the guard made herself scarce with but the briefest of glances my way. When she exited, the Materna locked the door's bolt after her. Then, still cradling my sword as though it were an infant, Valeria studied me.

"You are a very strange slave," she said. "Very informal. Most newly registered slaves can hardly look us in the eyes when stripped naked."

"Not as though I chose to be divested of my clothes, is it, Materna? Nor of my blade."

With a slight smirk, the priestess turned away to lay my wrapped blade upon a nearby table. "I suppose not. Some clothes should have been delivered for you—a fresh tunic and breeches. More will be acquired soon. Once you have overseen my bath, you may wash yourself as well—I'm sure you're quite exhausted from your journey here."

The idea of this exquisite elf bathing her smooth, dusky skin before me inspired a certain very natural twinge of lust. I resisted the urge to politely fold my hands before myself and instead crossed my arms. "Less exhausted than I am curious."

Her great green snake poking its head from beneath her long white locks, the Materna lifted a hand and stroked the elongated barrel of its body without looking down at either it or me. "I suppose you do not know much about our people…we are a very secretive race for a great many reasons, even among the elves. At least you will have much time for finding answers."

"It's a good thing, because you're right—I do have many questions. I was told you will decide where I eat and sleep."

"You will eat with me," she said, gliding past me while wearing the affect of a woman entranced by things mere mortals could not see. "There will be instances when my duties require solitude or separation from you; but by and large, you are expected to serve as my footman as much as my bodyguard."

Footman to a beautiful durrow! Now, that didn't sound so bad when compared to the lot of those men tasked with slaving over endless swords, shields, spearheads. I drew myself upright, assuring her, "It would be my honor to assist you in your day to—that is, bloom to—why, what are you laughing for?"

She had been laughing, at any rate, her teeth bright white pearls against the red cast of her lips. At my question—my demand—her laugh took a darker tone. "What an impudent question…you will learn how to speak to your betters in time, Burningsoul. Until then, I'd might as well humor you. I'm laughing at you, of course…your routine."

I scoffed lightly, hands folding before me. "What routine is that, Materna?"

"You know what I mean. This willingness to serve. This paladin of Weltyr, rolling over and showing the immediate obedience of a dog. You think you're so much smarter than us…don't you suppose other men have tried such things before, attempting to gain our trust to earn freedom—or, at the very least, privilege enough to steal their freedom back? It doesn't work. It never works. You saw this city. How long did it take you to traverse it? Most of the bloom, I would wager…and it's dark now. Not the finest time to be moving through the Nightlands. Not as a human, anyway."

"Surely you understand what I did to the spirit-thieves within their own den of sin."

"And surely you understand that we, as the keepers of slaves, have long-since developed all number of systems and social constructs to keep those slaves. In other words…your compliance until now has been very much appreciated, but ultimately unnecessary and far more duplicitous than showing your frustration would have been."

"I'm not frustrated. I owe my life to Odile and Indra; if anything, I'm frustrated that I won't be able to fulfill the favor I promised them when I was in their service."

"Oho, I see…this use they had for you in the city was attractive, was she?"

After considering the wadjita in my mind's eye, (and the expectant face of the durrow before me prepared for another lie), I decided it was best to confess the truth. "I did find her curiously beautiful, I admit, but it's more a point of honor. They offered my services as part of a deal on some heathen relic they were melting down; without me, they'll be cheated."

"I see. Well"—the Materna sighed and slunk into her bedroom, shrugging the great python from her slim shoulders and draping it over the branch of a tree growing, to my surprise, along with a great many other aboveground plants in a little garden to one corner of the room—"those two are trouble, but they have done me many favors in the past…your presence is but one of them."

While this high priestess looked tenderly upon her snake as he settled on the branch where she'd set him, I had the opportunity to examine her profile as close as I dared. In the dwarvish lighting and soft tapestries of the room, Valeria's gray-blue face was kissed by tinges of pink—a soft blush to her face, a hint of color upon the tip of her nose. It echoed the color of her mouth, those lips contorted in thought; my heart sped in my chest to behold her until, as she turned to face me, I averted my eyes to the snake.

"I will look into loaning you back to them for a few hours somebloom soon. But I must confess, Burning-soul…what talents could a paladin of Weltyr have in such matters?"

Another twinge of lust overcame me. Though I strove to keep my mind and manner professional, my undressed state made it difficult to hide my interest in her. "Plenty of talents, Materna. I have never been a man who was above learning what it is that women want."

"My, so it would seem…you are very charming."

Though she, like her sisters, had no pupils I could perceive, I nonetheless could tell her eyes were linked fully with mine. That phantom's gaze seemed as though to see my very soul, and now knowing her as I do I wonder if perhaps she could. As she looked into me, her hands lifted to the clasp of her cloak.

The fabric slipped from her shoulders and left her in the clinging priestess garb that was like nothing any holywoman of Weltyr ever would have dreamed of wearing. It was barely a loincloth and a bodice, in truth; without her cloak, her body's every curve was lain bare before me, dark against the white fabric of her vestments. These were thin, and the play of light upon them was such that even my insensitive human eyes could make out the distinct patterns of what lay beneath.

And all that lay beneath was soon lain bare for my eye, as the Materna of the durrow reached behind her neck to unclasp the hook of her gown. With barely more than a serpentine wiggle, the scraps of gilded white cloth fell to the floor at her feet. My new mistress stared me down through those haunting, steady eyes: my own whipped wildly from the pouring mane of thick white hair that half-obscured her sumptuous breasts; to the small cotton thicket of pubic hair, slight but barely visible upon the tip of her pubic mound; to the broad curves of her thighs and rear compared against the tight bow of her waist.

"Let your new mistress decide how talented you are in the matters of pleasing a woman…then I will make my final decision as to whether or not you are worth lending out."

Unable to help myself but cure the empty palms that itched to fill with her, I closed the distance to the sound of her brief gasp of erotic surprise. Her hands had lifted instinctively and I caught her wrists. Valeria gazed into me, her eyelids fluttering, her lips parted to show the tips of white teeth against the red petals of her mouth. Beyond that, a shimmering field of tongue.

She relaxed in my grip. I released her arms to pick her up by the waist, provoking a better-natured gasp followed by a quite astonished laugh. "Oh, my! You really *are* an impudent one…I knew I'd like you, oh—"

Her body was so warm and soft and fragrant to hold over my shoulder that I hated the thought of relinquishing my grip on her. All the same, I threw her down upon the thick spread of her bed, a well-pillowed love nest that splayed from the wall in a semi-circular shape and took up easily a quarter of the room. She gasped, landing upon her back, her thighs spreading to reveal a glint of excitement at the apex between.

"You're certainly making the most of your slavery, it would seem." One hand lifted to hide her mouth, her fingers poised against those ruby lips. The other hand ran over her breast, toying with a dusky nipple to increase the ache that I let her see without compunction. Anyway, it was impossible to avoid: I knelt between her splayed legs and ran my hands over her thighs, an act that left me uncovered for her gaze's greater pleasure. At the sight of me, I swear her legs spread wider into my touch.

"Weltyr guides us down strange byways in life—it is not up to us to argue, Materna, but to throw ourselves into our circumstances and see what comes of them."

My caressing thumb brushed over her gently parted lower lips, her delta's slight blossom of arousal revealing a pink valley amid the lovely ashen mounds. She gasped softly, shifting slightly as my thumb's tickling grew more deliberate but no less teasing, trailing up and down the button of her greatest pleasure.

"I feel much the same of Roserpine…my Lady warned me of you, Burningsoul, oh, in a dream just three darks ago…"

The feminine nectar of her lust poured in earnest now: I parted her labia to admire the tight, oozing source. The tip of my finger teased against this soft, warm burrow and she shuddered, her voice rising in a moan as I lowered my head to work my tongue over her center in time with my digit's probing. Each time I pushed in just a little deeper, and each time I ached all the more; I resisted relieving it, devoted solely to the pleasure of the exquisite woman before me. It was more than having something to prove—it was a desire from the start to give her pleasure. A real desire to learn about her, caress her, make love to her, that I felt from that very first time.

"I didn't know it was you, of course…I won't say more about it because—oh, because you're not one of Roserpine's chosen—but oh, oh! Oh, slave!"

She gasped, the hands that had been roving over her breasts reaching up to grip one of the many pillows behind her head. I lapped at her all the faster, my middle finger plunging into her soaking altar of Roserpine as deeply as my manhood ached to stab her. Ah, to be so lucky as that finger!

No matter. Just that touch rendered her momentarily speechless, her keening high and loud as she dripped hot feminine lust around my tongue and finger. "Slave, slave, yes, yes, you're very good…good boy, Burningsoul, oh, goddess, what a good slave…I was worried, you know—worried, worried the dream meant something else—worried that you wouldn't work out…by Roserpine's eyes, oh, I had no idea paladins were so versed in the bodies of women—yes, yes—"

While I suckled and teased and toyed with her, Valeria's body tightened sharply around my fast-working finger. It curled up in pursuit of the spot that I had found, in most women, to be as reliably sensitive as the more traditionally utilized external nerve. As many did, she cried out in shock to have it touched; unlike many, however, she did not protest that it was too intense for her. No—she only moaned with relief, with joy, crying out, "Oh, yes! Burningsoul, yes, faster, faster, oh—oh—"

Her widespread legs tensed on either side of me, her back arching into an exquisite obsidian bridge. I watched her as best I could, my eyes flickering toward the rest of her while my tongue increased its pace as fast as possible. Soon she clenched and released a veritable flood of desire, her body rocked by a moan that rattled through my brain and surely made it to the ears of the guards outside her quarters.

"Oh, yes! Yes, oh, Burningsoul…"

Her hands ran wildly over her body as she climaxed, her violent shuddering easing to something less rattling when I lifted my head and removed my hand from her glistening valley. She moaned, biting her lip and running those hands up into her streams of white hair. I realized after a belated seconds that she was staring at my cock, straining miserable and stiff against my stomach like a dog leaping up for table scraps.

"Maybe you do serve me happily after all," she said, her voice still breathy with shortened breath and low hums of pleasure. "That was very good, slave…oh, very good. Wretched thing—aren't you embarrassed that you've gotten so hard?"

"It's only the natural thing, Materna…you are the most beautiful woman I have ever bedded, to say the very least."

"Aha! You are a wretch, oh, my…you think your sweet words will be rewarded, do you? Think that if you're very good I'll let you satisfy yourself in this very same temple you just pleasured? Such a reward is only for the finest of slaves…the bulls we breed with, the concubines we favor. Your cock's satisfaction means nothing to me, nor will it to any of the women I permit to use you."

"It is more than enough to lay hands on you and suffer the aching weight of this desire."

"Is it?"

Watching me carefully, the Materna sat up and rolled to the edge of her bed. A shelf there was displayed with, I quickly realized, a number of differently-sized phalluses of a number of different materials. The ivory one she chose was nearly my size (only nearly) and almost as white as the pubic hairs near which its head lay when she settled back in the pillows again. In time I would have a chance to look around and consider that the whips and straps and other instruments of cruelty lining her chamber's walls were not intended for punishment, but pleasure. For now I was simply as surprised as I was aroused by the sight of my gorgeous mistress with this ivory dildo in her hand.

"So it's enough to watch me fuck myself with this, is it?"

Valeria moaned low to ease the cool tip of its head up and down her shimmering slit, working it slowly against herself before sliding it down toward the tight entrance of her body. "You don't mind that no matter how badly you want it, I'm not going to let you take me just yet?"

"Of course, it drives me mad...but the decision is yours, Materna. I am your slave."

"How your cock jumps to admit it! Oh...Burning-soul, oh—"

The ivory head had begun to push just inside her body, and I ached to be so lucky but strove not to show it in my face. Her wicked grin expanded. "Yes, that's right, watch me...oh, I like the thought of you watching me. Will you be able to stand to watch me use other slaves before your eyes?"

She was a tease to say the least, and the wildest woman I had ever known. Not even Branwen—like most aboveground elves, was very liberal with her so-called love—had been so avidly filthy-minded of tongue and daring of deed. As Valeria slowly worked the dildo into the confines of her wet valley, I dared to slide a hand along the smooth flesh of her shin and caress even high as the middle of her inner thigh—the only torture I dared offer her in revenge.

"If I am your slave, Madame, then I am to be your property. No more worthy of release or attention than this toy here. If you choose to use other slaves before me, I can stop you no more than I could stop you from lending me out to please your friends and comrades."

"Good, good...oh, good...I like a slave who genuinely has a good attitude. I like a slave who likes to watch...oh, you do like to watch, don't you?"

Her bare foot slid into my lap, the arch working against my aching member while she slid the toy rapidly in and out of her tight-gripping body. I groaned, buck my hips against her foot while I pressed down upon her ankle as much as I dared. "I would watch you do anything, Materna, lovely as you are…it is no imposition to watch you tease yourself with your toys, or a slave, or some lovely durrow companion of yours."

"You sound so hopeful…oh, and this prick of yours is so hard! Keep it hard…oh, yes, I want to see it straining for me while I'm bathed. I want to see how desperately it wants me…oh, Burningsoul, oh, this thing is so hard, so deliciously hard…I wonder if you can take me half this hard…"

"Odile and Indra can both attest that if you like it as rough as I think you do, Materna, then I am the best-suited slave for your needs."

Honey dripped from her swollen nethers and around the circumference of the rapidly working tool. All the while my mistress watched me, her lips parted, her toes sliding up and down the shaft of my engorged member. "Maybe that's true…maybe that's true…go on, slave. Use the toy on your mistress…make it quick, it's nearly time for my bath…"

Eager to please as ever, I took up the flat stand of the dildo and eagerly continued the task she had begun. At once she gasped, moaning even more wildly than before, her head thrashing back and forth upon the pillows while I pleasured her like I wished I could have with my own body. All the same, it was a sheer delight to see her bursting with pleasure, more uninhibited than any female I had ever encountered. It wasn't very long before she was climaxing again, her body bucking up against the toy in my hand as she soon enough would against me.

"Yes, yes! Oh, slave…slave, you'll fit right in. Praise Roserpine! She sends to me the sweetest dreams…oh, dear. Don't let me fall asleep, Burningsoul. Give me but a moment to recover, and then we'll to the baths…hold me, though, would you?"

6

THE PALACE BATHS

TRUE TO HER word, my mistress delivered no release to me once she had found her own. After making use of my embrace for a few moments, she simply pushed me away, told me to fetch her clothes, then sprang up to dress while commanding me into my own. Once I had put the tunic on she reached beneath, clasping me in the cool grip of her soft palm for a few long tugs while she stared into my suddenly glazing eyes.

"Remember what I commanded, Burningsoul...I want you to stay nice and hard."

Somehow, I didn't think that would be an issue. Leaving her cloak for someone else to pick up, the Materna led the way in her skimpy priestess garb without the least thought to her nearly nude state. I suppose, since I had just been led around literally naked, I ought not to have been shocked by that—but, owing to my raising, it was somehow more surprising to see a woman so thoughtlessly audacious in her dress. Now I realize how different it was there in the Nightlands, where durrow lived without the subjugating gaze of men always upon them: lusting, scheming.

Not to say slaves did not lust—but if a slave stared too long, or in the wrong ways, he was really looking, at best, at a public beating in the middle of the street. Maybe even execution, depending on who it was. Things were different there, and durrow women did not dress, as aboveground women did, to defend themselves from predators.

This differentiation between the sexes to which I was so used was perhaps why I was somehow shocked to find the baths were technically mixed sex, at least in terms of servants. Men and women both served durrow mistresses amid the thick mist of hot spring saunas carved out in one of the sub-levels of Roserpine's Palace. A few delicate elves of Branwen's kind, lovely maidens from aboveground who had at some point in their nearly eternal lives been taken belowground to live and serve among their cousins, stood chatting in a corner, free of obligations and able to gossip.

Each one of them was completely nude.

I would quickly find that this was true of all the slaves working in the baths. Every once in a while I would glimpse, on the way back to the Materna's private bathing chamber, another dressed guard in a similarly torturous position to myself, but over all the baths were a place of perfect security and civil business discourse to most durrow living in the central tower of the city.

There was precious little need of guards, therefore, unless someone was exceptionally paranoid—whether they had a reason to be, or not.

Upon seeing my mistress, the elfin trio cried out in simultaneous delight and hurried over to greet her. Each bowed with the grace of a dancer, then set about quickly stripping her of her clothes, speaking rapidly in the language of the aboveground elves. The blonde one peered coyly over at me, grinning a bit when she happened to look down to my beltline. By the time her eyes had flickered back to the Materna, my mistress had been divested of her clothes by the silver-haired elf and was now being led by the brown-haired one to the far pair of doors to which I followed.

"You speak many languages, Materna."

"I have been a long time living, slave...a long time, spent learning many things."

While the blonde elf threw open the doors and the silver-haired one caught up to us, the brunette led the way inside and gestured to the warm crystal pool pre-arranged with a tray of oils, stones, sponges, creams, and all manner of other things about which I had absolutely no conception. Valeria stepped into the water while ignoring the offered hand of the brunette, saying to me, "With so many slaves from so many different regions aboveground, it is important to be able to communicate with as many as possible. You would be advised to learn a few more languages, too. If only to communicate with your fellow slaves."

As Valeria slid into the bath, her body extending beneath the waves of the almost perfectly clear water, the brunette elf hurried to capture her hair. Gathering the thick mane of lovely white locks in her hands, the slender slave produced a sort of crown atop Valeria's head to keep her hair free of water. Then, looking pleased to do it, she accepted a palmful of oil from her blonde fellow and rubbed the substance into Valeria's neck. The Materna sighed and moaned, her head sagging forward just so while her arms outspread along the edge of the pool.

"Besides...if ever we have foreign visitors—rare, though it has been known to happen—I may offer your services to one of them, and a shared language makes it seem like less of a chore."

Though the elves attending to my mistress were quite a sensual show to behold, the rich, deep glow of the ring upon her finger caught my eye. She had worn it in bed, too, and I nodded at it.

"You never take it off," I commented, an observation more than a question. Valeria laughed lightly, a dry chuckle, and studied my neck with those phantom eyes that already haunted me.

"And you never take that tattoo off. Each one means the same thing...service to the divine. It is my duty to bear Roserpine's ring and endure her many burdensome gifts."

"Burdensome gifts?"

"You cannot imagine what it is like to know as much as I do, Son of the Wanderer. Trust me when I say that some things are better left unseen in this life...there are times I envy, oh, everyone who is not me. Not as aware as I am."

She had lifted her ringed hand to contemplate the stone upon it. Now her fingertips drifted toward her mouth, resting there, worrying. She glanced from me, the tips of her nails lightly scoring her kissable lower lip.

Ah! *Would* she let me kiss her? My mouth itched as had my hands—never had I been so taken with a woman on first sight. It was something about her, a heartfelt innocence and deep conviction behind her every uttered thought, that made Valeria appeal to me.

It made me see that there was no show here, not in the ways of conjurers or heretics. There was real fear in her tense face, and not just owing to the string of assassins about which I'd been warned. I pitied her.

"I've heard it said that Roserpine is the goddess of madness."

Even without visible pupils, I was growing used enough to the movement of durrow eyes that I saw her look back over at me. "Perhaps to your kind, to worshipers of Weltyr, her teachings can only seem as madness. To us—to me—she is the goddess of liberation."

"You don't look very liberated to me."

Laughing, shifting, Valeria sighed low as the elf rubbing her neck and shoulders gradually expanded her range to include the sumptuous breasts whose nipples barely peeked above the water. "What part of my existence does not seem liberated to you, exactly, slave?"

"Why, all of it. You live like a bird in a cage on a stand, your high apartment up in this tower. You're clearly powerful, yet you're so frightened by threats of violence and fears of overthrow that you need someone like me. By Weltyr, you don't even bathe yourself—you let others do it for you." I lifted my brows, leaving it at, "Not a very independent existence at all, Materna. Not very liberated in my estimate."

"While it is apt to say I am a slave to Roserpine, Burningsoul, I must point out that I mean a different kind of liberation. A spiritual liberation by way of knowledge, which can only lead to true physical liberation at the end of one's relationship with the mortal plane. Until then, all the money in the world, all the respect, all the obligation, is just another way to hide true knowledge. To soften it. But for me it is not softened. There are no illusions remaining. I have many years of life ahead of me, and I will have to live them all in the perfect, crisp awareness of what it truly is to exist in this physical realm."

"This is why the Church of Weltyr is structured in the way it is, Materna…no one, human or elf or any other, should be burdened with the direct knowledge of any facet of the godhead. The linear mind is fragile…most of us cannot perceive the sorts of things to which you refer for a reason."

"Yet you seem to speak as though you understand."

"I am fully devoted to Weltyr, and there are many sacred mysteries that are revealed for the illumination of such paladins as myself. We are not encouraged to meditate much on the matters of the gods, but we do learn some important things. That mind and body together coordinate in the production of the soul, which is more still than either for it also encompasses all of eternity. I would imagine that, if one were to be too aware of one's soul, it would be very preoccupying indeed."

"To say the least."

"This sort of thing is why I enjoy a good battle," I told her, turning my tone out of my serious concern for her mental health as a result of the cult of Roserpine and into a more merry, easy-going attitude. "Such matters of the body keep a man occupied with earthly things, with the issue of preserving his life."

"Sex does the same thing," advised the durrow priestess, sighing while the elf massaging her bosoms kissed the tip of her dark ear.

How much I had to say on that matter! Sadly, our flirtations would have to wait. The door to the chamber opened and a shadow fell across the floor. I turned at the first hint of it and found, still clad in her dark robes, the vizier called Trystera.

Coolly, the vizier assessed me, then said to her queen,

"I see you are already adapting the new slave to his lot in life."

"Naturally," answered Valeria. "These things must be seen to from the very first day...no one likes it when a slave is confused as to his purpose."

"Yes, well, that's just it—one of the guards at the place gate said Odile and Indra had some...choice things to say about you, and sent this note..."

From the dark sleeve of her robe, Trystera drew a hastily rolled scroll upon which I could easily imagine Odile angrily scribbling...or, perhaps more likely, angrily dictating to scribbling Indra. The vizier cleared her throat, then read, *"Dear Marm, With all due respect we humbly request use of your slave as soon as possible."*

While she read, the other elves took up the task of massaging what parts of the Materna could not be reached by the brunette. As this most eager elf toyed sensually with the sighing priestess's nipples, the blonde waded into the water with her and slid between her splayed legs to massage the flesh of her powerful thighs. Up and up and up, those lovely elfin hands raised, and I ached to see just how high their caresses drew. While the silver-haired elf massaged her hands and arms, the vizier went on as though nothing at all were happening. Clearly, I was experiencing a little culture shock.

"Our honor is dependent on this, and while we appreciate that you have been very lenient to us despite our mistakes, we humbly request a boon for just one day so as to make good on our pre-arranged bargain. You know our district, Odile & Indra."

"Oh...those two..." Moaning openly now, her legs splaying as the blonde nymph of a slave-girl sensually massaged the labia beneath that little tuft of white, the Materna tilted her ear into the lick of the brunette elf's sweet pink tongue between lingering kisses. "They really are very audacious...but yes, I have just heard something of the same from Burningsoul. He does seem like a man of honor, I will give him that."

Ignoring that comment as effortlessly as she ignored the penetrations of the slave girl's fingers into Valeria's swollen pussy, Trystera rolled the note back up and stowed it away again. "That may be so, but you can't think it wise to send your slave away so soon into his training; nor when you are so in need of protection."

"Oh...oh, ah, yes, well—it will be a fine opportunity to see if he comes back. Yes, yes, yes, oh, by Roserpine... but he *will* be back. Just look at that hard prick under that tunic, Trystera, oh, my! He does love to see me satisfied."

With a light sniff and a sidelong glance at me, the vizier looked forward again and asked, "Are you looking for a guard, Madame, or a bull out to stud?"

"If I were in search of the latter, who better than the slave responsible for my life...at any rate, it was not my choice. It was Roserpine's." Contemplating the ring again, then sighing as the sweet blonde slave suckled gently upon a nipple, the priestess leaned her head upon the purplish stone at the back of the pool. "I have faith, then, that things will fall into place with accordance of her will. Send a message back assuring our little sisters that they may borrow my slave's services two blooms hence."

"Very good, Madame."

"You know, Trystera—" The vizier, who had been turning away, paused and looked back at the watchful high priestess. The Materna lifted her head again to assess her inferior, all while writhing and shuddering beneath the multiplicity of caresses sliding across her flesh's every inch.

"I have made many invitations to you over the years of your employment in my service...there's no call for you to be jealous."

"Your overtures have been flattering, but I assure you, I am not jealous. Enjoy the dark, Your Majesty."

Nodding, then turning with a pair of eyes that stared through me as though I were a chair or a rock, the vizier strode out again. The door rattled slightly upon its hinge. If she wasn't jealous, then she was mad about something. And maybe it did seem absurd or even crass to accuse someone of envying a slave...but then I turned back to see Valeria, her head back to accept the swirling tongue and suckling kisses of the elf-girls upon her mouth, and I had to wonder if there was a being on Urde who would not have envied me in that alarmingly erotic second.

The fever with which she filled me was immense. Even the most sensual and erotic of surface women, whether human or elf or dwarf or any other, was a prude by the standards of decadent El'ryh. At least, by the standards of decadent Valeria. The sensual priestess of hedonism cracked open her eyes to make sure I watched her exchange a kiss with one of her girl-toys. The elves switched positions and the lovely silver-haired creature proved herself quite possibly not an elf so much as some kind of naiad or merfolk—really just a cousin of the land-dwelling elf as much as were durrow. Her silver hair floated out behind her like lunar seaweed while she dove beneath the waters to explore her mistress's swollen labia and sensitive bud of pleasure with her tongue.

I held my breath, waiting for her to come up for air. Long before she did, I was gasping with the burning of my lungs. Hands moved all over Valeria; hands and lips and tongues, and soon entire bodies. All three elf servants (for who could really be a slave when they were so willing?) now joined her in the water. The two land-dwelling elves ground against her. Massaging and suckling her breast, kissing her mouth, holding her thighs apart for the benefit of their water-breathing sister, the elf-girls laughed and exchanged affection with one another in between lavishing sensual caresses upon the body of their mistress.

Then, suddenly, I remembered myself when Valeria once more locked eyes with me. For an aching handful of minutes I seemed to transcend spacetime while watching the caresses of these sylphs upon a goddess, and when I returned back to earth it was only at that goddess's behest. "Remove your clothes, slave," she commanded, then saying something to the blonde one. The elf nodded, expressing something back in that sonorous language of her people. Valeria waved her hand and, elegantly smiling, the golden-haired elf who had been so taken with me left her comrades and swam through the water to me.

"I want to see how that great rod of yours works in the service of your talents before I decide whether I should bother letting you use it on me. Lira here has volunteered her services...she's had her eye on you since we arrived."

"I noticed...hello, Lira." As she rested her arms upon my side of the pool, I reached down and offered her my hand. A sweet dimple appearing in the edge of her cheek, Lira accepted my invitation and permitted me to let her pull her out of the water. While the naked elf girl stumbled to her feet, I cradled her svelte body in my arms and kissed her soft mouth. It was perfect and silken, yet it seemed to me as though Valeria's would be infinitely more soft when at last I had the chance to taste its love.

But, though Lira was not the Valeria I desired, I had no qualms with her. Her body already shimmered with desire when I caressed her backside, fondled her thigh, grazed her sensitive labia. She moaned, then again all the more when she saw I was looking not at her but Valeria. For her part, the Materna was now being fingered by the silver-haired slave that had emerged from the waters to kiss her. The subservient elf-girl in my arms moaned and lifted her leg, hooking her thigh against my hip to offer her pussy to me. I teased around it, tickling the tip of her most frayed nerve and letting her suffer the same proximity of my straining manhood that so pained me.

"This serving girl of yours seems to take great delight in being ignored."

"They love being reduced to sex toys...we put all the happy, pretty sluts in the baths. Especially when they don't speak the common tongue well...you wouldn't believe how slaves gossip...oh, yes, but I love a gossipy slave...any excuse for a whipping, you know, Rorke...oh, just wait, just wait..."

Never had the thought of punishment made me so throb with desire; yet her promise of a whipping did just that. Perhaps it was the obvious relish she held for the idea. Perhaps it was the thought of submitting to a woman who I could have physically overpowered in a battle but who was versed in magic and social graces far in excess of anything I had until then been acquainted with. Whatever the cause, I was swept by a ferocious storm of lust. Soon I eased the elf-girl upon her back and made sure Valeria watched while I slid my member into a tight little hole that was absolutely drenched with excitement. Lovely Lira almost screamed at once, gasping sharply, her body's glovelike embrace second to none.

Except, I knew, for Valeria. It was her embrace I wanted most of all; so, to earn that embrace, I watched Valeria's pleasure while I impaled her blonde maid again and again. The elf-girl moaned and trembled, bracing herself down against the rocks and offering her hips up to me. I rose upon my knees and rode hard into her, using her body at the pace her eagerly bucking hips determined. Soon I caught her by the pelvis and her slender legs wrapped around my waist, linking tight around me to deepen the plunge of a blade meant for Valeria.

"Oh, Burningsoul…she certainly likes it, doesn't she…"

Valeria's fingertips, after trailing over her collarbone, soon glided down her body. She spread her labia and the eager silver-haired elf dived below the water, her tongue lashing back to work in tandem with her fingers. She moaned into the lascivious kisses of the brunette elf who was subjected to the occasional tweaked nipple or slap on the backside and seemed to love every last second of it. At the sight of such casual wickedness from Valeria, I redoubled my pace within the sacred halls of the pretty blonde elf. My partner was soaking wet and desperately tight; Valeria moaned with pleasure to see it all, commanding me, "Harder, slave—ride her harder. Give it to her rough, very rough. That's what she's begging for…oh, that's right, look at her, look at how much she likes it…"

It wasn't very many more strokes before Lira reached a noisy climax that made her body ripple rapidly around me. She cried out in that musical language again, touching herself and pawing at me. When I ignored her, she moaned and shuddered with such violent pleasure it was like a second orgasm.

"You had ought to let me give you a firsthand demonstration, Materna."

Chuckling, moaning, still evidently not having peaked to an orgasm yet, the Materna looked closely at me and said, "Take it out of her and bathe yourself, then put on your clothes."

Such a command was unbelievably cruel at such a moment. After all the rapturous torment of watching her pleasure, I was very close to relief. She knew it. She waited for me to complain or to argue. Instead, head dizzy, I forced myself out of the whining elf who pawed and kissed at my chest. After applying a tender kiss to the corner of her mouth, and let Valeria watch me bathe and dress. She moaned at the sight of my shining cock bobbing in the air and I willed her to have mercy, to invite me into her side of the pool and into her; but the wicked priestess of Roserpine only smiled, waiting, and eventually I dressed in silence.

By the time I was back in clothes that felt like they ought to have combusted on contact with my body, blonde Lira had long-since dove back in the pool and rejoined the orgy on the other side. I watched, amazed at the completely altered set of mores I beheld in this, yes, very sexually liberated society of women. Perhaps it was only the manners of the decadent upper society of the durrow; I could not yet discern, for my mistress was obviously permitted many luxuries and privileges that no other Nightland elf could have been said to enjoy. One of those luxuries was forcing me to watch, full to bursting, as the three elf serving girls caressed and massaged and licked and kissed and penetrated her to a slow-building but ultimately quite explosive orgasm. Her long cry of ecstasy rattled my bones; I shuddered, desiring her more than ever as a consequence of her exhibition and cruelty.

After coming out of her climactic stupor, the priestess moaned and stretched and said something in that elfin tongue. The slaves all laughed, then chattered happily as birds while they set about letting down their mistress's hair to be washed. Our mistress's hair, I supposed then.

Yes—somehow, she was my mistress, too. And that

seemed like a very odd sort of privilege in and of itself, though I could not then fully imagine why. I only knew that my body desired her as ferociously as the plains cat its hoofed prey. She did not address me further during the baths; she only studied me absently, as though I were a work of art, while the women with whom she cryptically conversed washed her body, then anointed her with oils and creams.

When she at last stood outside of the bath her body gleamed with attention and euphoric vigor, each plump inch of her flesh flushed and looking warm to the touch. My prick still throbbed. Valeria smiled at it while she crossed to me in the fresh gown she had been given for the dark. Although the cut was somehow more modest, the dress in itself was literally translucent across her stomach and so short that I glimpsed a hint of the shining flesh hidden within the shadows of her thighs. Agonized, on the verge of explosion, I bowed to her and felt as though I may well have passed out if I bent any lower.

"You have been extremely patient, slave," observed my mistress, who accepted the sheer negligee that enclosed her little dress. While her hair was combed down her back by one pair of hands while another pair of hands braided a few sections of it, she reached forward beneath the tunic that was my only defense aside from my boots. Into my breeches this cruel hand slipped to grab hold of my struggling manhood. While I choked back a gasp, she moaned to pull on me, her fingers trailing up to the head that she then teased with the tips of her cruel, cold fingernails.

"Let's retire for the night. You've proved yourself so reliable so far that I think I might even let you watch over me as I sleep this very night…what a big, hard cock my new slave has! Oh"—she moaned, her eyes boring passionately into mine as she released me and turned toward the door—"maybe I do need a bull...one's line is important to consider after a time, after all..."

I had never given much thought to siring children, truth be told, but the mere idea of filling Valeria with my seed and seeing her belly grow with children sharpened the thrill I felt in looking upon her. By the time of our departure, the baths were full of a great deal more lovely durrow—all of whom hastened out of the way or bowed from where they stood on Valeria's passage. My mistress ignored them all, her negligee rippling behind her like the train of a gown.

Transit up the tower in that box felt the task of centuries. Valeria leaned against the back wall, her eyelids heavy as she assessed me steadily the whole way up.

"Will you tell me," I chose to ask her to ease my own tension, my own overwhelming desire to crush her body beneath the lust of mine, "about this dream that heralded my coming?"

She smiled somewhat thinly at me upon such a question. "You are very inquisitive, Paladin of Weltyr. It reminds me...I do not think I have heard a servant of Weltyr speak on the matter of Roserpine with the respect you showed during our discussion in the baths."

"All gods are due respect and veneration, Materna... because all gods are, like the world itself, lesser emanations of Weltyr."

Valeria laughed, her teeth a white flash behind her lips. "You do have interesting ideas, slave."

"As do you, Materna. I may not agree with your interpretation of the godhead, but the passion with which you believe is admirable to me."

"It is my entire life," she said, studying her ring once more as the box stopped its rumbling and its doors slid open. The guards in the hall stood at attention while we emerged, Valeria leading the way to her chambers' doors without looking. "Roserpine has given me more than sufficient proof that she shepherds my existence. And now that you are here, slave, that is only more evidence."

Within the privacy of her chambers, the priestess sighed deeply and slid her negligee from her shoulders. It fell to the floor and I held my breath at the round nates peeking from beneath the hem of her ultra-short gown. While she made for her bedroom, she waved a hand at me and said, "I'll have a mug of mead from the bar over there."

Somehow, though we were the only two in her apartment, I didn't fully realize she spoke to me. Perhaps it was because I was not then used to getting women drinks as though I were a barkeep; but, as rattled as I was by this intense desire for her, it was a pleasure to fetch a mug and fill it with the contents of a bottle I de-corked. The honey wine's sweet elderflower aroma made my mouth water, but I resisted stealing a sip without invitation. That was a classic nursery tale error when a man was brought to faerieland, and the Nightlands seemed most certainly to be that.

When I found her in the bedroom she stood again amid the plants of her private garden, focused on the snake that happily scented the air from the branch where it lay. I pressed the mug into her hands, watching the serpent with her. "I'm not sure I've seen a python so closely. It is beautiful, I must admit."

"He is a good-natured snake. Prefers resting to anything else in the world...I don't know that I really blame him. What else is there to do? We keep the tower too clean for mice to long dwell here, so he's not much of a hunter."

"You just think that's the case…maybe he's doing a better job than you perceive he is."

Valeria laughed at that, knocking back a swig of the mug while trailing away from me and once more reclining in her bed. I held my breath from the distance of the garden, my eyes lured constantly to the flashes of shimmering flesh between her sometimes parting thighs.

"That could be so," she said, spreading her legs more willfully when she noticed the direction of my gaze. "So, Son of the Wanderer, how is it that you've found yourself in the Nightlands as the slave of durrow?"

"I descended into the earth with three companions— an old man, an elf, and a dwarf—in pursuit of the Scepter of Weltyr. The spirit-thieves had long since plundered it and perverted it for their own cryptic rituals, and I was tasked with retrieving it. The Temple granted me a small sum of gold with which I assembled a team. Hildolfr— the old man—was our guide, the elf called Branwen did the task of taming and calming the wild creatures we encountered, and Grimalkin…mostly got into arguments with me."

"And where are these companions of yours now?"

"Wherever the Scepter is, assuming they have not already pawned it off to whomever put them to the task of swiping it from under my nose. They betrayed me in the den of the spirit-thieves; all three of them, even Branwen, turned against me."

I could not help the great pain—the insult—that showed in my face at the thought. Valeria smirked lightly, her fingertips trailing back and forth over the swell of one lovely breast. "I take it you were laying siege to this Branwen elf during your travels together?"

"Aye, and much too blinded by her charms to wonder at the aims of her seduction. All three were hoping that

I might agree to sell the relic for a higher price to another bidder. They found me disagreeable and attacked me, leaving me for dead and taking the relic with them."

"Small wonder you are so accepting of your new lot in life as a slave to the durrow…at least we are forthright about our tendencies."

"It does seem as if subterfuge is something of a pastime here…yet, it's not all fun and games with you, Materna. I see it in your eyes—hear it in your voice when you speak of this dream that showed me to you."

"Dreams," she corrected, "plural."

Though I arched my brow at that, she set her mug aside and, to my aching thrill, drew the hem of her night dress up the curve of her waist. "Undress, slave."

After setting down Strife, I hurried to obey her. My prick stung to feel her eyes, my body on full display for her lascivious interest while she sat naked at the head of the bed. She moaned to simply see me, her hands running over her body and back up to her neck. "What a splendid example of manhood you are, Burningsoul…pleasing to behold, every last inch of you. I thought about forcing you to wait longer to put that rod of yours to use, but after seeing the fucking you gave Lira, why, I'm aching for attention."

"Surely not near as much as I am, Madame. Never in all my days have I seen a woman so uninhibited. So sensual. Powerful."

Her hands had swept back down over her breasts and one now fell between her legs to slowly massage the glistening labia still swollen by the attention of the elf-girls. I held my breath, dizzy with lust while she idly teased herself and looked upon me. "And I have never been so eager to use a new slave…oh, my. Now that I think of it, it's been much too long since I've had a man in me. I usually just have a girlfriend or other slave help me with a toy, or do it myself…but I'd much rather have you for a toy, Burningsoul. Come here"—the splay of her legs widened and she spread herself with the tips of her fingers—"put that mouth to use again."

Even before I touched her, she dripped with arousal: but from the moment my lips made contact with her most aching nerve, her body was rocked with moans that echoed through every room of her apartment. Encouraged from that fiery start, I took up the task of keeping the petals of her body parted wide so as to allow my tongue to batter against her smallest center of lust. She moaned, trembling instantly, her nails tickling over my scalp and down the back of my neck as she held my head against the musky incense of her temple. I nuzzled her, my tongue lashing up into that sacred delta, throbbing with a desperate desire at the simple taste.

I ignored the organ throbbing against my stomach. There was no way for me to satisfy myself when this cruel woman splayed before me, moaning, panting, gripping my hair and scratching at my back. "Oh, Burningsoul! Why, slave, oh, there has never been a new acquisition of finer quality in all this tower…oh, yes, yes, oh, that talented tongue—your fingers, give me your—ah!"

My middle and ring finger slid into the tight embrace of her cunt and she twitched around me, her channel fluttering much as her legs tightened about my wrist. I had lifted my head and now looked boldly into her face while my fingers pumped in and out, rapidly beating against the spongy surface of her dripping cavern. She squeezed around me, gasping, thrusting, rocking her hips up against my palm and toying with the purplish peaks of her nipples. While I lowered my head to suckle one, my tongue battering its stiff surface as my fingers battered the inner chamber of her cunt, Valeria ran her fingers down my back and lightly scratched at my flesh.

"Burningsoul, oh, sweet fuck! By Roserpine's love, you are as I dreamed you—oh, so talented, oh, Son of the Wanderer! Is that great prick of yours aching for me?"

"The agony you provoke in my body is greater than that of any woman I have ever known. I would be a slave to you for all eternity to have your body just once, now. How you flow!" I marveled down at her, at the sight of my soaked fingers sliding so easily in and out of her body. "It seems you are denying yourself as much as you are denying me."

"Oh, oh—I get everything I want, slave...if I don't deny myself sometimes, who will? Oh, Burningsoul, permit me to taste your mouth—"

My breath hitched and I lifted my head, working my fingers in and out of her until she pushed my hand away. At the same time, she kissed me, the soft silken pillows of her lips enfolding mine, her spry tongue weaving in against my aching own. I groaned at the sweetness of her breath, at the hot and fast stimulus of her gifted tongue; so enchanted was I that I hardly realized she had eased against my shoulders until I was on my back, at which point she straddled my hips with her shimmering apex suspended a mere handful of inches above my pulsing desire.

"What sweet kisses, slave...what a fine weapon. No wonder Odile and Indra were so reluctant to give you up—amazing this Branwen fool spurned you as she did."

"Amazing, perhaps, but I'm relieved now to know that she did...I would rather be tormented by you than satisfied by her, Materna."

Chuckling, the priestess lowered until the dripping lips of her body barely brushed the head of my pleasure. I felt on the verge of swallowing my tongue, so unbearable was the ecstasy she inflicted upon me. The smooth river between her lips flowed while she worked herself upon me, moaning to grind her aching nerve along the shaft of my member. I twitched with lust every time she permitted me to approach the moment of penetration, but never to truly enjoy it; she might take my tool in her gentle hand and ease it against her demanding burrow, but I was never permitted more than a quarter of an inch's probing within before she shifted me away and used me to stimulate her nerves elsewhere. I groaned, aching, my skull feverish with the need for release.

"How fun you are to tease, slave…I think I'll do this and worse to you all the time. You certainly did enjoy watching me in the baths, didn't you…"

"What man wouldn't? Fain would I see you caressed and kissed by any lovely slave-girl, your fellow durrow, even another man. You are so eager, so receptive and commanding of attention, that I find myself absolutely enraptured by your body."

Chuckling, the Materna looked down at my member already gleaming with the perfumes of her body. With a glance back up at my face, she commanded, "You are not to release until I give you explicit permission. If you do, I will whip you senseless."

The idea was far more thrilling than it was deterring, but all the same I nodded and managed to dryly produce the words, "As you wish, Materna."

At last—after what seemed like a century of teasing, though it had only been an hour and a half at the absolute most—the wicked elf lowered herself upon the staff of my passion.

Her eyes widened along with mine, that smooth forehead of hers furrowing at the lift of her white brows.

"Slave! Oh, Burningsoul—Roserpine herself never had a lover half so sweet, never—"

Moaning, completely exposed to my eye while her hands lifted into her hair, Valeria took to riding me with a sensual series of all-body ripples that seemed to my eye reminiscent of her snake's motion. Her satin lining was, as I had expected, the softest and best-fitting I had ever felt—not to mention, the wettest. She had worked herself into such a frenzy of sensual excitement that she had flooded with lust, and as her body squeezed and tugged at me, she grew only wetter by the second. Her eyelids fluttered as she pounded herself down upon me, moaning high, bracing back against my legs while her hips slammed down, arched up, slammed down again.

"Oh, yes! Oh, slave—oh, I've dreamt of this, this big, hard blade, those lovely hands. Touch me, slave—touch me, Burningsoul—"

From her first command, my hands had been leaping to her firm thighs. While I squeezed and stroked them, reaching back to massage her rear, her moans only increased in low appreciation. "Paladin! Oh, nevermore accept that title—you were born to be a stud for me, sweet slave, yes, yes, ah, I think I may well use you for my breeding—oh! Oh…"

The tip of my finger had grazed against the puckered hole between those grabbable cheeks, and as her noise of surprise transformed into another moan of desire, I teased and brushed it whenever I could. Each time, her body twitched wildly around me; each time, her thrusts down upon me grew faster, harder. The wet slap of her flesh against mine filled the room like the scent of our mingled arousal; when at last she descended upon me and drew a long kiss from my mouth, I felt her body's tension and knew just what it meant.

Accordingly, I slid my arms around her hips and held her down against my lap, my feet bracing into the bed to permit the eager thrusts of my pelvis up to hers. She gasped, moaned, whined with pleasure while I pounded into her. Her mouth open, she looked down at the tool working between us as though in astonishment. Then, soon, she exploded in an almost shocked scream that rattled the room and was accompanied by the quaking grips of her desperate body. Moaning, hammering herself home upon me, she tangled her fingers in her hair and cried, "Fair Roserpine, oh, thank you—thank you, thank you for sending him to me—"

It was no small wonder that Roserpine was the goddess of madness when her high priestess was so seemingly mad herself. At the very least, emotional, and so closely connected with her goddess that she would not have permitted a little thing like the presence of other people stand between her and divine conversation. Even once her orgasm faded, Valeria seemed incapable of the least hint of self-consciousness. She dismounted me with a shuddering moan, then lay upon her back with her legs outspread and her arms open to me.

"Give me a taste of your power, Burningsoul…let me feel all the hard male energy that will be put to better use than warfare now."

With a groan of desire, I pushed myself up and knelt between her legs. Her body's embrace was the sweetest thing I had felt in my life and I eagerly made myself at home in it again, taking her by the hips only to be swallowed by pleasure when she bucked up to meet me. I plunged into her to the hilt, then took her with all the vigor I had shown for delicate Lira.

Valeria seemed infinitely less fragile than the slave. Teeth gritted, her voice rising in a scream of feminine pleasure, Valeria clutched the pillow behind her head and braced her feet against the mattress to keep her hips easily accessible to me.

"Oh, goddess—a bull, indeed, yes, a real stud. Oh, yes, yes, use that big thing, please your mistress—ah, Burningsoul! I'll have a few girlfriends up soon and show them your prowess, won't you love to take me in front of my lesser sisters of Roserpine..."

"I'll please you in private or in company, Madame... the unrestrained mores of your culture are—ah, I admit, quite exciting prospects."

"Some slaves are very offended...I prefer ones who embrace their new lot in life—and you're showing such splendid attitude, oh, yes, yes you are...what a good slave, what a good toy—"

Gripping her all the tighter, I bent down to boldly take a kiss from her mouth without invitation. She gasped, but her eyes fluttered shut and her breath exuded from her honeyed lungs in a soft moan. Our tongues intermingled, caressing one another while I pounded as deep within her as I dared to fit without harming her holy anatomy.

I was exhausted after the many ordeals on my travels, still preoccupied with licking the psychological wounds of betrayal at the hands of my former companions, my shoulder yet burned with the same sigil of slavery that instilled in me the urgency to escape the Nightlands and return aboveground—and still, with Valeria in my arms, her body around mine, our tongues intertwined, I had no troubles or obligations at all.

There was nothing outside of that bed—nothing outside of our two bodies, our two spirits intensely connected in ways I could then hardly comprehend. I only knew that from first sight I had fallen into dangerous obsession with the woman who was to be my mistress; and I only knew how grateful I was that she felt the same, for else then I would have been the one driven to madness.

"Oh, Burningsoul—yes, yes, deeper, bruise me with it, yes—"

"You do love it rough, don't you, Materna...you're quite a woman to want to be taken by your own slave, used in such a way as this..."

"Oh—oh—oh, your pleasure is incidental, mongrel— if I didn't want to feel your hot seed drip out of me, I would consider denying you an climax just for that remark. But oh, yes, that's what I want...I want that strong life of yours deep inside me, slave. Ah, goddess! I'll loan you out to friends and let you inseminate them, I love this tool of yours so much...yes, yes, oh, yes, I want to see it struggling with lust and dripping with seed all the time—"

"Materna! Oh, sweet Valeria, are you really sure you want it inside?"

"Yes! Yes! I need it—breed with me, fill me with all your sticky human cum. I want it, I need it, release inside me, oh, yes, yes—"

Well! I never have been a man inclined to argue with a woman. Now wasn't the time to start. Pushing her leg up, gripping it around the thigh flesh of her thigh, I impaled myself as deep and fast as I could apply myself to the task. She looked almost shocked, then threw back her head in an animal moan: the thought of the guards outside able to so clearly hear all the pleasure I provided her gave me an extra ebb of lust, but it was the sound of her elegant voice so crudely demanding, "Yes, slave, yes! Defile your mistress's pussy, oh, go on—yes, very well, use my cunt as no other man would dare," that pushed me over the edge.

I groaned, bending down to catch another kiss from her while she screamed my name in an orgasm of her own; we came together, pulses of pleasure surging out of my body and into hers to fill her to the brim with the result of her steady campaign of sexual torture. I groaned into her mouth, the rapid, rhythmic embraces of her pleasure so unbearably sweet that it seemed my climax would never end. When it did, it was gradual; a slow and steady coming back to earth from which she likewise seemed to take her time. Her breast still rose and fell with rapid panting. As she recovered, she stared at me in absolute amazement. Her hand lifted to run along my face.

She looked at my mouth.

I moved to kiss her.

She came to her senses and leaned casually away before I could make contact.

"What a fine acquisition you are," she said to me, plucking her cup of mead from the stand beside the table and raising it to her lips for a sip. "Your quarters are one room over. Because I am sure you are simply exhausted after your journey here, and a rested slave is worth more to me than one who falls asleep on his feet, why don't you sleep the dark through and worry about seeing to me only starting tomorrow."

"Sure you don't need me around to keep intruders out of your bedroom?"

"I'm not so helpless that I need your supervision at all times, Burningsoul…and, at any rate, I don't want you to be confused. You are my slave, my property—not a lover, or a friend, or anything like that."

"You had more than a few loving words for me just now."

"Affection and love are two different things. Rest well, paladin."

She set the cup aside and turned over, waving a dismissive hand through the air. The lights dimmed by some magical means and I repressed an amused scoff. Well! I'd heard of men who were this way with women, but I'd never known such mannerisms to work both ways.

Yet, whatever she said—I knew it was calculated. Without a doubt, her sensual astonishment and in-the-moment enjoyment had been genuine. Whatever dreams she had been given of me, she seemed to believe that they really were of me. Owing to her position as Materna and the strict standards enforced for women of her position when it came to interactions with slaves, she could not openly share any passionate feeling she may have had.

And I could not believe that, after all that happened between us that first night, she did not feel the same passion for me that I found myself feeling for her.

DREAMS OF DESTINY

TO SAY I had not slept so well in years would have been an understatement. I was well-worn from the day and, as this sleep in a bed was my first since departing on my journey to reclaim the Scepter, all elements of reality conspired to tranquilize me as soon as my head hit the pillow. Weltyr blessed me with a thick, dreamless sleep that night—a great black void that saw me come back to consciousness the next bloom with my first thought one of disorientation, and my second thought one of thrill for Valeria.

It was one thing to make love to such a woman, but another thing to awaken after making love to such a woman—better still, to awaken and still have her in one's future. Perhaps it was the religious scholar in me, but I was never much interested in casual one-time flings as a matter of course. When I liked a woman, I wanted her until she didn't want me…and just the thought that Valeria would surely want me again made my blood boil with anticipation through my every vein. Memories of her sweet mouth and fiery embrace made me ache to relive everything we had experienced. I lay in bed like a boy on a holiday, anticipating the moment when I would have no choice but to start time back into motion.

Sadly, the life of a bureaucrat's manservant did not make for a very sexually exciting experience a great deal of the time. If I did not have Valeria to look upon during the long hours of my duties, I would have torn my hair out—but she was a relief to me from the second she slunk out of her bedroom, a new immodest scrap of a priestess robe barely covering her breasts and shielding the apex of her thighs. The lucky snake slithered over her arms, its white belly contrasting brightly against her onyx flesh.

"How your eyes move over me, Burningsoul…be careful how you look upon me in front of others. Your impudence is amusing in private, but cannot be permitted in mixed company. Don't worry…as pleasing as you were to me last dark, I expect the manner in which I intend to use you this dark will be even more satisfying to us both."

It was some consolation for having to stand around in her throne room, dying of boredom for the next eight hours of my life…only some. The truth is that I have never been interested in formal events and find myself far closer to Weltyr in battle than in Mass. This meant that I had little interest in the political and formal lives of the durrow. Valeria's primary duty was not, I would find, the assessment and appraisal of new slaves; in fact, that was but a small subset of the concerns that were brought before her. She seemed an arbitrator of conflicts, a giver of advice, on oracular seer to whom durrow brought their hopes for better careers or pressing relationship dilemmas. I gathered gradually, as I had only lightly gleaned the day before, that Valeria was by far and away acknowledged to be the wisest woman in El'ryh.

If she was as painfully bored by the mundanities of her work as I was, she did not show it. She only gazed dreamily into the middle-distance whenever she was not being directly addressed, and sometimes when she was. Her hand would trail over her breast or along the body of her snake, and I often swore I could feel her body pulsing with the desire to turn her head and look upon me. So far as I was aware, she always resisted, and in fact went so far as to never look at me at all. The amount of effort— and constant thought of my presence—this must have required was flattery in and of itself. No, she did not look at me at all, yet while we were separated by a fair distance in a room full of other people, the tension of sex rose between us like the thunder of a chorus. I was feverish with desire for her by the time the day was done, but to my great annoyance there was still more to be accomplished.

Dinner—well, I supposed I could appreciate that. Having been given only a small ration of food that morning, I was famished, and much to my relief my mistress explained to me that favored slaves in the tower ate nearly as well as any durrow with a few exceptions. A banquet had been arranged in a dining hall to which Valeria led me, and after instructing me to find us both food, she went to recline in a longue that was quickly surrounded by a bevy of lovely hangers-on.

Perhaps this might have been an opportunity to get to know my fellow slaves—an ideal chance to begin sowing the seeds for how I would find my way out. Yet, seeing Valeria surrounded by her lovely comrades, I thought of the baths the previous day and decided I couldn't miss a moment of my mistress's moving about the world. I hurried back with plates burdened with food, my own meal far lower priority than the one I held for her. My first instinct was to hand it over; then I remembered my present rank and knelt beside the edge of the longue, resting my own plate upon the stone floor while balancing hers upon my knee. I fed her a handful of sweet purple berries while she smiled in approval, the brushes of her lips across my fingertips like the searing of dragon's breath.

"Isn't he a fine specimen," she enthused to her favorite courtiers once she swallowed her mouthful of sweet fruit. "It's not often one acquires a slave with so much enthusiasm right from the start…their pride usually keeps them from admitting what a pleasant time they're having, at least for the first few months."

"He does seem very eager to please," agreed a long-limbed durrow with an aristocratic nose and a high white up-do constructed of elaborate curls that were pinned in place with a spider-shaped gem. "Wherever did you find him?"

My mistress repeated the story of Indra and Odile while I contemplated her other three friends. All the durrow I had seen were beautiful, without exception—it was the way with elves, I had found, that their faces and features were like unearthly caricatures of human ideals—but there was not one among them who was half so searingly gorgeous to my eye as Valeria. The natural pout of her contemplative lips, the hint of ruby in her cheek that echoed her lovely tongue, the sharp and watchful scrutiny of bright eyes to indicate a mind always at work—I longed to kiss her even there, in front of that mixed company about which she'd warned me. Instead I settled for pushing nuts into her waiting mouth. She chewed, and watched me, and once she swallowed she said, "And he has many more uses than just killing spirit-thieves."

"Oh," gasped a durrow with short hair sculpted back upon her head, "have you already used him? What's he like?"

"Very fine indeed. I thought perhaps you lot should come over tomorrow—he has one last bit of business that I have agreed Odile and Indra are owed, and thereafter he'll be fully mine. You all must come try him out, oh, there hasn't been a concubine so fine in El'ryh for decades."

"How exciting," enthused a curly-haired, somewhat curvy woman who sat at the priestess's feet and had gazed at me with open appreciation for most of the conversation. "I'm glad to know he serves like he looks."

"Just wait…even better than he looks. It's so refreshing to encounter a man who can handle both kinds of swords. Thank you, slave"—she took the plate from my knee before I could offer her a bite of fig—"go on, eat your food."

I did, anticipating I would need a great deal of energy that evening. And, as you may imagine, I was right to show prudence. Once we had returned to her chambers, my mistress called on me again; this time, her kisses were more liberal, her affections all the more hotly whispered. And whatever she said, her attention and enjoyment of me never felt like the excitement of an owner for a new piece of property. In fact, that second night of my employ with the durrow of Roserpine, she told me when I came to a panting finish, "You may rest with me for a time, if you would care to…but sleep lightly if you fall asleep. I would hate to think of you failing in your intended purpose because my leisure uses for you sap your strength."

"Far from it, Madame…making love to you is a tonic for the nerves, yes, but an expedient for my strength. You make a man feel like an ox."

Chuckling, patting my chest with a condescension that somehow reminded me she was a century older—maybe more—my eternally youthful lover stretched out along her side of the bed and drew the red sheets up over her waist. "I should think you need no help feeling such a way as that, Burningsoul…I do look forward to hearing my friends' reports."

"How strange to hear you say such a thing! Aboveground women's heads would spin to hear a female of any race express such a thought."

"Well? You liked seeing me in the baths, didn't you? Why should I feel any differently?"

"I suppose that's a fair enough point. But—I suppose I'm also something of an exception to the rule. Most men are far more jealous than I."

"Because they have too much pride…a little pride is a healthy thing in a man, but that transformation into arrogance—now that's the danger."

"That's just what I like about you," I answered teasingly. "I took one look at you and saw an arrogance that was just palpable."

"Arrogant! I'm no such thing, slave."

"All your kind are. It's all right—I find it appealing when a woman knows her worth, since so many of the nuns and nurses who raised us were humble. Docile. I'm quite shocked at how thrilled I find myself by this world of yours, Materna, but I cannot help what I feel."

"At least you're open to it. Some slaves never adapt to society and must be consigned to roles toiling in smithing or masonry or some other tedious, body-destroying task." She propped her cheek upon her fist and turned to look at me. "Are you still planning to try to escape, I wonder?"

I had spent the whole day so awash with thoughts of her body that it had hardly crossed my mind. The greedy mortal in me craved to take advantage of my time among the durrow as a kind of vacation; the warrior-priest in the service of Weltyr and his own immortal soul, however, could no more lie to her than could it be satisfied with a slave's lot in life. "I would be a fool if I did not dream of freedom, Materna," I decided to tell her carefully, studying the beautiful arcs of a face I soon caressed. "But after only one full bloom of your company I find myself dreaming of freedom with you, rather than freedom from you."

Her lips parted, shock mingling with the splendor of new love while she searched my face for the truth of this statement. I meant it. She smiled slightly, then turned her body and face away from me to stare off toward her lush green garden. "Tell me of your home, Burningsoul. Whence do you hail? Your features are most refined— you must be of noble blood."

"If I am, I have no way of knowing. I was brought to my Order as an orphan, no parents to be named. A small babe, not yet a year old. My childhood home was Weltyr's monastery on the outskirts of Skythorn, and when I came of age I was sent to work the city's central Temple. I was only formally accepted into the Order as a paladin this past year; in order to be confirmed in the role, I must carry out the duty assigned to me while adhering to the principles of Weltyr's service."

"The retrieval of that Scepter, you mean."

"Yes, Madame."

"What does it do, precisely?"

"The Scepter? I can't say for certain it *does* anything; only that it is a relic said to have been crafted by Weltyr himself, a symbol of the just rule of the First King who oversaw the realms of men. It was lost eventually, and in its duty to re-collect and restore all the relics of Weltyr, the Temple took a recent interest in rumors of it having fallen into the hands of the spirit-thieves. Turns out the rumors were accurate…and my colleagues didn't feel they were paid enough."

"No matter," said Valeria to me, reaching back for my arm to draw it around her body. I smiled to myself while folding her in my arm, embracing her to me while she stared out across her plants. "Tell me more about what it's like to be aboveground."

"I couldn't even begin to know what to say…it's blue. Very blue, because of the sky. Have you ever been aboveground?"

"Goodness, no. I've never left the city."

"Never! Never left the city—never seen the sky, save for that simulacrum on the ceiling of your throne room!"

I had asked her if she had been aboveground in a casual way, not ever expecting it possible for the answer to be 'no.' To hear her say such a thing utterly shocked me. A being her age, never having seen the sky with her own two eyes? I could hardly comprehend it—then, as swiftly as the shock had come upon me, swifter still came the realization that perhaps this was the way with most durrow. Humans spent entire lifetimes barely leaving their provinces. Why should even long-lived elves be all that different?

All the same, I was amazed, and I told her with the great, unthinking delight of one lover for another, "How thrilled I would be to show you the sky! Oh, the stars! Valeria—you would love them."

"Roserpine has shown them to me in dreams more than once. Little moth holes of light through a dark

112

curtain. I long to see them with my own eyes, my physical eyes. I long to see the aboveground world that I've read so much about in books and heard spoken of on the lips of our wanderers and slaves."

"You would love it." There was an opportunity here. I felt it immediately but, not willing to spoil it by seeming to seduce her away from her people, I continued on with an innocent gesture toward her garden. "I see you've an interest in horticulture; oh, there are more plants than you could possibly name upon Urde's surface. And the flowers, Valeria!"

Her breath hitched and she turned to look at me, a lock of white hair falling across her faintly blushing cheek.

"I love flowers from aboveground. Those who wish for my favor and know me will bring me living plants to grow. Fruits and flowers are my favorite things. Is it true that there are great masses of trees?"

"Forests? Oh, yes, there are many forests, and of many different kinds. North of Skythorn is Klexus, which was where Hildolfr and I met Branwen and Grimalkin; a region blessed with beautiful trees of rich red wood that live at least as long as elves, if not longer. They tower higher than any other tree I've ever seen, and grow to be far wider, too."

"How wonderful! Oh, I should love to see such a thing. And it rains, yes? Water falls from the sky?"

What amazing minutiae of life had managed to escape the durrow priestess's most basic sets of experience! I could not help the faintest laugh as I told her, "That's right, Madame…it rains. And sometimes, when it's cold enough, the rain comes down instead as snow. Everything is blanketed with a soft powder as white as your hair… lovers frolic and people happily warm themselves by the hearth, waiting for the next holiday to brighten up the winter days."

"How truly lovely you make it sound, Burningsoul...I almost feel a certain shame at the thought of keeping you from it."

Not wanting her to feel any negative way concerning me, yet also not willing to discourage her from experiencing that very shame that might eventually lead to my liberation, I stroked her hair and assured her, "I feel a certain shame of my own to think of you missing out on the glory of the sunshine, the brightness of the moon. Maybe someday you'll get to see it...maybe someday I'll get to show it to you. You *have* at least left this tower, haven't you, Materna?"

"Why of course I've left the tower—do you think I was born on Roserpine's doorstep? I'm not a girl, you know...I've lived longer than you have."

"It happens that I was just marveling at that fact... anyway, I didn't mean to offend you, Materna. I suppose I'm just surprised to have found you so evidently sheltered...you are so open and eager—worldly, some would say—in the expressions of your sexuality, that one would have thought you had traveled everywhere, done everything."

"Not at all. I have too much to do here at the tower. My intimacy with my body comes because I know so little of the world from personal experience. My freedom of expression lies in my sexual life. Everything else I do is done in service to Roserpine...and, sometimes, not even sex is exempt from her edicts."

"Like the sex between you and me, Materna?"

A smile lit her voice.

"Good dark to you, Burningsoul," she told me, waving her hand in a gesture that put out the magical lights in the room and plunged us both into the dark.

It was truly maddening to love a priestess! Perhaps the experience should have helped me develop a bit of empathy for Branwen, who was a child of the forest with absolutely no interest in my theological discourses whenever matters of discussion were more abstract than the subjects of warfare or business. The difference was that unlike Branwen, I was interested in what Valeria had to say—what she felt—in matters of the divine.

There was no doubt in my mind that Weltyr was the superior god, but it also seemed to me that anyone who approached any portion of the godhead with the lifelong dedication of the durrow high priestess was surely in possession of some esoteric secret, some metaphysical lesson, that would benefit any member of any faith to know.

And I knew that Valeria possessed such information from the way she earnestly refused to speak about it. It was not a coy playfulness with which she denied me details on, say, her dreams of me prior to our meeting. Rather, there was an apologetic tinge to her smile whenever she had to patiently refuse an elaboration. As if it truly was a matter she believed better kept between herself and Roserpine.

That mysterious nature of hers was surely what made her so appealing to me. She and I both shared a spiritual core and each side longed to connect with the other, but neither faith could fully permit such concord. She thought much and refrained from sharing all things except those bits that were absolutely necessary. I wished to observe firsthand the workings of her elegant mind, the driver of those wandering eyes that drifted around the room within the depths of her pondering or the pit of her sleep.

She was beautiful when she slept; beautiful when she was awake. I had yet to see any sign of danger in the well-guarded Palace of Roserpine, but regardless of whether or not her life was truly at stake, I was glad to put myself on the line for the opportunity to admire her beauty with the innocent appreciation as she dreamed the dark away. Her gentle features were always sharp with a commingling of stress and serious duty while she was awake; when asleep, they were so limp and peaceful that she looked almost happy. Certainly less pained by the contents of whatever knowledge she held.

Yet even the Materna's sleep was not wholly uninterrupted. I spent several hours of dark lost in thought, contemplating the garden of the high priestess whose regal status belied an unexpected sensitivity. I should not have been surprised to find a woman in the service of any goddess to be a dreamer full up with longing for other worlds. All the same, I felt pleasantly shaken by her confessed longing to experience the surface. There was more to her than beauty—more than the intense magnetic attraction that provoked a kind of lightning to fill the air between us since the first time we set eyes on one another. As we grew closer to one another, surely I would find inroads to her heart. I was no great seducer, but I was confident that, with the chemistry already between us, it was possible for me to woo her sufficiently to at least earn my freedom.

But how could I be freed of this woman for whom I was now to serve as protector? I was just thinking of settling in to rest my eyes for a few hours when Valeria, who had been shifting in her sleep, mumbled into her pillow at a volume too soft and incoherent to parse. Her limbs twitched beneath the sheets and her eyelids fluttered rapidly; I tried to discern whether she was enjoying a sweet dream or a nightmare when she clarified that for me. Aside from many repetitions of the word "No," her muted screams were utterly lacking in meaning but full of desperate urgency. I hurried to her side, my hands running over her shoulders and across her brow in a touch that seemed to instantly snap her awake. Her final "No!" aborted very suddenly, those pale eyes of hers snapping open in the dark. Beneath my touch, her body relaxed, and she turned slightly to peer up at me.

"Burningsoul," she said, sighing low, turning to examine the hand that I let lay upon her cheek. "How embarrassing...thank you for waking me."

"It's my pleasure, Materna...do you have such nightmares often?"

"Often enough that you will find one of your most frequent duties to be waking me from them, I'm afraid. Oh! Roserpine." Sitting up, Valeria ran her hand over her face, then looked at the ring resting heavily upon her finger. "I suppose my mistress feels that she does so much for me in my waking life, she has no need to care for me when I am at rest...but I do go on. How is it with you that I feel so inclined to share my thoughts, slave?"

"I'm a patient listener," I assured her, chuckling as I knelt at her side. "Besides...if your goddess has been sharing dreams of me, perhaps she has good reason for wanting you to trust me. The aims of the divine are cryptic to us for a reason."

"You have no idea how true that is..."

Those bright eyes seemed to glow in the dark of the room, searching my face for something before continuing the search around my chest. She leaned forward, her hand resting upon my tunic, the sheet falling from her bosom while she bit her lip to look upon me. "Remove your clothes. Rest with me, slave. You will have a busy

117

bloom tomorrow in the service of Indra and Odile, and then will have to turn right around and entertain my guests on your return. Gather your strength."

"As it pleases you, Materna."

I rose and, beneath the steady assessment of her eyes, undressed before sliding into the bed with her. The soft flesh of her long, powerful body caused an immediate renewing of that dreadful fever she inspired, her limbs extending in a tigerish stretch that was punctuated by a splendid shudder.

After resting an experimental hand in the crook of her waist and finding she settled back against me, I embraced her there in the bed and arched my hips forward to let her feel the throb of passion she produced. She moaned lightly, the soft hillocks of her luscious backside rubbing back and forth along my length.

"How you fire my blood, slave! Such excitement had ought to be beneath me...yet, like a girl with her first love, all bloom I found myself thinking ceaselessly of your body, and my own body's intense craving for you. Feel how my heart races!"

Her slender hand fit to the one I rested on her waist. She guided my touch to her bosom, closing my fingers around the orb of soft flesh and moaning slightly at even that simplest contact. While the arch of her back caused her ass to rub against that spasming source of my lust for her, I caressed and teased the breast whose flesh dimpled with her anticipation. "Aye, Madame"—my words were a whisper against the tip of her ear, each sound I produced a puff of air that made her shudder and sweetly moan and led me to kiss her in this sensitive region between my thoughts—"aye, I can feel you nearly trembling even now...surely you're not afraid of your own slave, Materna."

"Only of the feelings you inspire…only of this fire roiling inside of me, a more furious and dangerous blaze than any I've felt. Oh! Burningsoul…"

Her leg lifted and hooked back around mine, this act of feminine flexibility leaving her splayed and ready to be touched. As I was occupied, she did it herself, thrilling me with the artful hand that trailed between her legs in the dark. "How excited I am to be near you! It is indecent that I should think of a man your status in such a way—yes, indecent—"

After rolling her stiff nipple between my fingers, I let my caress trail down the slope of her taut stomach. There I rested my hand to enjoy the twitching of her torso, her whole body affected by the source of pleasure she nursed with a teasing index finger. I worked myself steadily against her, my aching prick only all the more tortured by the perfect fit of her soft rump against its length. While she touched herself and rubbed against me, I kissed her ear and teased her with the proximity of my hand.

"I like the thought of tormenting you the way you torment me," I told her, lifting my head and kissing the side of her softly gasping face. "I confess, Materna…I have been obedient since my coming here out of some misguided hope of escape, but how quickly all those hopes have left my mind! Now…now, I crave this body this yours. Crave to be used to your pleasure. How sweet it is to be commanded by a woman this beautiful, this powerful!"

"Oh, it will not always seem sweet to you…and perhaps the reality of your circumstances will wear thin on you after a time."

"You sound like a woman assuring her new lover that he will tire of her."

"Isn't that what this is?"

"I don't know...is it?"

"It's not proper," she corrected herself with a gasp, "no, not proper for you to think of yourself as my lover...oh, no, you're a toy, a pet..."

Valeria moaned as my hand lowered further, trailing just over her pubic mound and worsening the teasing impact of the proximity. Finally she lifted her hand from its work and caught mine, pushing me down and guiding my fingers between her spread labia. While I groaned with appreciation to feel her so ready for my attention, she arched her hips in small circles against my fingers until at last I picked up the rhythm. As I saw to the pleasuring of her slickened body, she moved against me, her leg still folded around mine and her body still splayed open. "How many lovers I've had...one such as you should mean nothing to me..."

"Perhaps there's a reason we feel so attracted to one another," I suggested, kissing her jaw.

"Like what?"

"Like a love spell...some potion of seduction that was used against us without our knowing." While she laughed softly, then soon dissolved into another spate of moans, Valeria rocked in my embrace and let me go on joking, "Anroa herself has convinced Weltyr and Roserpine to bring us together for her amusement."

"Then I will offer her libations, oh—Burningsoul, yes, that's right, please your mistress, oh!"

She gasped when I sat up and pushed her legs wider apart. As I lowered my head, her body trembled; my kisses soon applied themselves to the pink flesh peering wetly amid her dark folds, and while she moaned at the gentle but rapid coaxing of my tongue, I was rewarded. Her hand extended out to the member throbbing near her side, those long fingers furling around me to tug sparks of pleasure down out of my mind and through my every inch. I spread her wider, kissing, nuzzling, teasingly licking between while she trembled and played with my aching life.

"Most men from aboveground refuse to use their mouths in such methods without a strict beating first— oh, Burningsoul, oh, what a good slave...how violently this thing of yours twitches when I call you a good slave! You really do enjoy working in the service of your mistress, don't you?"

In answer, I bent my head more closely against her and plunged my tongue as far into that wet little hole as it could get. She moaned, and to my great delight the regal high priestess of Roserpine tilted her mouth against the base of my anatomy. Her lips and nose nuzzling against me, she applied longing kisses, extended her tongue for a few teasing feline licks, blew torturous puffs of air along the surface. Gradually, her lips folded around the tip of what was by then my entire mind. There she suckled and licked, the tips of her nails teasing up and down the shaft while I groaned against her body's holy center.

Desperate for her, desperate to be close to her, I gripped her around the thighs and increased their pressure around my face. Then, folding an arm around her spine, I rolled with her until I was upon my back and settled her lovely body down upon my face. She moaned, grinding against me, the wet velvet of her flesh marking my lips with her scent.

I throbbed for the durrow who sat on my face, my nose buried in her luscious backside and my tongue working against her valley all provoking the envy of that far more desperate organ. It was this that she teased, leaning forward from her throne to resume her tender suckling.

"I'd ought not to let you be satisfied before I loan

you out to Indra and Odile," said my mistress, her hand folding around me to slowly work me over, each pump a torturous journey of her delicate hand. "You'll be gone all the longer if you're not ready to go from the start...I think I'll just make you nice and hard before I go back to sleep, and then when bloom is here and it's time for you to go, you'll be perfectly ready to satisfy whatever lucky durrow has earned your services."

"It's a wadjiti woman, actually," I informed her in a murmur against her labia, provoking a laugh while her keen ears picked up my muffled words.

"A wadjita! Look at you, Burningsoul...not even a few days in the Nightlands and already availing yourself of its benefits. Wadjiti women are very sensual, indeed. I'm sure you'll enjoy fucking her...how you twitch to hear me mention it! Well, you must tell me about your conquest later so I can make use of this nice, stiff condition."

"I've never known a person so foreign to jealousy..." Gasping at the way she strangled my very existence, I gripped at her flesh in response, nuzzled her and indulged my tongue for a few penetrations before murmuring against her, "How curious it feels to be told by a woman with her hand around me that she'd like to hear of me put to other use!"

"It's only natural...think of what a status symbol it is for a durrow with a popular stud. One becomes godmother to a bevy of promising young ladies, the next generation is secured, and it is all thanks to one's good choices. I love the thought of you pumping my friends full in the name of breeding them... Oh, oh—speak of love potions, Burningsoul, I'll give you a love potion that will keep that rod of yours eager all night so you can satisfy each one of us before the dark has ended."

"By Weltyr, your wickedness is so utterly captivating

to me—yes, Madame, as you will, I am happy to serve you in any way you command…"

"Then please me, slave, go on, oh—oh! Yes, that's it, faster, faster—yes, yes, Burningsoul, oh!"

There was nothing sweeter to me than Valeria's bright, crying climaxes. She trembled around me, her body stiffening against mine, her feminine heart rubbing against my mouth and the stubble of my jaw. The elf woman groaned and worked my length for a few avid strokes before releasing me, her quivering body still grinding against my lips until the orgasm had completely passed her by. Then with a low, almost playful chuckle, she dismounted me and said, "You may hold me while I sleep, Paladin, but anything more you do will be at the risk of your own health."

I laughed and folded my arms around her, my head swimming with unsated desire but my honor bound to obey her commands. At any rate, there was a sweetness in that obedience. I could not understand it, but I meant what I said about the pleasures of a gorgeous woman's commands. It was surely as baffling to me as the emotions she experienced were to her.

To me, the love-feelings were less baffling but certainly ill-advised and far more powerful than anything I had experienced. We knew so little about one another—she, I suppose, knew some things about me, though only by virtue of her dream interpretation. Therefore we were relative strangers, yet our bodies communed with such natural passion that the answers to what questions we did ask one another occurred to us as a form of remembering, rather than learning.

It seemed somehow to me that she was reminding me about herself; about things I had never and yet always known.

Therefore, when it came time for her to depart for the bloom without me in her shadow as I'd been the day prior, I felt a pang of reluctance—an oddly genuine worry. There was no reason for it. She had been perfectly fine before my arrival, and was surrounded by other, longer-standing durrow guards all hours of the day. Yet I had to coach myself into believing that she would be fine and that I would clap eyes on her again soon enough. Ignorant to my strange strain of worried thoughts, she drew her cloak around her shoulders and adjusted the embrace of her snake.

"Odile and Indra have been instructed to collect you from here," said my mistress, looking me up and down with a languid smile of pleasure. "Serve them as readily as you would serve me."

"Yes, Madame."

"Oh, and leave that sword of yours behind."

I scoffed, looking from her to Strife at my hip. "I'm to move through El'ryh without a weapon?"

"It's not relevant to your duties, is it? The sword will be here when you return…rest assured, it is better you should be without it than risk it being confiscated by the city guards because you are out and about without your registered owner."

Grimly assessing the weapon and then, with a sigh, shaking my head, I removed it from my hip and told her, "I suppose I have no choice."

"Oh, come now, no need to pout…why, it isn't as though you were going to try to escape or anything like that, right?" Valeria winked at me. I said nothing and upon seeing that she laughed, turning to exit and telling me, "I will see you this evening; a few slaves will be helping us at the party, and I'll have that potion for you."

"That wasn't just dirty talk?"

"Worried?"

"Excited, maybe," I confessed to her. Her teeth glinted with her broader smile and she reached out, pawing at me through the fabric of my tunic before making good her exit from the chambers.

How she ached me! My head swam and my body yearned to follow her. Never had I dreamed a woman would so obsess me, but oh, this priestess of the durrow was so different from anyone I had known! Her sensuality captivated me; I wished to please her, not just by making love to her but by exciting her friends, by following her every command to the letter, by earning her trust.

And then?

Then, would I still be able to escape?

Barely two days had passed since my arrival to the Palace and my induction into this new life of slavery, however pleasurable it seemed it could be. The scar of my brand had not yet healed. I barely knew anything about Valeria as a woman...yet knowing her at all made me feel light and bright, as excited and hopeful as I once was when first being inducted into the Order. I buzzed with happy possibility and somehow feared spoiling what felt like an opportunity of some kind. An opportunity to what, I wondered?

I did not long ponder before the door to my mistress's chamber was thrown open by one of the guards outside. "You, slave—Mistresses Indra and Odile are here to collect you. The Materna has already discussed the matter with us."

While I thanked them and stepped out of the room, my ears were soon pierced with a shriek of delight. "There he is," cried Indra with the excited tone of a girl recovering a lost dog. Odile watched with her arms folded while her companion hurried up to embrace and greet me as a friend. The more seasoned of the two adventurers looked pleased to see me despite her reserved expression.

"Hail, Burningsoul," said Odile, raising a gloved hand in greeting when Indra had released me. "How goes your new life as a slave to beauty?"

"Thusfar it is a far sweeter slavery than any man deserves," I assured them, laughing, reflexively smoothing my hair back upon my head before gesturing toward the lift. "I'm glad to see you both again, though. Good thing Valeria seems fairly reasonable; she didn't put up much argument about loaning me out for a day. A bloom. You know."

"A good thing, too." Sighing as we piled into the lift car together, Odile slumped against the back wall and said, "I was having terrible dreams about not being able to get my money back from that wadjita…they're ruthless creatures, even by Nightlands standards."

Given how ruthless I had heard durrow to be, I admit I had a new sense of over-confidence when it came to my way with women and my ability to find a kernel of feminine ego in any of them. Surely, no matter how ruthless this snake-woman was, she would melt in my arms the same as any female. My confidence was even such that I looked forward to my meeting with her, the journey back through the city with Indra and Odile seeming quite an overlong march between me and the exotic new experience to be had. All the while the durrow accompanying me discussed many things, making small explanations of this or that aspect of durrow culture when I thought to ask. As we neared the district where lay the smithy, I inquired, "My mistress—"

The women looked at me in curious anticipation: I realized right away that I was the slave of the hottest source of gossip in all El'ryh. I therefore tempered carefully my choice of language and my tone, saying simply, "Valeria is quite a stupendous woman—I never expected that I would find myself in the service of such a lovely and intriguing mistress. How is it that she doesn't have a guard already?"

"Oh, I think she's employed more than a handful of personal guards through the years..." Shrugging, Odile resumed leading the way and said, "She's had a lot of problems lately, though. I think her last one was killed while trying to delay and assassin who managed to get in through her window—did his job long enough that she managed to do the deed of her own avenging, but obviously, his life was lost in the process."

Surprised to have learned this, I searched Odile's face for some hint of humor before deciding she wasn't kidding. I had been wondering about these vague murmurs of subterfuge, but had yet seen no evidence. For some reason the thought that I had a predecessor in my lady's defense did not occur to me until this anecdote was shared. Had Valeria had loved him even half as much as she loved me? Based on her unbridled passion, she did not seem like a woman in mourning. Surely if she were grieving anything like a death, I would have been able to determine it.

I pondered this warily while Indra and Odile led me to the façade of the shop I remembered only vaguely amid the blur of my arrival to El'ryh. Standing on the stoop, the women exchanged a look and Odile said, "You wait here."

Then, leaving Indra behind, Odile pushed me into the shop just as the wadjita emerged from the back room with a glance over her shoulder. Her slender neck snapped into position when she realized she was not alone. The burning golden snake eyes set within the pale mask of her face trailed over us, searching only briefly before finding recognition. "Well, there you are! As promised...how good it is to see you again, Odile."

"Yeah, and you. Do you have our gold?"

"All ready to go, once I've had a chance to amuse myself with your man."

"Oh, he's not ours anymore...Valeria laid claim to him." The wadjita's eyes widened and leapt back up to me, assessing me closely while Odile went on with a wave in my direction. "Sounds like he's poised to be the next big thing around the Palace, so enjoy him while he's new... he's going to be too in-demand to be of use to anyone on our level."

"Is that so? Well...he must be quite talented to already be so well-regarded after a few days."

"Rest assured, he certainly is...we'll leave you two alone for a couple of hours. When I come back, I want him and the gold, both."

"Of course, of course...see you soon, Odile, thank you for keeping your word."

"I hate it when people thank me for doing the decent thing, like they didn't expect it of me!" Shaking her head, Odile slipped past me and back out into the street.

Alone with the wadjita, I turned to appreciate her serpentine beauty and found her leaning forward to assess me more closely from the other side of the counter. The scales of her white bosom glittered in the low light of her shop from within the fabric of her bodce; I wondered about the rest of her anatomy and how it was related to the long tail that was her only means of movement.

"Valeria's stud, are you? Well, this should be interesting...come along, slave." Throwing open the board at the side of her counter to gesture me through, the wadjita watched me every step of the way before drawing back the curtain to the second half of her shop. "You and I will have a very pleasing hour ahead of us, if only you will let it be."

I was about to banter back the assurance that there was no way an hour with a woman so intriguing could be anything but pleasant, but the words disappeared from my lips as I was ushered into the wadjita's back rooms. Stepping over the threshold and into her private home, I faltered, reached instinctively for Strife's handle, then remembered I had been obliged to leave it back in the Palace.

A pity! It would have been useful against the spirit-thief towering before me.

AL-LISTUX

ONLY IN RETROSPECT did I consider I ought to have recognized the fishy rubber smell of the spirit-thief before I ever saw it. Then I may have been slightly more prepared to turn the corner and find myself face-to-face with that hideous tentacled visage, the demon's blazing eyes sickly yellow within the slimy pink flesh of its face. I leapt back, my fists raised, my eyes scanning the walls for one of the wadjita's many weapons even as the spirit-thief's voice rattled through my head.

Do not fear, Paladin. I have not met you here to punish you for your crimes against my people, as perhaps I had ought.

"You might be able to try," I advised it.

Ignoring my furious glance, the wadjita who shut the curtain behind us and looked unconcerned at the spirit-thief in her house. "You didn't tell me that this guy was Valeria's slave...now I understand."

I have told you many times before, Kyrie, that you are better off not questioning my judgments. All things piece together as we will them.

"As Weltyr wills them, heretic."

Far less patient for matters of theological discussion when it came to a being such as this, I remained at the ready and kept my eyes plastered upon the predatory features of the tentacled demon. "Tell me why I'm here, if I'm not meant to kill you during your attempt to avenge your brood?"

Your swagger is very amusing, Paladin. It is one of the things that lured Valeria to you; it is one of the things that you can exploit on our behalf.

"Exploit on *your* behalf? Help you, you mean? Why would I help one of your kind with anything?"

Because I am willing to overlook your crimes against my people in exchange. Because I am willing to free you in exchange. At the slight relaxing of my tense arms, the tentacles on either edge of the writhing bunch at the spirit-thief's mouth curled in the hideous approximation of a smile. *That's right, Paladin—freedom. Your liberation from slavery, accomplished with one very simple price before you even fully adjust to being a slave.*

"Go on," I said. "What's the trick here? I can't believe I'm actually considering a bargain with a spirit-thief, but I'll hear you out."

What I want is very simple—a task not even in conflict with your values. After all, it is your duty to kill heretics whose teachings run counter to the faith of Weltyr, correct?

It waited for me to respond and, eventually determining no answer was forthcoming from my lips, it simple told me, *All we ask is that you kill that mistress of yours. We will be able to ferry you away from danger and back up to the surface, if only you would accomplish this one little thing.*

"Little!" I balked, the thought of plunging a blade through Valeria's heart or killing her with some insidious poison a worse crime to my soul than any I had heard proposed in my lifetime. "It's no small thing to take an innocent life," I warned the spirit-thief as well as the wadjita who seemed to be in league with it. The slithering tentacles of the spirit-thief twisted around one another with its scoff.

Surely slaying this woman is no more important to you than ending the lives of my many family members back in our desecrated lair. You have only just met her. Is it really true that humans attach themselves so quickly, even to those who would subjugate them?

"It has nothing to do with being human—all I know is that Valeria has treated me with kindness, and so far as I have seen she has done nothing against me. Nothing immoral at all."

Aside from engaging in slavery, of course. The spirit-thief's eyes focused on me for a long moment before its rectangular pupils trailed over to the wadjita. *Surely, this slave is in enamored with his lovely mistress. Would you see if you can break this spell over him, Kyrie? I suspect all that will be required is reminding him that the embraces of other women do exist.*

"With pleasure," answered the snake woman, her arms weaving around my neck in a sweetly scented jingle of bangles clattering upon one another.

While her cool body slithered up against mine, I did my best to ignore her caresses and kisses. In fact, I did not look at her at all while telling the hateful demon before me, "It is not a matter of attachment or other women—not anything like that. I simply cannot accuse my mistress of being unjust toward me. Not within the context of durrow social structures, at any rate."

Listen to how readily he would justify his own bondage! 'My mistress,' he says…already, he has adapted to his role too much to leave it.

"That simply isn't the case. Rather, I'm sure if I serve her loyally—"

That she'll free you? What a foolish dream that is.

As the wadjita's long tongue lashed against my throat, her slim fingers trailing down my chest and under my tunic, I stared down the spirit-thief. It mocked me by going on. *Perhaps, in forty years, she'll tire of having you around. You'll be a mere sixty-something by then, Paladin…still with a few good years left to savor on the surface.*

I gritted my teeth as the wadjita's nimble hand fit down against the bulge in my breeches, inevitable with the lascivious performance of this female serpent. And serpent was indeed the word; I looked coldly upon her as she lowered toward the ground and put her mouth to work on me, an act that I suppose would have meant more to a slave who hadn't already had such promising interactions with his mistress. Ignoring her, I demanded, "What cause have either one of you to wish Valeria's life?"

Oh, the durrow have never gotten along with anybody… surely you know that.

"Has something to do with their habit of slavery," suggested the wadjita, her surprisingly soft lips lifting from me to permit her breathy speech. "And genocide."

Just so. No doubt your extermination of my fellows meant you were among the most well-regarded of slaves from the outset, and this has something to do with your clouded judgment. But, just look at them. They subjugate men of all races; they enact a haphazard form of eugenics with their attempts at breeding. All the while, they wage war on everyone around them. They give no space for spirit-thieves, wadjiti people, berich dwarves, or any other species that wishes to peacefully live near or even among the durrow.

"So you're a selfless revolutionary?" I couldn't keep the derision out of my voice and stared with hateful skepticism at the wadjita operating upon me, her enthusiasm unfeigned but my body's reaction motivated far more by spite than by any sense of pleasure. I'd heard it said spirit-thieves had no sex organs. If I couldn't kill the one before me, the next best thing was to remind it that its perception of reality was wretched and incomplete. All the same, I could barely focus on what I was there to do to the wadjita when the spirit-thief was making such ridiculous propositions. "The durrow founded this city," I continued. "I may not agree with the culture, but it's their culture."

"They kill with impunity, slaves and visitors alike. No one is safe here; everyone is an assumed or suspected criminal. Rest assured, you'll find in time that even your pretty mistress has a very cruel streak."

While she spoke these words, the wadjita's slender fingers curled around me. I stared into the face of the hideous squid-monster without regard to her, saying as I did, "You're hardly exempt from such accusations, demon. How many good men and women have spirit-thieves killed long before their time, only to have a new skin to wear about?"

It's only in our nature…perhaps that's why Kyrie and I get along so well.

"That's right!"

The wadjita laughed, her eyes glittering bright like gold coins within the smooth scales of her face. "Wadjiti shed our skins…spirit-thieves make themselves new ones. It's only natural we should together be interested in overthrowing the durrow stranglehold over both our people."

While I caught the wadjita by her dark hair and pulled her upright, she hissed and reached up toward the clench of my fist. "Are Indra and Odile involved in this?"

"We were going to try to work their skills into this arrangement, seeing how much time they spend going back and forth from the Palace of Roserpine to trade in slaves and pay the occasional fine...but then they brought you around, and my friend here assured me that you were really who we were after."

"And your friend's name?"

Al-listux, answered the demon, that terribly cool voice trailing into my mind yet again. *It is only a name to ease communication between myself and mortals. Among my people we are one.*

I sneered. "And how is it that you came to deal with this demon, Kyrie?"

"Al-listux is hardly a *demon!* Every being wishes only to live, Paladin...Al-listux and I both want the same thing. To live and to thrive without being trapped under the thumb of Roserpine's race."

Come now, human...you must know that if you turn this bargain down, you will never see the sun again. Never be a free man again. This is an opportunity to save yourself before your servitude has even properly begun.

The wadjita was pawing at me still—I pushed her away, off toward the spirit-thief that caught her in its arms. "It cannot be the will of Weltyr for me to change my circumstances in such a way as that. When the time comes for me to regain my freedom, I will accomplish the task in a way that brings no harm to the woman who has done no harm to me."

No harm yet, anyway. While the pouting wadjita pushed her disarrayed hair from her face, then turned to cling to the squid-faced monster as though it were her lover, I barely restrained my disgust. The spirit-thief embraced her in return, saying, *You must be truly hypnotized by these durrow if you would turn away from Kyrie's embrace.*

"Not to mention foolish...even non-durrow females are worth more amid their race than you, Paladin. I could have you killed for rejecting me—could kill you myself and pay a small fee to your mistress to get out of it without legal judgment."

"Then do it, or let me be. I'll have no part in your sordid plans, however they might benefit me." While, before me, the squid-demon's hands began to explore the wadjita's body, I repressed a shudder of horror. How I longed for Strife! "So you must be part of this string of assassins making threats upon my lady's life."

"More than one faction in this dreadful city would like to see your mistress overthrown, slave." Moaning while the demon's hands cupped her breasts through her leather bustier, the wadjita thrashed her tail against the floor and stared at me through heavily lidded eyes. "Surely the organization with which we are employed cannot take responsibility for all of them, but yes, one or two, perhaps we have sent one or two missionaries to the cause...oh, Al-listux..."

The demon pushed away the leather and bared the plump mounds tipped by dark green nipples. As its slimy fingers trailed around them, tugged and teased, I admit a certain throb overcame me at the sight. Particularly as the wadjita, inarguably lovely, ran her hands over her body and slowly drew the shimmering tassels of her bejeweled gold belt away from the smooth white scales of her pelvis. Beneath I glimpsed a pink slit shimmering with anticipation, an opening in those serpentine scales that somehow repulsed me as much as thrilled me. While she moaned to touch it, the spirit-thief watched with an expression that remained, to me, completely unreadable.

Think harder on this matter, Burningsoul, before you make a choice…your freedom is not the only thing at stake here. Your very life will be endangered if you insist on remaining with the durrow and taking up the mantle of Valeria's protector—a role for which you will never be repaid or rewarded.

"Not by the durrow, perhaps," I agreed.

That is just it. The longer you are down here, the longer you will be separated from your culture—from your temple and your god. Who is to say you will not someday be stripped of all your powers? And that is the best case…that assumes you will survive.

While the tentacles of the spirit-thief's mouth trailed over Kyrie's cheek, grazed her ear, curled about her neck, she moaned and thrashed and touched herself before my hungry eye. I ached, remembering the early wakening with my mistress and her talented caresses. She had not permitted me to reach completion and now I throbbed with desire to use the very slit the wadjita fingered, one long digit working in and out of her shining lips while the spirit-thief gradually lowered to its knees.

Worst case, human, you will be killed when we send some-one to destroy your mistress…or you will simply be killed by one of my kind in exchange for what was done to my brood.

"Sounds like you would be happiest if it were you who did such a thing."

I can hardly deny that I would take great pleasure in see-ing to your death…but we all must make sacrifices now and again in the name of a greater cause, and working with you would be a small sacrifice compared to the victory that would come to us if we might but overturn the power structure of Roserpine's Palace.

"And why, exactly, would her death be any kind of victory? For all you know the next priestess of Roserpine will be even more cruelly disposed toward other races of the Nightlands."

Because some durrow of the palace are sympathetic to our plight…some know how much there is to be gained by cooperation, or can be convinced to see it.

Gently pushing the wadjita's hand away, the spirit-thief leaned toward the shining pink that gleamed amid white-yellow scales. The purplish tendrils of its mouth lifted and the wadjita moaned with anticipation, her hands upon her breasts and sometimes sliding up into her hair while her partner teased her. Al-listux's tentacles trailed over the plump labia of the snake-woman's genitals, these petals parting like a flower beneath the ultra-light touch.

Two tentacles eased between, one sliding into her soaking channel and the other slipping back and forth against her sensitive nub of nerves. She moaned and shuddered, the sound producing another sharp throb through me. I wasn't sure how much longer I could resist her—not when the pleasure she received seemed to afflict her so acutely. She reminded me of the elf-slave Valeria had bade me to use in front of her, and the memory made me eager to see my mistress again; to protect her from this heinous conspiracy against her life.

Come now, human, look at how splendid Kyrie is…surely just as splendid as your mistress, or any other durrow. She has committed her body to me out of fondness, but I would happily lend her to you for your use if only you might do this favor for me. We would give you so much! Your pick of the women in the city…why, if you prefer durrow, rest assured you will have every durrow slave-girl you like.

"Did you not just say that slavery was foremost among

the durrows' sins? Yet you would turn around and engage in the same practices!"

I would enact justice, and balance the scales that have been too long tipped. The durrow deserve punishment for the years that they have subjugated other races, mine included. Some generations of slavery should set them straight...perhaps then, when it is time for them to be free, they will be prepared to interact civilly with people of other species.

The wadjita, meanwhile, gripped a shelf of weapons behind her and panted wildly as the tentacles of the spirit-thief worked in and out of her body. Her tail thrashed and she moaned, eyes finding mine as she begged her master, "Oh, yes, yes, Al-listux, Al-listux! Yes, use me—ah, how dexterous your tentacles are, my liege...oh, yes, yes, ah—"

Another tentacle joined the one that penetrated the trembling wadjita. While these two tendrils pumped in and out of a channel spread wide by others, her bare stomach contorted with the gasps that panted from her fanged mouth. Aching, I ran a hand over myself through my tunic and soon enough, no longer able to resist, made my way over.

While I slid my arms around her body, the wadjita moaned with desire and wove her fingers around the back of my neck. I kissed her fiercely, not without plea-sure, and found her forked tongue eager to slide against mine. The spirit-thief removed its tentacles from her and towered to its full height while I pushed her against the shelves, my hands working quickly over her body.

Face it, Paladin...the Nightlands are a completely different world from the surface. As the wadjita's hands hastily pushed away my tunic and ran along my length, the spirit-thief stepped away to watch through watery alien eyes. *We are cut-throat because we must be...because the beings of the surface have banished all our kinds down here, and forced us to structure our lives out of desperation. They withhold the plenty of aboveground nations so we all must take what we can get—but the durrow have taken too much, and order must be restored.*

I groaned, half-listening at best while my throbbing member plunged into the wadjita's welcoming embrace. She screamed with absolute pleasure, her tail slapping wildly against the floor, then curling around my body while I took her as hard and deep as I could. It was no substitute for Strife, but the satisfaction of stabbing the wicked creature time and time again was truly immeasurable. She gasped in astonishment while running her fingers through my short hair and down the back of my neck. Gritting my teeth, I worked her all the deeper and told them both, "Whatever the durrow have taken or done, I hold no quarrel with anything but their slavery, and their heresy. Neither one of those things will be eased by Valeria's death."

But your power will be immeasurable. And you need not even kill her with your own hands, if that will prove too trying an experience. I could give you something to help you—a poison to slip in her wine, a wand to paralyze her lungs. The choices are limitless.

"And if I fail? If I'm found out and captured?" The spirit-thief said nothing and I pushed the wadjita's body back all the tighter against the wall, the slap of my flesh against hers echoing through the room even louder than the rattle of wood against brick. "I can't imagine your organization, whatever it is, would be able to assist me then."

Don't be so sure, advised the spirit-thief. *We have many connections all throughout the city, and the Palace itself. There is no shortage of those who could be sent to retrieve you in exchange for a job well done.*

Though I was very skeptical on that point, I could not argue with the demon that much more. Swiftly the pleasure closed in on my consciousness and I, breath almost held for the sweetness of it, worked my hips fast and hard against the wadjita's body. She screamed with ecstasy, arms and tail intermittently curling around me, then releasing to permit her shudders of delight. All the while that slit squeezed, dripping wet and almost as greedy as Valeria's. My cock ached for release and I hastened the speed with which I buried myself in her, each penetration another stab of pleasure that rattled through us both. Her scaled brow furrowed, her yellow eyes plastered upon mine, the wadjita came first with a high-pitched cry and a series of rapid squeezes around my tool.

The rhythm of her pleasure was so fluttering that it drew me over my own edge. Groaning, I jerked myself swiftly out before I spilled. A gasp tore from my lips as the seed of ecstasy splattered across her stomach and over the scales at the base of her tail. Each burst was thinner than the last, each note of pleasure lighter than the one that came before; soon these echoes of bliss vanished and left only the faint sense of displeasure, of sticky disappointment, of horror and disdain for the being that tried to seduce me into its hateful service.

"I won't do it," I told the squid-demon, wiping myself off and fixing the fabric of my clothes to once more protect myself. "Find someone else—and do it knowing that I'll kill them myself rather than see them do the least harm to Valeria."

So be it, consented the spirit-thief with a wave of its gnarled hand. *Just remember, Paladin…I gave you a chance. When you come to your senses, find a way to see us again—if you can—and perhaps we will be merciful toward you. Perhaps we will give you another chance.*

Another chance to ruin my life, maybe. Another chance to betray a woman who had done me no wrong.

Never—I could never dream of such a thing. Senses restored, my fury was borne anew. Moving quickly, I snatched up the mace displayed upon the shelf and raised it high, ready to bludgeon the hateful demon's soft head with it. Kyrie cried aloud and grabbed a dagger, ready to defend herself against me, but as my eyes fell upon the spirit-thief, I instead stumbled back a step.

Valeria stood before me: proud, naked, glorious.

Her—its—voice was a perfect emulation. "Is this body all that you want, Paladin? We can give it to you. Whatever would please you would be yours. You might kill Valeria for us and have her still."

Though I knew the image before me was not real, I nonetheless lowered my mace. "So the interloper in the ranks of the palace is a spirit-thief."

"Whatever gives you that idea?"

Shaking off the vile illusion, I looked the replica up and down. "I've heard it said that the spirit-thieves all share one great mind, and that when one spirit-thief looks upon a man, his image is forever stolen by the entire species. From then on any spirit thief can, at will, appear as that same stolen image. But that's all it is—an image. It's a difference I wouldn't expect a thing like you to understand."

"How small-minded," hissed Kyrie, attempting a slice at my left arm and instead having the dagger knocked from even her strong grip. As she cried out in pain, gripping a fist that must have bruised beneath her scales, I returned my attention to the spirit-thief in its captive form.

"I don't love Valeria for her body. Beautiful though she is, all durrow are beautiful—all elves I have ever seen. It is her mind, shrewd and ceaseless, and the mystery of her interest in me: these things are what draw me to her, far beyond anything concerning matters of the flesh."

I wouldn't be so sure of that...

While the image before me smiled far more cruelly, its flesh pulsed. Before my eyes, the gray-blue of Valeria's flesh transfigured cell by cell until the spirit-thief stood before me in its true form. I remained at the ready even as it extended an arm to Kyrie, who slithered into its embrace and allowed her hand to be held for the demon's investigation. The scene before me, rather than recalling a pair of lovers, reminded me of the priests and their pets up in Skythorn.

"Surely there are other ways to achieve your goals. If it's equality you want, the task should be accomplished socially rather than with violence."

Show me in history where slavery has ever reached a peaceful resolution, Paladin, and I will make you the very governor of El'ryh when we have claimed it...

While one hideous tentacle slithered over the snake-woman's hand. As its saliva soothed her pain, the demon's eyes lifted toward me. *However, if you find yourself so ensorcelled that you cannot bear to take Valeria's life— even if we give you the means to do so painlessly—there is perhaps one more way for us to come to an agreement.*

"And that is?"

The ring.

Images of that brilliant indigo gem rushed through my mind. Loathe though I was to betray my mistress even in this way, I listened on—if only because I was unequipped to successfully skirmish with the beast in such close quarters.

Without the gem she bears, Valeria is worth no more than any other durrow in the Nightlands. The durrow believe that when the gem falls into new hands, it is the will of Roserpine that a new Materna be recognized upon the palace priestesses. If you can acquire the ring and bring it to me, the attempts on Valeria's life will come to an end. You and she will be permitted to exist in peace.

The notion was somehow very tempting to me, if only because I found the idea of continued security for my mistress a relief. What life would there be for her, though, without her goddess? Perhaps this was what Weltyr wanted—an opportunity for the priestess to be separated from her divinity so that, in Roserpine's absence, the true spirit of the divine might enter into her heart and soul.

"How can I be sure that you won't go back on your word?"

As you so cleverly mentioned, Paladin, the god-mind of my race hears and sees all that I do; and all my siblings hear and see what the god-mind hears. My betrayal would be noted among my fellows. I would be ill-regarded.

"So I'm to put my trust in the ethics of an entire race of demons? Forgive me for remaining unconvinced."

Just consider it, Paladin. If you acquire the ring, meet me here.

"Easier said than done!"

Yes, said the spirit thief at last, releasing its healed charge and making its way to the rear door of the room, *it is almost as though it would be far easier for you to kill her and wait for us to release you from the dungeon. Think my offer over, Burningsoul. I will not make it again.*

AT HER PLEASURE

THOUGH IT WAS not long before Indra and Odile came back to collect me, the wait seemed eternal. All I wished was to return to the Palace of Roserpine and see my mistress, over whom I now worried in light of the spirit-thief's aims. What had occurred in my absence? What would I find when I returned?

"You're so quiet now, Burningsoul!" Odile laughed and slapped me in the arm. "Whatever happened in there couldn't be so bad, could it?"

I did laugh with her, albeit darkly. "It's true, Kyrie was a very attractive woman...perhaps I'm only feeling a twang of guilt. We humans are not used to such—liberation."

It was useless, I knew, to bring up the spirit-thief to Indra and Odile—useless, or maybe even dangerous.

The last thing I wanted was for the lives of the women who saved mine to be put at stake. Therefore, I kept the knowledge of Kyrie and her so-called friend to myself. Easy enough to blame my odd mood on odder feelings about my mistress—and Odile believed me, laughing and shaking her head with even more enthusiasm.

"Oh, Burningsoul…you're a gentleman, all right. Rest assured, if your mistress didn't like the thought of you in the arms of another woman, she wouldn't have sent you along with us and would have instead left us high and dry, or even paid us the difference out of her own coffers. We like to share here in El'ryh—men, at least."

"Apparently."

Although I tried to ignore the poisonous thoughts of the spirit-thief, I could not help but find new criticism for the society among which I was staying. Now I looked around me with a colder, more judgmental eye. All around me, slaves—men and women both—lugged goods as I had only a few days before, or sold wares in exchange for money that they would not be permitted to keep for themselves, or (more than once on that trip back to the palace) received a public thrashing for some slight, real or imagined.

Regardless of whether or not the spirit-thieves were at all to be trusted, I could not help but admit its proposed position on the institution of slavery was correct. However long it had been maintained, the durrow's method of securing cheap labor and genetic material was unacceptable…and I was a part of it now. Yes, I had gone along peacefully, telling myself I had done so as part of the bargain made in exchange for my life—but did I really have a choice? I had not been in any position to refuse such an agreement; and in my condition, if I had found some justification by which to break with the deal, they just as easily could have killed me before I fully recovered. So, whatever I told myself, my lot was the same as the lots of all these men and women brought to the Nightlands to serve the long-lived durrow. I was only better off by virtue of my mistress's affection for me; only by grace of her kindness.

Somehow, I thought it might be best if I left a proverbial door open for myself.

"Will I see either one of you again?" I glanced between my saviors, who exchanged a look of their own at my question.

Indra in particular frowned. "Perhaps, by chance, if Roserpine is generous."

"We live south of the meat market," Odile said with a general wave, "so if your mistress ever sends you out that way, ask around and find your way to our home. Most people around there know us."

"The meat market? I don't know that my mistress will ever have cause to send me on an errand for the kitchens."

The women found that the funniest thing I had yet to say. "It's slang," explained Odile. "The auction quarter— where slaves are most often bought and sold."

"Ah," I said, somewhat coldly again.

"Come on, Burningsoul, lighten up! Your mistress won't be mad at you, no matter what you did in there. For all you know she's spent this whole time aching with desire for you…she'll greet you home again with open arms and eager lips, reward you for all the time spent out paying our dues for us like the honest man you are."

Honest—yes, honest. My circumstances were changed, but if there was still one thing that could be said of me, I certainly was honest. Honest, and loyal. It was terribly strange that after just a few days by her side I could feel such a deep connection to Valeria, but there was no helping it. Beyond her generosity to me in those first few blooms of our acquaintance, she was a well of sincere feelings like one could rarely find on the surface, let alone in the Nightlands.

Not to mention the lightning that always seemed to strike between us.

After I parted ways with Indra and Odile at the palace gates, a guard accompanied me up to Valeria's quarters. I was not expecting, despite my mistress's warnings, the commotion I found inside, nor the slew of beautiful durrow females arranged along with their favored female slaves throughout the sitting room. All manner of giddy noises rose to the ceiling and I, stunned by the beauty of the paradisical sight, stopped short in the doorway and had to be pushed within by the guard.

"Your man is back, Materna," called the guard, interrupting a whispered conversation between Valeria and her vizier on the other side of the room. My mistress stood with her arms crossed and a few locks of radiant white hair falling around her flushed cheeks; seeing me, Trystera's already tight expression tightened all the further. She turned on her heel and strode around the party, once more ignoring me although we passed each other in the process.

Meanwhile, in the conversation pit at the center of Valeria's living room, the women produced excited whispers to see me. I recognized most from the dining hall the previous day, though a few were unknown to me. Certainly I had not seen any of their slaves before, lovely pale elves and one or two humans already half-undressed (or simply dressed in customarily skimpy garments that shocked me with their novelty) who lifted indolent heads and exchanged hungry glances.

Valeria turned to greet me and glowed with approval

as I knelt. "There you are, slave. Were Indra and Odile satisfied with your performance?"

"Not as satisfied as the wadjita, I would think, but pleased with my obedience, yes, Madame."

"I'm not surprised…stand, Paladin, be at ease. Here"— the sensual priestess waved her ringed hand to indicate for the elf-girl near a glittering pitcher of some bright pink fluid—"let's get you comfortable. Drink up and stay by my side. It will surely be boring for you to be exposed to all this chatter, but I promise, things will be interesting soon."

That was to say the least—although nothing could be further from boring than standing by Valeria's side. To simply do this much filled me with such a fire that I feared I might combust, and these thoughts had me drinking the cloying potion I'd been handed with true thirst. While my mistress reclined in a chaise longue and laughed with nearby women about this or that anecdote from politics, the Palace, or the world outside El'ryh, I admired her and all those who had been invited to the evening of debauchery ahead.

Indeed, it would seem that the debauchery had already begun. While some bantered casually, a pair of durrow exchanged the occasional lingering kiss, their eyes heavily upon one another whenever they were forced to separate to add to the conversation. The short-haired one I recognized from the dining hall had her hand inside the gauzy silver gown of the friend nearest her, the lovely creature with the intricate and glamorous coiffure that had since been rearranged to let a few delicate curls tumble before her sweeping ear. Each studied me frequently, as did all the others in the room—and somehow, it only occurred to me belatedly that no one had brought along a male slave.

151

Finally, the banter returned to me. Some teasing comment was made: I missed its context along with the comment itself, but tuned back in from my distant thoughts at the sound of explosive laughter coming from all the durrow. Valeria smiled patiently on, and then the short-haired durrow boldly asked to know, "So, Valeria? Will you put him out to stud for slaves as well as noblewomen?"

"I've thought about it, but this one's seed seems so valuable...not to mention this tool of his." She set her goblet down upon a nearby table and turned to me then, blithely lifting my tunic and further commenting, "I must say, Burningsoul here has been exceptionally patient when it comes to learning about our ways."

"I can't imagine why," quipped the well-fed woman who, much like my mistress, openly admired my rear. "Given the chance for a mistress like you, Valeria, I think we'd all be slaves..."

"Well, Burningsoul?" Ignoring her friend as Trystera ignored me, my lady propped her elbow against the back of her seat and turned toward me that fiery pair of pearls. Her furred robe slid open at her breast and I let her watch my gaze fall this time. She smiled slightly when I regained eye contact, asking me at the same time, "You must have thought of a few questions to ask about this world."

"Only the names of these lovely ladies before me," I said, "and how they'd best be pleased."

"How quick you are, Paladin." Though the women around us giggled, my mistress appeared unamused. I nonetheless smiled at her, especially as she pressed, "A quick study, yes—but, surely there are some things you wonder about. Here we are in the company of all these durrow. You don't have a question?"

"Well, I suppose. Is it normal for a slave to be put to this use?"

"Normal, yes...but still uncommon. It just depends on the situation. You don't apply for every job in every field when looking for an occupation, do you? Don't fall in love with everyone you meet." She paused, thinking something to herself, looking hard at me. I looked back at her and knew we felt the same things. She went on, "It's a bit like that with pleasure-slaves. Sometimes, you acquire one that simply...suits your needs."

"And do slaves that suit your needs end up beaten in the streets for their troubles?"

A few durrow tutted and exchanged disapproving glances. Valeria, nonplussed, asked drolly, "I thought humans kept animals."

"We do. All species do, even yours."

"Yes. We keep animals, too." The high priestess into whose clutches I had fallen leaned forward to afford me a scintillating look down her gown...what little of it there was to look down, at any rate. "And are all owners of animals universally good? Do all animals owned by human beings, dwarfs, surface elves, gnomes—do they all, each and every one of them, go to bed with full stomachs, well entertained, well at-ease?"

I said, thinking honestly on the matter for a few seconds, "No, of course not. Would that it were so."

"Would that it were so. Precisely." Valeria plucked up her goblet of ruby wine and looked me over, saying somewhat thinly, "Would that all men and women were treated well within the confines of their households. Would that slaves were, in practice, something closer to indentured servants. Would that many things were different, Paladin...but they aren't. This is the culture."

"The culture can change," I said to the woman who

clearly did not feel like she was, in her full heart, part of that same social construct that had begun to weigh so heavily upon my conscience. "Anyone, anything can change."

"Much like a slave when well-beaten," chimed in the merry, curvaceous woman, who laughed and glanced toward the friends sharing in her mirth. "Come on, Pally, a bit of whipping is good for your soul. Always sets my Ernani straight."

"Some slaves actually like being beaten," agreed the short-haired durrow still fondling the bosom of her elegant friend. "Coral, come."

With a rotation of her free wrist, she summoned forward a buxom gold-haired elf who looked pleased to be called upon. "You like a good bit of flagellation now and again, don't you, Coral?"

The slave blushed wildly at the question. "If 't would please Madame to hear my wicked thoughts, then I must confess a certain glee upon the well-placed strike of a whip or nasty little scourge."

"Don't we all," agreed Valeria, glancing at me sidelong before saying to me, "Go fetch the scourge from the wall above my bed."

Very dramatic. I understood her reasoning for orchestrating such a thing—knew why she felt like demonstrating the power she had over me, to make me helpless while I watched he savage beating of an innocent woman I did not know—but I had no eagerness to witness the imminent events even if consensual. As a consequence I stared her down for a long few seconds before I turned to do as she commanded.

Perhaps the spirit-thief had been right about this poisonous institution and the violence required to overthrow it. Perhaps there was no peaceful route that could be found when it came to dismantling slavery.

When I returned with the scourge, the elf, flushed and lovely, had stripped bare to her pale flesh. A pulse of pleasure swept me and I averted my eyes, not willing to see her and titillate myself when I was about to witness such a heinous act. Weltyr's will at work again; I struggled to keep my face neutral and out of a deep frown of displeasure as I tried to hand my mistress the flagellum handle-first.

"What are you waiting for?" She gazed at me with those lustful pearls from behind the goblet pressed against her lips. "Whip her."

I struggled to make out what she had just said amid the sudden drop of blood from my head, and could only repeat dumbly, "You want *me* to do it?"

"Go on."

Valeria nodded toward the splendid elf-slave, who had gathered her thick blonde tresses over her shoulder and now petted them in some nervous habit. The gentle slope of her back was a snowy hill that terminated in comely twin domes. A pair of precious dimples demarcated the shift, and while my free hand grabbed and held the tips of the handheld whip, Valeria settled back in her seat to watch properly. "You'll see that she likes it...we're not all such disgraceful, cruel mistresses as you would think."

More frightened of myself than the women around me, I glanced at the implement in my hand. What was this bright wave of excitement on considering the elf before me, who waited with her back exposed and her breath quickening in anticipation of the so-called punishment?

"Go on, slave," repeated Valeria, impatient in the face of my hesitance. "We don't have all dark to wait."

"Fain would I take the lashes of the cruelest scourge

you could provide," assured the elf, looking over the pale curve of her bare shoulder to regard me with plump lip bitten and bright eyes all the brighter amid the glow of her face.

Exhaling, I looked once more at the weapon, then steeled myself for the act.

"Turn around," I told her, amazed at the relief this one second of power provoked in me. I was not a man accustomed to giving orders, but after spending any time in the clutches of the durrow, the act of giving a command seemed to restore some inner sense of balance—especially when the command was obeyed, and the elf called Coral turned her face away. She sat upon a bench and, feeling the eyes of the durrow upon me, I strode over and took her by the arm. The elf gasped as I drew her to her feet, then again as I gazed into her eyes. No hesitance there at all, remarkably.

Finally, satisfied that I was committing no crime against another sapient being, I took several steps back and gathered the lashes of the scourge in my free hand. The leather thongs were many in number, each one terribly small—and anyone who has ever been hit by such a thing can attest that small lashes somehow manage to sting all the worse. Perhaps I was so sensitive to the idea of slaves being whipped because I had known the lash more than once as a boy prone to ill behavior. But seeing how the elf responded from that very first blow changed something in me: at the very least, my perspective on corporal punishment.

I drew back my arm, struck forward with the whip. The durrow around us gasped as though with desire, but none near with so much pleasure as Coral. Her breath hitched and, by Weltyr, she moaned upon the sharp slash of the cruel thongs into her back's radiant flesh.

"There, see?" Valeria's voice was sultry with approval while, somewhat amazed, I experimented with striking again, lower, and received only a lower note of desire from the elfin slave. "It's not so bad, is it."

The lash snapped down a third time and, with this new moan, pink marks from the first blow faded into the elf's skin. She swayed upon her feet, wiggling back and forth as though eager to be taken. Had the other slaves had been plied with that same expedient of pleasure that had been handed me, and that the durrow sipped while watching the unfurling performance? Whatever the case, Coral seemed unfeignedly pleased as I applied the lash to every inch of her back, her buttocks, her pretty pale thighs—all soon glowing pink with the attention of my implement.

"He is very talented with that thing," said the short-haired durrow approvingly.

"I had a feeling he would be." Valeria's voice was breathless with pleasure to see all this unfold before her. I glanced over my shoulder to see her hand rested upon her bosom, slowly and unconsciously massaging while she watched. I redoubled my efforts, throbbing with desire at the thought of my mistress taking such hedonistic glee in all this. Coral, meanwhile, moaned and begged for more, crying out, "Oh, Paladin! Yes oh…it's been too long since I was beaten by a man, please—harder, harder, don't be shy!"

Jaw set, I obliged her, the scourge cracking in the air before thudding sharply against her flesh. Now she screamed, gasped in pain, but still it was edged with pleasure and her mingled tones only increased my ache. I yearned to bury myself inside of her right then and there—especially as, moaning to observe the sight, my mistress called over one of the nearby elf girls. While

Valeria drew high the gauzy fabric of her barely-there gown, the nubile elf knelt between her splayed legs. Soon the slave was at eager work, lapping and teasing and fingering the priestess's shining glory while I hammered the scourge against the tender skin of Coral.

Inspired by the sight of my mistress, the durrow spread around the chamber called upon their own slaves—more avidly caressed their friends, kissing and pulling away clothes that were already by and large mostly removed. Even the elf-girl I whipped began, whimpering, to touch herself, unfazed by the thought of doing so before the entire room. If anything, the audience seemed to urge her on as it did all the other durrow; as it did my arm.

"Harder," begged the elf girl, panting amid the caresses of her fingers and the hard strikes of my lash. "Oh, yes, Paladin—"

"I can't do it any harder," I told her, snapped somewhat to my senses. I lowered the device. "I can't—I'll truly harm you."

Someone in the room made a noise of displeasure—above and beyond Coral, that was, who whined quite beautifully—and I looked helplessly toward my mistress in an ill-advised attempt to find some sympathy. Instead the Materna gasped, pressing the head of the elf all the more tightly against the apex of her thighs while looking me right in the eye. "Felina," Valeria managed with a glance toward the elegant durrow being fondled by the short-haired one, "why don't you show my new slave that a hard whipping can be very pleasurable indeed."

"Oh, happily—I'll be back in a moment, Junia." Kissing her short-haired friend, Felina stood and extended her hand for the whip. The elf, still swaying, stumbled toward newly-freed Junia and fell upon her knees at her mistress's side. While I passed the whip to exquisite Felina, she looked upon me with almost savage delight and told me, "Strip."

With one more, far quicker glance toward my mistress, I obeyed; soon I stood naked, my desire for the women around me exposed, my muscles wound tight with the tension of the whipping in which I had been engaged. A few of the women produced noises of approval and Valeria in particular let me see her eyes upon me while I stared down lovely Felina. The durrow tried the lash in the air and, with an audacious other hand, reached out to tug a few times on my length.

"I would say your slave already knows the virtues of a fine whipping, Materna," said the durrow, laughing gaily, glancing at my mistress. I gasped, not yet adapted to being used by other women before her, and feared to look upon her reaction—yet, to my relief, she seemed only the more pleased by the contact, moaning low and spreading her legs for the slave's work. Upon releasing my cock, Felina gestured toward that same bench where Coral had once been seated. "Kneel," said the woman. "You're too tall, slave. I can't do a proper job while you're looming over me…come on, hurry up."

I obeyed her, the thrill of being compelled to obey such a delicate woman truly one of a kind. Prick aching for another touch, I folded my hands behind my head and offered my back to her. Her bare feet padded upon the ground and came to a stop some three feet behind me. With very little delay, the first blow came.

Again, perhaps it was that beverage I'd been given—but I was shocked to find the bolt of pain rushed right to my groin and instead became pleasure. Amazed as I was, I hardly managed to catch my breath before the second blow rained down. Beneath her measured arm lay a tender balance of pleasure and pain that few other things could match—and amazingly, the pain but sweetened that pleasure. When I gasped again, Felina laughed and demanded to know, "Do you like it?"

"I— I—"

My mistress commanded my tongue into action, moaning, "Speak, slave! Speak. I'd know how well my friend applies the lash."

"Very well, Madame," I told her, pressed by her command. "Each blow has a loveliness to it— ah—"

I clenched my teeth while the lash struck again, again, again. My cock throbbed insatiably, not just with the pain but with the thought of my mistress receiving pleasure from the elfin slave. A few other durrow moaned beneath the caresses of lovers or slaves; I shut my eyes and focused on staying still between the strikes, which were sometimes beyond the boundary of pleasure and only painful.

Yet, the pain was not always unwelcome. The durrow doing the beating sometimes stepped forward and ran her fingertips lightly along my back, her nails grazing cruelly the edges of the brand and then more kindly the welts her whipping raised on me—far larger, I couldn't help but estimate, than anything I drew out of Coral's tender flesh.

"Isn't that lovely," praised Felina, stepping back again and laying hard into my backside. "Yes, oh, I do love a man who can take a beating from a beautiful woman."

"Hear! Hear!" said one of the women around us, inciting a few others to laugh.

"What an aching weapon," commented Valeria meanwhile. "Coral, relieve him a little."

With a gasp of pleasure, the elf girl hastened over to obey. After moving the bench aside, she knelt elegantly before me, then bowed her head low and gently took my manhood into her hands. Grunting, I savored her dreamy smile as she caressed me up and down with those fair palms, then lowered her head and parted her pink lips to take me between. Her tongue swirled over the aching purple head while I groaned, my hips easing slowly against her mouth as the durrow lashed all the harder.

I must admit, my mistress knew what was needed to persevere. The sensual prowess of Coral's warm, wet mouth made even the hardest lashes not just a joy to take, but an expedient to pleasure. Soon each stinging strike was not painful at all, but erotic as the sight of my mistress climaxing beneath the tongue of the slave. Coral's tongue was just as talented; but when my mistress called, "Enough," relief surged in my heart. My desire, more than anyone, was for her.

"Come to me, Paladin," demanded the priestess, sliding out of her gown and displaying her naked body upon her chaise. Legs falling wide, she spread her glistening body for all to see—most especially me. My cock throbbed as she said, "Satisfy your mistress, oh, I must be filled—I want all these lovely companions of mine to see you dripping from me. Go on…show them how fine a stud you are."

By then I was at her side and bent to kiss her mouth. She moaned, releasing herself to instead fold her arms around my neck. I glanced away only to gauge the distance needed to draw her hips to the end of the chaise. Then, with her backside just over the edge, I pressed against her.

The warmth of her embrace was so immediately intoxicating that I groaned to penetrate her, my head swimming in the passion of Valeria's body. She moaned, too—almost screamed, really—and arched her hips in welcome while I buried myself in her.

"Oh," she cried, looking into my face, "oh, yes, Paladin—Weltyr himself couldn't take a woman so well—"

When we were situated, I drew one limber leg up and draped it over my shoulder. The other wrapped around my hip and with this posture she was well spread, her pussy completely open and eager for the hard penetrations of my cock. Each slam deep into her caused another jiggle of her voluptuous breasts, and while my mouth enclosed around a peaked nipple, my hands reached down to clutch the flesh of her marvelous backside. The durrow around us moaned and commented their approval, elegant Felina having returned to her friend and now lying with her legs spread to take the explorations of nimble fingers. Coral, striped from my blows, knelt beside them and assisted in Felina's pleasure, suckling her nipples and kissing her neck.

"What a wild animal he is," commented the curvy durrow with approval, having drawn up her skirts to pleasure herself while she watched us. "You must let me have the next turn, Valeria, oh, please! I need a good, hard fucking."

"Of course, Myrtale, of course, I'd be glad to give you the next turn—oh! By Roserpine, he *is* something…see how deep he gets? Look, look, oh, his cock his so big! Harder, Paladin, harder—oh! Yes, yes, yes, yes!"

Valeria's brow furrowed as though she were on the verge of tears while I leapt to obey her every declaration. My hand shifting to her hip to apply some downward pressure, I slammed up into her and watched in satisfaction as her eyelids fluttered. The open appreciation of Myrtale for the conjunction of our sex organs made it all the sweeter, and I impudently admired the self-caresses of my mistress's friend while working myself into a high pressure frenzy amid the ecstasy of the scene. Every inch I pounded into Valeria was another spate of pleasure, and every cry of bliss that rose up past her lips made me only harder, only closer to the end. I moved faster as a result, and her body trembled with joy to receive me.

"Oh, Roserpine, oh, goddess! Harder, Paladin, harder, I'm close, I'm so close—hurt me with it, Burningsoul, oh, fill me with your seed!"

Groaning, I stared into her beautiful face while I obeyed. Her entire body seized with tremors; it was not very long before Valeria clenched tighter around me than ever, and her eyes widened in shock. She screamed, extolling, "Oh, slave! Finest of slaves, finest of men, oh, Burningsoul!"

The sheer bliss of her voice was more than sufficient to drag me over the edge along with her. Her name fell from my lips and I kept up the pace until the pleasure burst from me with an almost vicious energy. Teeth clenched, I worked deep into her, the pulses of joy now yielding the fluid of love's passion for my mistress. I filled her with more cum by the thrust until, groaning, I drew myself from her. The last few strands of the stuff oozed from her, distinct against her dark flesh. Valeria moaned, shuddered, looked down at herself with a noise of appreciative lust.

"Oh, Paladin…you filled me to the brim. There's so much of it!"

"How sexy," moaned Myrtale, scrambling up and over to see her friend.

"He really *did* fill you," marveled Felina between her gasps. "Oh, I can't wait for my turn, ah!"

Myrtale, meanwhile, knelt between my mistress's legs while I steadied myself upon my feet beside her. Amazingly, I still throbbed with lust: I remained overwhelmed by the rage of desire, the need to be buried in the flesh of a beautiful woman. The potion, no doubt—and its effects were only intensified by the sight of this lovely durrow exploring my mistress anatomy, spreading her labia and moaning to admire the dribble of my semen down the folds of her flesh.

"Yes, oh, that's so nice…I wonder if he'll get any of us pregnant today."

Looking pleased as could be, Myrtale reached forward and reverently smeared my semen across Valeria, working it into her skin as though it were some kind of lotion. She leaned forward, then, the tip of her tongue tickling against the surface, a hum of pleasure raising from her throat. "Oh! By Roserpine, he tastes so fine…I must have you, Paladin. I want to be filled with you! Sit down there where I was, oh, I would love to breed you…"

While I did as she'd bade me, seeing as my mistress was clearly comfortable with whatever orders they had to give, Myrtale rose unsteadily to her feet and amid a great jangling of jewelry stripped off her gown. Then, still decked in bracelets and necklaces of all kinds, the sumptuous elf straddled my lap and lowered herself upon me with a high moan. "Roserpine! Oh, Valeria, he's so big—"

"He certainly is," commented my mistress, enjoying the scene, smearing the rest of my seed into the delta of her pleasure before sliding a few fingers inside. "I love the way he stretches me, ah, he's such a tight fit…"

Nodding, her lower lip trembling with passion, Myrtale braced herself back upon the pillows littering the conversation pit and began to piston her hips upon me. I groaned, my hands audaciously lifting to explore her broad thighs, her wide hips, the soft swell of her stomach and the far larger mounds of her breasts.

While my hands enveloped these, she moaned and said, "Yes, yes, oh, Paladin, do I feel good?"

"Wonderful, Madame, ah, you're so wet and tight—durrow bodies are the finest in the world—"

While the aristocratic women around me giggled, Myrtale smiled and worked herself upon me all the harder. "Oh, good, that's good—you'll be getting a lot of us, I think! Yes, yes, oh, Roserpine—you want to breed with me, Paladin? You want to fill me with that human warrior seed and make me nice and pregnant? I know you do, oh! Oh, yes, that's right, stud—that's right, give me a baby—"

Bracing against her hips, I worked mine up against her and provoked a shriek of surprised pleasure from her unready lips. She moaned, the noises hiccuping from her with the pace of my thrusts, her soaked anatomy tighter around me by the second. Each strike of my second head against the soft walls of her body sent another streak of pleasure into my skull, and seemed to please her just as much. Soon I focused on the same spot each time and her eyes appeared as though to roll into the back of her head. Her tongue lolled from her mouth, opened to emit a chain of moans that were higher all the time.

"Slave, slave! Oh, what a good stud, yes, yes, take me as hard as you want, take me, breed me, flood my pussy with your human cum, yes, yes, yes!"

These durrow women had a way with words. A groan of my own on my lips, I caught her in my arms and pushed her down into the pillows where I could more effectively take her...and watch my mistress. Valeria moaned just to make eye contact with me, her leisurely toying with herself evolving into the slide of two fingers into her when she saw I watched. We admired one another, my mistress fingering herself and me taking her friend, each of us knowing we would have preferred being together.

Not that I was one to turn down a woman as beautiful a Myrtale. The durrow keened and writhed in my arms, bucked her hips up to mine, and finally climaxed with a shattering orgasm that left her quivering in the pillows. My own, coming on the tail end of hers, produced a shocked cry from her lungs and engendered a second orgasm in a sensual chain. I smiled, only barely able to bite back my laughter for these lovely women lest they mistake my appreciation for contempt. It was just so marvelous to see a group of exquisite women who were so very pleased by the thought of being bred my me. What man could help but enjoy the praise?

Soon, panting, I drew myself from Myrtale. She moaned and ran her hands up into her hair. "Oh, again, again! Take me again, slave!"

"But it's *my* turn," whined Felina, a girlish pout contorting her lips. She turned over upon hands and knees, her dripping body offered to me beneath the swell of her lovely rear.

"Come, Paladin. Let me feel you dripping out of me…I would love to be bred by a big, powerful stud like you. Let me have it! See how wet I am from watching my friends take your tool?"

"I can think of no finer honor than having so many splendid women eager for my seed," I admitted, now permitting myself a low chuckle as I knelt behind Felina's splayed legs. Sensing they were a pair, I glanced toward Junia to gauge her reaction. Truly, this was a very different culture. Junia seemed quite taken with the image, and though she held hands with lovely Felina, she hardly seemed inclined to interrupt. I slid into the woman's tight embrace and felt my entire body pulse with desire at the depth of her prolonged moan.

"Oh, Paladin, Paladin! You're so big, it makes me feel small—oh, Roserpine, you make me drip, yes, oh, plow me nice and hard, give me a baby, what a good stud you are…that's right, that's right, oh, slave, slave!"

Judging by the quickness of sensitive Felina's orgasm, she was perhaps the readiest of all of them for my attention—all except my mistress, who moaned with her own climax to see me leave her friend senseless. It wasn't long before I once more came, the vigor of the potion unflagging.

One by one, the rest of the durrow took their turns with me. At the end, with my tool wet by the lust of all these lovely women, Valeria pushed me down and mounted me anew. As others dozed or pleasured themselves or each other, she gazed into my eyes with her hands poised upon my chest and worked herself upon me.

"Best of servants," she praised me, "finest of slaves… how hard you still are!"

"Only with the hope of serving you once more, Madame."

"And serve me you do—oh, Burningsoul, oh, Paladin! It twitches for me so sweetly…fill me with this sacred seed of yours, go on, go on—oh! By Roserpine—"

She bent her head and kissed me, uncaring who watched or how improper it was.

Soon even my magical endurance reached its limit, and the party wound to a close. Worn, enmeshed in the pink afterglow of sex, the friends of my mistress made their exits. Each time someone left my heart grew all the lighter.

Why was it I, from the very start, so thrilled at the thought of being alone with my mistress? Why was it that she had this hold over my heart more than even over my body? I couldn't have begun to explain; not then. I could only savor my joy as the final party-goers left us alone.

Valeria, sighing with satisfaction, shut the door behind them.

"How exhausting! I'm glad to have them by, but it's always a relief when they leave…"

As though realizing to whom she talked—not a husband, but a slave—Valeria blinked herself back into awareness and looked up into my face. "Clean up," she told me, waving her hand toward the conversation pit, its many pillows and goblets and golden plates of food still lying in disarray after the orgy. "Then you may join me in bed, much as I hate to make it a habit…but I found you very comfortable to sleep beside this morning, Burning-soul."

"It would be my pleasure, Madame."

While she sauntered off to her bedroom, I busied myself with the task, bending with a sigh to collect bejeweled goblets by the fistful.

I was only able to lay hands on a few before Valeria's scream pierced the air.

10

A FOILED ATTEMPT

WHEN I BURST into the bedroom, I could not quite comprehend the scene before me. Valeria's robed body was wrapped in some kind of green vine that thrashed wildly in the room's corner, as though one of the plants there had come to life and developed a taste for flesh. Only on closer glance did I recognize this was no plant by any means, but the snake that my lady carried throughout the palace as a pet. The beast had grown to enormous proportions, a pet serpent expanded into a jungle python either in my absence or during the course of the party.

Valeria reached for me, gripping my arm in hopes I might manage to pull her out. Meanwhile the tail of the snake whipped across the floor, its girth bludgeoning me even as I caught it and tried to force it to unwind. It hissed, its great head twisting in my direction and its mouth opening to reveal fangs practically the length of Strife.

"Hold on," I told my mistress, sprinting back into the sitting room where Strife had been mounted upon the wall during my absence. I tore the blade down and charged back to the source of the commotion: there, the snake had only tightened around Valeria's body. Her robe had fallen somewhat open and the pressure of each coil gave her flesh the appearance of being ready to burst— more alarmingly, her dark face had adopted a notable purple-crimson hue. My heart surging with passion to protect my mistress, I drew the blade from its scabbard and set against the beast at once.

Such things were easier said than done, however. I swiped at its great head and, as it reared away from me, I realized how easy it would be to hurt Valeria instead of the creature assailing her. Cutting away the coils might endanger her body, and missing the beast's face might still so aggravate it that it began to bite either Valeria or myself.

Instead, I sank Strife's blade into the end of the serpent's tail, cutting the tip clean off while it hissed in terrible agony. The coils tightened further for a few seconds and Valeria gagged sharply, gripping at the one around her throat; then, as the pain passed into the instinct to escape its assailant, the snake unwound from its would-be victim and slithered away to regroup. Valeria gasped sharply, clutching her throat with her ringed hand while I bent over her to inspect her body. The dark shadow of a bruise stretched across her neck and another trailed over her ribs, but she seemed to be breathing steadily.

"Burningsoul," she rasped, her free hand gesturing behind me.

I whirled to find the snake had gathered its senses and was on the attack once again, rising high above us both and clearly intent on lunging at me. Strife stood between us, my only defense against the monster's lengthy fangs. When at last the serpent sprang forth to bite, I met its fangs with my cold steel and swore I felt the impact rattle through its skull. With a lower, all the more hateful hiss, the serpent lunged again. I poised the blade forward.

Its already thin pupils shrank to dull lines as it realized it had impaled itself upon Strife's vicious point. Though the snake reared back once more, it knew the end was nigh as much as did Valeria and I. Finding itself unable to remove the blade from the vertebrae through which it had penetrated, the beast collapsed forward in a heap upon the floor. Breathless, I jerked Strife from its throat, then made short work of severing the creature's skull from its body. The stump of its tail gave one more wretched thrash, blood splashing across the floor, before it died.

Panting, assessing my unexpected prey, I lowered Strife and turned toward Valeria with an expression that reflected the solemn feelings of my heart. "I am——"

My lady dashed into my arms, even her brave body trembling after such an unexpected ordeal. "Rorke," she said, my first name precious on her lips for its rarity there, "oh, Rorke! I'm so glad you're here—if not for you, that might have been my undoing. Hold me—please, hold me!"

Strife tumbled to the ground while I embraced Valeria, wrapping her safely in my arms and kissing the temple of her fragrant forehead. "It's all right," I told her. "I swear, Madame, I will let nothing happen to you. You're safe now. I am so very sorry about your pet."

While she wept into my chest, I found myself quite surprised. As cool and collected as the priestess was, in the aftermath of her distressing assault she was more sensitive than I had imagined her ever being. The Materna wept softly against my heart, her fingers sinking into my back while I cradled her, then gradually led her in the direction of her bed. We sat upon its foot together while she said, "Even my sweet snake—oh, even the creatures I love are embroiled in this awful conspiracy against me! I'm so tired, Burningsoul. Yes, so tired of living this way!"

"It is the curse of those who are most valuable to society," I told her, "that they should attract the jealous violence of those far lesser than they. You are a powerful woman, Valeria—a powerful woman among powerful, power-hungry women, and that is a dangerous situation in which to find yourself."

Nodding weakly, Valeria wiped the back of her hand across her face and said with a shake of her head, "It is a terrible burden—I always knew my time as high priestess would be this way, but I just never realized how exhausting it would be. How discouraging. I can't trust anyone, Burningsoul…oh, I feel so terribly alone."

"You're not alone, Madame…you have me."

Her smile was faint as any I have seen. I held her hands in mine and kissed them, eyes shut: when they opened again, I found myself eye-to-eye with the indigo gem of that glowing ring.

The conversation with the spirit-thief again rang in my ears. My hands tightened all the more around hers and I looked deeply into her distraught features.

"Materna," I told her softly, my thumb worrying the edge of her palm, "I had ought to tell you something about what happened today while I was in town in the service of Indra and Odile."

Gently, I released her hands, then folded my own—still stained with the blood of the serpent. I began with my arrival at the smith's shop and watched her face as I explained the whole ordeal; it changed quite swiftly, the sorrow fading away to be soon replaced by deep, dark fury. By the time I was finished she had turned her expression away, her gaze trained around the corpse of the snake upon which she evidently meditated. I was not even sure she still heard what I was saying until, when I finished, she asked softly, "And you believe what this—this creature said? That there is subterfuge at work in the Palace?"

"I can't say for certain, Madame—only that when you left me in the bloom today, your snake was of perfectly average size for one of its species."

Rising, first stepping toward the dead snake and then drawing back away from it, Valeria gazed out the window and said after another moment of silent contemplation. "Fetch the guards and tell them I wish this body removed and respectfully buried. Lithnor was a noble serpent, a good companion to me before you came into my life. My heart is so unspeakably heavy to think that this was done to—"

Her eyes squeezed shut and her hand flew up to press across them. "When you've finished and the task is seen to, come to me in the northern room here in my chambers. I cannot stand to be alone at all this dark. Oh! My heart."

I reached out to touch her, but she hurried from the room on fast-moving feet that left me plagued with guilt. No doubt, I had done the right thing—the only right thing that there was to be done—yet I could not help but see myself as little more than the murderer of an innocent animal. Weltyr, however, spoke in my soul to bolster its resolve. I knew beyond a shadow of a doubt that protecting my mistress, not some snake, was why I had been handed the challenge of this servitude.

Of course, it was not always easy to remember that such a thing would ultimately be to my benefit.

The guards were visibly shocked upon taking in the new size of the snake, clearly not having believed or understood it when I expressed that the creature had grown to such massive proportions. They looked carefully at one another, then at me. "You killed this thing for the Materna," observed the one who had seen me into the chambers on my first arrival.

"Naturally—I would not dream of seeing her hurt."

"They must be putting some kind of binding magic in the brands now," said the other durrow with a shake of her head, exiting to fetch more help in the task of the removal. "It's not every bloom you see a human so loyal."

We were halfway through working out the task of coiling the snake's massive body up around itself to make the moving process easier when a commotion drew my attention. Trystera burst into the sitting room of my mistress's chambers.

"Materna," cried the vizier, looking wildly around.

"Calm yourself, Madame," I called to her, admittedly forgetting my station in that second. "She is abed after her frightening ordeal."

The vizier's head whipped sharply in my direction, her eyes narrowed to irritated slits simply to hear my voice. "If I have the faintest desire to address you, slave, I will."

"Speak to him with a little kindness, Trystera," urged the most sensible of the durrow guards, rising with a clinking of her armor from where she knelt beside the serpent. "It was he who slew this beast and annihilated yet another threat to the Materna's life. We owe him gratitude, slave or no."

Sniffing to have been remonstrated by someone whom she felt to be clearly beneath her station, the vizier nonetheless spared me a displeased flicker of her lilac eyes. "Yes, well—very good, human. I am glad the Materna is wise enough to know a suitable guard when she sees one. Tell her I asked after her, won't you?"

I looked very carefully at the vizier just then, thinking of the notorious body-snatching powers of the spirit-thieves. Just what had the second in command been doing in Valeria's quarters when I arrived after the termination of the meeting? It would have been a fine time to put some enchantment on my lady's snake, or engage in any other bit of deadly mischief. I would have to ask Valeria if Trystera went anywhere within the chambers by herself.

"I'll let her know," I assured Trystera, nodding respectfully in her direction. "I'm sure she'll be glad to know she still has friends."

Trystera nodded once, looked at me as if she still had something more to say, then decided it was better to keep it to herself. She turned and was gone, back out the door, and I and the guards were left to attend to the remains of the snake.

I wish I could say I found my lady sound asleep after the serpent was removed from the scene of the crime. Sadly, that was not the case. Still awash with the invigorating chemicals of her near-death experience, the powerful durrow nonetheless trembled in the covers of her bed as violently as might a human in the frigid winter tundra. Frowning, I stripped off my clothes and slid into bed to embrace her firm body. Even still, she trembled, an automatic process that would only be soothed with the moving forth of time.

"Were they gentle when they moved him?"

"Very gentle," I assured her. "They took a sheet and—"

"I don't want to know."

"Very well."

We fell silent again for a time, until, lifting a hand to trail her fingertips over my chest, Valeria said, "I'm so grateful you're here, Burningsoul. I do wish—well. Wishing is worthless. This is the only way things could have happened. The only way I could have met you. But... when I hear about the way things are done aboveground, I find myself envious. Just a little. There is something very sweet about the thought of being swept off one's feet, as I've read you people say of romance. We are very different down here in the Nightlands."

"You are," I agreed, pushing a few locks of bright white hair from her pensive features and back behind the point of her sensitive ear. "But not so different inside, I think. Not you, anyway...not Indra and Odile. We're all just people, whether owner or slave."

While she nodded softly, I continued my caresses, smoothing the frayed hairs of one of her delicate brows. "You said before, Materna, that you knew you would someday be in the position you're in...high priestess."

"Did I?"

"Just now—perhaps you don't remember because it was so soon in the aftermath of the attack, but you said something about how you knew things would be this way when you became Roserpine's high priestess."

"Oh." Shutting her eyes, her lips upturned in the faint unsmile of a woman with good humor caught at something harmless, the Materna said, "I am usually better at thinking before speaking, but I admit I was somewhat rattled after that...the prophetic dreams my Holy Mother sends, they have come to me since I was a very young girl. Since menses, or thereabout."

"How fascinating," I said, looking carefully into her face.

A connection made itself within the dim halls of even my brain then. Studying her features more closely, I asked her, "Is it possible that these prophetic dreams also included me from a time so long ago? Is that why you become so coy when I inquire about them?"

Laughing in slight surprise, Valeria shook her head and confessed, "You're too smart for a warrior."

"Weltyr's gift...it's why I'm half a priest, rather than all barbarous fighter."

"So I can tell...indeed, Burningsoul. I have dreamt of you, the man with the sun blazing upon his neck, for years and years." Her laughter faded but her smile remained, softly warming her lips as she ran her fingertip down the edge of my neck. "As soon as I saw you with my own two eyes, I recognized you from my dreams...what a way to meet you! What a way."

I could not imagine what it must have been like for her to see me—what a shock. I've heard it said that, for those unaccustomed to the tangible magic of the gods, such stories of prophecy are met with strong skepticism. However, in my life, in our time, having seen with my own eyes the raising of skeletons out of the earth, or the scuttling of gigantic spiders summoned from green smoke, or great balls of fire produced by seemingly powerless old men, I could personally attest long before meeting Valeria that the least of the gods' powers were divinatory in nature. I believed her completely—saw her honestly in her face and, more importantly, heard it in the tone of her voice—but could not help wondering if the source really was Roserpine.

Among other things, Weltyr was said to be a god of prophecy.

I kept my opinion to myself and instead told her, "If the gods have given you foresight of our companionship, this must be a very important time in your life."

"Hopefully not because it's the end," she said, her grim expression visible to me even in the dark.

My hands enfolded her beautiful face. She gasped softly, then relaxed into the touch and even shut her eyes.

"I won't let it be," I promised her. "Nothing will kill you so long as I am alive and in your service."

Her lower lip disappearing between her teeth, her cheeks warm beneath my hands, gentle Valeria murmured, "Thank you," and shut her eyes once more to doze.

She slept restlessly that dark, her tossing and turning keeping me up if only to be there to awaken her from the pits of some horrific nightmare. Remarkably, she did not seem to have any nightmares at all until the very early hours of the bloom; when at last she did begin to gasp and cry out in the dim bedroom, I was still awake and pondering the events of the dark prior.

I pressed a hand to her back while she struggled with some unseen threat. On contact with me, she faded back into a blissful slumber. The tips of my fingers curled against her flesh and I marveled that a being so ancient might still have skin so impossibly soft. I kissed the nape of her neck and dozed for an hour or two until she stirred, pushed herself out of bed, and went about the course of her duties.

Now I observed her schedule more carefully, interested less in my place in it and more how she went about hers. That bloom, of course, was an exception, for on her waking she almost at once wept with the memories of her lost python. Once I consoled her and she picked herself back up, she stretched, anointed herself, and prayed in the nude. I had never seen so earnest a person in prayer aside from myself.

When praying, Valeria sat among those verdant plants, face covered by her hands, her body rocking with her avid recitations and sometimes bowing forward completely to press her forehead to the floor. I had seen such rocking before, in certain sects of Weltyr, and was surprised to find its like reflected in the priestess's communion with her goddess.

Somehow I had it in my head—as did many surface dwellers, I would think—that worship of Roserpine was all nude dances around a fire and elaborate sacrifices using the hearts and sweetmeats of men. Instead here it was, displayed before me in its one true form: prayer. Yes, here were those dastardly pagan rites I had sworn to fight against. I turned away, unwilling to disrupt the beautiful scene but unable to leave her completely by herself after the events with the snake.

Finally, when she was dressed in a short silver gown with a surprisingly high neckline and a cape that was clearly more for fashion than for anything else, Valeria said to me, "I would like you to be prepared to speak at Court today."

"About what?"

"What happened last dark—and what happened when you were out with Indra and Odile. It is important that the traitor, of it is someone close to me, understand what I know now."

"Perhaps the spirit-thief wanted you to know," I posited, unsure whether it was wise to tip our hand just yet. "Surely it understood that I am a servant of Weltyr and bound by oath to be honorable in word and deed. To conceal from you the truth of the mole would break my sacred bond with my god, and I have no doubt the demon knew that when revealing information of any kind."

"Then it probably has some means of passing information to the mole in the Palace," she said firmly, draping her wrists in bangles arranging pins in her hair with a certain curt air. "And the mole, then, is well aware of your knowledge, and your propensity to tell me."

179

"It needs no way of passing information if the mole is a spirit-thief in disguise."

While she absorbed that thought, I went on to warn her, "Speaking our awareness aloud may provoke conspirators into action, if only because increased awareness of the conspiracy throughout the Palace will endanger them—and, anyway, I made it seem as though I were somewhat open to the idea, if only to get out of the situation alive. I wish I had been permitted to bring Strife."

"Sadly," she said with genuine compassion, "that is not an option here."

"But say you and I must leave the Palace together?"

"Depending on context, you may be permitted to bring your sword...but by and large, you will have to do without it. I am sorry, Burningsoul—I know it isn't what you're used to."

This was all part of a trial of Weltyr's design.

I moved on, "Be that as it may, the spirit-thief seemed to think it really could get through to me in one way or another. While it knew the task would be ultimately fruitless, I knew better than to shut the door in its face. We had ought to have a damn good reason for revealing what I told you. I think we'd ought to save it."

While she lapsed into silence and seemed to genuinely consider my opinion on the matter, I did a brief bit of thinking of my own.

"Say we announce a gala of some kind," I told her. "A public gathering designed to tempt the assassins into making their move. Say it's to prove to the individuals involved that you won't be so easily cowed into silence."

"An interesting idea...meanwhile, we debrief the guards—"

"That's right. A few people who need to know can be

informed of the dangers—and you'll always have me by your side."

Drumming her fingers upon her dressing table, Valeria at last stood in a jangle of jewelry. "Very well, Paladin. Let's continue with the announcement about what happened last dark, and save all mention of proposed spies for the future. A big party, all those people circulating publicly around me...yes, I would be very surprised if any conspirator could resist such an opportunity."

Soon she sat in the throne room while I stood customarily apart from her. Valeria looked curiously exposed without the snake to which I had already grown accustomed. Each individual who entered was given cool assessment by her eye as well as mine, and together we silently pondered. Which of these people could it be? A guard? A servant?

The vizier hurried in at the end of the daily procession of people, producing a noise somewhat like a sigh as she reached the bottom of the platform upon which the Materna's throne was situated.

"Majesty," said Trystera, hand upon her heart, her head bowing. "I am so glad to see you up and about."

"Did you expect me to be put out by a little thing like a brush with my own snake, Trystera?" Valeria waved her hand, those same fingers soon reflexively landing upon the thick, bruising line that had disappeared after two swallows of some dark red potion. "I can assure you, I won't be prevented from serving Roserpine by a little thing like that."

Soon, at the nod of Valeria's head, the doors to the throne room shut. My mistress rose from her seat. As her cool eye swept the room, those that knew the events of the dark prior stared grimly on. Others looked with more confusion at the doors until she declared, "Another attempt was made on my life last dark, and though I very obviously stand before you in one piece, I'm afraid to say that my beloved serpent is no more. All of you here know how long he has been my companion, and my heart is heavy with the loss; I am grateful, however, for Holy Mother Roserpine, and this paladin she has brought into my service. Burningsoul—explain what occurred last night after the departure of our guests."

Though I was not exactly used to public speaking, formal settings such as Court were a bit different. Due to their similarity to religious services of Weltyr I felt matter-of-fact as I explained what I saw: from the scream that called me into the bedchambers to the final death of the serpent, I left nothing out.

All the while, Valeria searched the faces around us. When I finished, my mistress returned to her throne and crossed her legs, the short fabric of her dress riding slightly up her thighs. Ah, she was beautiful! I had to avert my eyes to keep from staring at such an inappropriate moment.

"As you all are surely aware, this is far from the first attempt on my life. I suspect it will not be the last. However, it also occurred to us last dark that perhaps the point is not necessarily to take my life, but to cow me into fearful submission and in some way impact our ways here in El'ryh. With that considered, I have decided that the only rational response is to throw a banquet at the week's end."

A few breaths of shock were expelled, and more than one voice in the scattered groups of two or three servants, bureaucrats, guards and recorders rose in concern at the thought.

But one voice that showed no real concern was the vizier, who had listened to all this very quietly from her customary place to the left of my mistress's throne. When Valeria had at last finished formulating her proposition, Trystera posited, "That is a very fine idea, Madame—perhaps then the conspirators will have a greater respect for your power, and might even accept somewhat that the status quo here cannot, will not, be shaken."

Carefully studying the vizier from the corner of my eye, I replayed again our two brief interactions from the dark before. How standoffish she was, even considering the way durrow tended to regard their mortal property! And how suspicious it was to have found her in the chambers of my mistress a few hours before the ordeal.

Yet...of course, many others had been in the chambers that dark as well. Not just durrow, but the durrows' slaves. A great number of women had been coming in and out through the eve, and though I could not think of a one I saw entering my mistress's chambers unattended, magic did not require such a contrivance as physical presence. There were magicians so great that they only needed peer into a seeing stone, identify the target of their hateful whims, and lay some enchantment from a distance. It was not required that anyone actually enter my mistress's chambers for her snake to be affected by a curse. It was not required for the vizier to have entered the bedroom for her to have betrayed Valeria.

After my lady's work was finished for the bloom, I joined her in the baths. The engagement was by no means as thrilling as our first visit. The elf-slaves who had so eagerly pleasured her before saw her tense expression and seemed to know she was in no mood to be trifled with even for her own benefit. Instead, no doubt having also heard of her ordeal the night before, they more solemnly led her to her private bathing chambers. There, before the slaves, we were free to speak unheard.

My lady brooded, thinking frequently aloud of the party, until she lapsed into silence again.

I took a chance.

"How long has Trystera been in your service, Madame?"

"Since before I was even in the service of El'ryh…she has been vizier to three high priestesses of Roserpine, myself included."

I whistled, astonished. That would put her over six hundred years old, easily. "And she has been loyal all these years?"

"To the best of my knowledge, she has been among my most loyal helpers. Of course—her loyalty is to the ring and Roserpine, and not necessarily to me. Trystera has no qualms when it comes to second-guessing my decisions, or steering me into what idea she thinks to be best. She is the ideal woman for the position of vizier. In all the Nightlands, there is none better."

I frowned, rubbing my jaw from where I stood near the steaming water, and considered the ring upon my lady's finger. "Has she ever shown you any envy? Perhaps slipped away for long hours without explanation for her whereabouts?"

At last gathering the aim of my questioning, Valeria looked up at me more sharply. "Are you implying my vizier is the conspirator orchestrating these attacks on my person, slave?"

As fond as I already was of her, and as pleased as I was by her praise, I was just as cut by the tone of her derision when she reduced me to little more than her property by only a word. Nonetheless, thinking of how she had just praised Trystera for pushing back against her ideas, I suggested, "You must keep open to the possibility that it is anyone, Madame. You just said yourself that for centuries—for the long lifetimes of three priestesses—Trystera has been adjacent to great power, but never possessed it fully for herself. Not to mention last dark. She was at the party when I arrived and was first to arrive after the attack. Aside from the guards, at any rate."

"Word travels quickly in the Palace," said Valeria, nevertheless thinking over my suggestions on this matter. Divine lips pursing as she glanced down at her ring, my lady closed her hand into a fist. "But you do make some interesting points."

"May I inquire as to the nature of her visit with you when I arrived at your chambers?"

With the note of a light, humorless laugh, Valeria rested her arm against the edge of the pool in which she was attended by the caresses of the elf-girls. "She has been, from the moment she set eyes on you, completely opposed to your presence. She thinks my guards should be enough and that you pose an unnecessary security flaw—that you are too easily compromised, have too many reasons to betray me."

"In other words, the same sense I get about her."

Valeria offered no reply.

"Once, when I was a lad, I loved a girl terrifically." The story came flowing out of me and as it did I sat upon a nearby bench, hands folded as I explained, "A maiden who was, like me, orphaned and left at Weltyr's gates. She was witty and funny and charming, and she loved me back in the way of first love—nervous, impassioned, and short. One day, without my understanding why, she began to accuse me of looking too closely at other women. Soon she was questioning my every move. Each absence had to be accounted for, and Weltyr forbid I was seen speaking with a priestess!

"Then, one day, I found her caressing another boy

from our temple. Everything clicked into place. She was jealous because she feared I was doing to her what she was doing to me—or, perhaps, she thought that by accusing me of these things, she might produce a smokescreen by means of which she could seem the blameless victim. I was shocked and broken-hearted. Like every young man experiencing such things, I vowed to never give my heart to a woman again." I laughed, and even pensive Valeria produced a smirk at that. "You can imagine, I was in love with another girl the next week."

"Youth is exceedingly fickle," agreed my lady. After staring into the indigo gem for a long few moments during which I wondered what she saw in it, Valeria sighed.

"Perhaps you're right," she announced, her fingers drumming upon the edge of the pool. "Perhaps Trystera does bear investigation…at the very least, to rule her out and ease my mind. Loyal though she may be, her loyalty does not exclude her from investigation. If we are going to be suspicious of everyone in the Court of Roserpine, it would be foolish for us to write her off on the basis of years of service."

I nodded, adding, "I hope as much as anyone that my instincts are wrong in this issue, but her eagerness to see us separated does concern me—until we can rule her out as a suspect, you would do well to avoid sharing too much information with her." With a glance toward the door, I confessed, "I must admit I find myself all the more frustrated by my condition as a slave, Madame. It would be far easier to investigate were I capable of moving about the palace with at least a modicum of freedom. Instead I'm left to baseless speculation…a thing I hate. The idea that I may this very minute be accusing an innocent woman of treason is a deep concern for me."

With a faint chuckle, Valeria shook her head out of fondness and rose from the water. While droplets sluiced down her curves and dripped from the tips of her plump breasts, she told me, "You are noble indeed, Paladin. However...there may be a solution to this."

Speaking in clipped Elvish to the slaves of the baths, Valeria permitted herself to be dried and dressed in a fresh gown. Soon she again led me through the halls of the Palace, but instead of bringing me back up to her chambers, we took a series of twisting hallways and soon found ourselves in a quiet series of offices. Without knocking, she let herself into one and surprised a durrow mage whose terse expression of interruption faded into shock. While the magic-user leapt from her seat, Valeria waved a hand.

"No formalities, please—I'm here only to give my slave a pass."

"Ah!" Looking absolutely relieved that she was not perhaps about to lose her job or in some other way be imposed upon by the most powerful woman in the city, the mage pressed a hand to her heart and leaned back in the seat into which she'd once more fallen. "Well! That's no trouble. For how long?"

While the magical clerk removed a blank sheet of vellum from her desk, Valeria glanced at me thoughtfully and said, "Make it seven blooms long."

In other words, until the banquet had passed. Such trust seemed particularly generous and bolstered my own resolve. Though I by no means thought I would be able to resolve the entire mystery of the conspiracy in those seven days, it seemed to me that we might make some headway on the issue of these vile attempts. By the time of the banquet I may have had the chance to acquire, if nothing else, a lead.

"Will it be for the city as a whole, Madame?"

"Just the palace," Valeria answered the mage, who nodded and made the appropriate adjustments to the symbol her quill quickly produced with ruby ink. Soon, pleased with it, the durrow said a few words: the sigil glowed, then settled upon the page as plainly as any other rendering. Smiling, the magus dusted it with a brisk coating of powder she then blew away. With the ink set, she then rolled up the scroll, tied it with a piece of ribbon, and handed it to my mistress. In turn, Valeria handed it to me.

"This scroll will burn up in seven blooms," she told me. "Until then, anyone who is presented with it will be compelled to let you pass through the palace unmolested. Take heed that you use it only in my best interests, Paladin…and in your own."

Nodding, pressing the scroll to my heart, I assured her, "I will see this issue put to rest—you will sleep more easily than you have in years."

A quite affectionate smile crossing her lips for me, Valeria nodded her thanks to the magus. We were then off again, neither one of us knowing exactly how soon that scroll would be of use.

It transpired that, as we stepped off the lift and into the anteroom of Valeria's chambers, the well-mannered guard perked at attention. "You just missed a visit from Trystera, Madame," the guard told Valeria, glancing at me and (to my surprise) offering a polite nod before she focused again on the freewoman who had become my charge. As my lady and I exchanged a glance at this new information, the guard went on, "Unfortunately, she was disinterested in waiting and made her way off again."

"Thank you for letting me know, Fiora. Burningsoul—" My mistress glanced at me, then at the scroll I had slipped into the belt securing my tunic and my Strife. "Would you perhaps be kind enough to use that new pass of yours and inquire about Trystera's intentions? Her apartment is on the 51st floor of the palace, at the end of the northern hall."

Understanding her perfectly, I bowed with my hand upon my chest. "With pleasure, Madame. I will be back as soon as possible with the information."

Without delay, I turned right around, slipped back into the lift, and looked carefully at the numbers. Much to my humiliation I, with no knowledge of Elvish, was forced to tarry to count the many buttons presented upon the mechanism before divining which was 51. Upon my finding it, the box lurched into motion made all the more discomforting for the fact that I was the only one within it. Bracing myself against the wall, the mechanism whirring around me, I shut my eyes and wondered if I would ever acclimate to this strange sensation of dropping—if I would ever acclimate to the strange ways of the durrow.

Maybe it was not the culture of the durrow so much as it was the institution of their slavery. While I was not exactly used to possessing any great power, nor was I used to being so completely powerless. As an orphan in the Temple of Weltyr I had been servant to many, but that was as a matter of education. Each task I carried out was designed to teach me something of living in the world, of maintaining a household, of interacting with my fellow men and women. There was a purpose to it that ultimately benefited me.

Now the tasks I completed—yes, even making love to Valeria—were assignments for my own good as much as the plow was for the good of the mule. I was a means to an end: an extension of my lady's arm and no more than that.

Well…no more than that to anyone but her. Though Valeria did her best to maintain a certain sense of social propriety between us, even when we lay in bed together, I could see in her eyes and feel in the tones of her pleasure-laden gasps that there was far more between us than mere ownership. Add to that her mentions of these dreams, and I sensed that what she felt for me was no mere possession—no mere lust.

I could not help but admit my feelings were similar. Once I had come into her service thinking I could find some clever means out of the Palace, El'ryh, and the Nightlands as a whole. How quickly that changed! Though I still wished deeply to see my homelands once again and free myself from this bondage amid the durrow, I found now that my priority before any of that was to see to the safety of this splendid woman.

Perhaps, also, to free her from a bondage of her own.

The lift jerked to a stop at the 51st floor. I stepped off into a hallway that was empty save for a pair of guards chatting at the end and a series of shut doors on either side. As they noticed me, then further noticed I was unaccompanied, the two exchanged a few more words and parted ways. One went left down the t-juncture where they had stood conversing, and the one who remained came directly for me, calling down the hall, "Halt, slave. Do you have a pass?"

I removed the scroll from my belt and let it do the speaking for me. The durrow took it from my hand, her mail clinking as she swiftly tore the ribbon from the vellum and unfurled it to see the sigil there emblazoned. Looking it over, then glancing quickly up at the symbol of Weltyr upon my neck, she rolled the pass again and observed, "You're the Materna's new guard."

"That's correct."

"Fiora mentioned you recently. What's your business on this floor?"

I had hoped to keep even the vaguest of my intentions concealed, but there was no helping it. Asked so directly, I was forced to confess, "Fiora herself just informed my mistress that she missed a visit from Trystera, her vizier; I was commanded to track her down again and discover what it was she wanted."

"I see. Take a left at the juncture," said the guard, gesturing me up the hall. "Is this your first pass? Well, be ready to use it. We're all on-edge after what happened with the Materna's serpent."

The guard really wasn't kidding when she told me I'd have to be ready to make use of the scroll. On the way through the halls of the 51st floor I was stopped no fewer than four separate times, each by another guard. Swiftly I realized that the kind of subterfuge I had imagined—ducking around corners and sneaking behind decorative plants—was not a possibility. As I ought to have expected, the Palace of Roserpine was extraordinarily well-protected for the sake of its sovereign. Moreso than ever, I suspected, owing to the recent spate of challenges to my mistress's life.

I was appreciative of the guards in some small way, though. For instance, even with Valeria's instructions, I would have struggled to find the vizier's quarters without people there to provide directions. Eventually I found myself before the light blue door of an apartment identical to all the others in the series. This one was different largely based on the palms that stood proud on either side of the doorframe.

Not that it was particularly reassuring to find myself there—with the guard watching from the corner of the hall and nowhere else to go owing to a dead-end, I was forced to knock upon the door and adjust somewhat my plans for subtlety.

Trystera's slave took a long while to answer the door. Hope briefly stirred my heart that the standoffish vizier was elsewhere and I might be able to slip away without having to speak to her. Sadly, this was not the case, and a pretty young surface elf opened the door with a polite smile—one that grew a bit more real when she saw on the other side not one of her masters, but one of her fellows.

"Good day—ah, bloom, that is. Would your mistress happen to be in, Madame?"

Giggling to be addressed so formally despite her station, the now blushing elf glanced over her shoulder and said, "Yes, friend, come in, wait here—may I ask your name?"

"Rorke Burningsoul," I answered, stepping just inside the brightly lit foyer. "I am Materna Valeria's—servant. My mistress asked I come see why Trystera came by her chambers."

"Very good," said the agreeable elf, glancing shyly at me once more before disappearing through a curtained doorway, "one moment, please."

Here was a chance. Left alone, I looked quickly around the room where I stood. A few stands held drawers that I quietly confirmed contained little more than scraps of note vellum, a set of keys that did me no good because I knew not what they were for, and a scroll that I glanced at and soon divined to be a pass made up for the vizier's slave.

I had just shut the drawer when a footfall alerted me. Barely containing a guilty leap of surprise, I turned to find Trystera with her arms folded before her ribs.

"I'm told my lady has returned to her chambers? I'll go speak with her, then. Thank you for informing me."

Her almost surprising (and perhaps accidental) gratitude notwithstanding, the vizier turned back toward her inner chamber with a dismissive wave of her hand. I cleared my throat and took a step toward her, saying delicately as I could, "Ah, well, Madame…it's correct that the Materna is back in her chambers, but—"

The durrow turned to assess me rather sharply while I continued, "She is not interested in further visitors tonight, and sent me to inquire as to the nature of your request."

"I do not speak to slaves," insisted Trystera.

With a glance behind her shoulder, I pressed, "Not even your own?"

A sniff of derision flared her delicate nostrils. "What an impudent creature you are—of course I speak to *my* slave."

"Well, I have heard it expressed that when a man is taken as slave to the durrow, he becomes a slave to the entire race—that the lowest-born durrow could command all unoccupied slaves whose ears could be reached by her order. Therefore, I am your slave as much as I am your lady's."

"I wouldn't be so sure about that," she said with a snort, albeit a somewhat chastened one. After considering my earnest expression, the vizier continued, "The Materna is the only one who could be said to possess all slaves, no matter to whom they belong…but I suppose from a certain angle of consideration you are rather correct. Very well," she said, waving me in one more room, "come along, we'll make it quick."

My heart beating with hope that I might find some clue in all this, whether it was whatever clumsily constructed lie she fed me on the spot or the contents of her home itself, I hurried after her and soon stood in the center of a small but very comfortable parlor where the elf-girl darned one of her mistress's cloaks.

"If we are, in fact, to be throwing a banquet," said the vizier, bending down beside the table in the center of the room to drag from beneath a hefty leather-bound volume of some kind, "and if it is to mock these would-be killers who insist on sending fool after fool to waste our time, it struck me we had ought to make it lavish as possible. I wished to consult with her on issues of decoration and guest list, but if she is in no mood to speak further this dark, I suppose I can understand. She suffered quite an ordeal yesterday."

"She did indeed," I agreed, accepting a tome that would have been over-sized even for an illuminated manuscript constructed in honor of Weltyr. Amazed at its weight, I took a peek inside while the durrow's back was turned on her way to her chaise. Illustrations of all kinds lay within, mostly depicting patterns of various sorts. Shutting the book before I could be remonstrated for my curiosity, I asked the vizier, "And she will know what this volume is?"

"Of course, it's just a catalogue…ask that she decide as soon as possible what colors she would like, and also whom she'd like to see invited to dine. Oh! Yes, and the menu, I nearly forgot."

Somehow, though these mundanities should have relieved me, I was instead deflated. Like a naïve fool—or an arrogant one—I had settled on the likeliest suspect and assured myself that with little effort I could resolve the mystery that had kept the palace at high alert since long before my arrival. The vizier proved me wrong, or at least did not automatically reveal the evidence of guilt I'd desired. Her command struck me as too mundane and too ready to be a lie; and the catalogue, if it was a prop in deception, very close at-hand.

Chastened somewhat, I nodded at the vizier. "I will relay your message, Madame. Anything else?"

"No, that will be all."

I delayed all the same, shifting the book in my grip to keep from dropping the unwieldy thing. "May I ask, Madame—"

She looked at me with an expression that declared I may not. I did anyway.

"Is there anyone in this palace who strikes you as being—involved, perhaps, in this conspiracy against the Materna's life?"

"Aside from a slave that came from nowhere, caught her eye and was thereafter invited at once to her bedchambers? No." Plucking from the surface of the table the same strange glass pane she tended to use in the throne room, the vizier busied herself by reading something upon its surface. "All the guards and staff are loyal to Valeria, or they would not be here."

Though I waited for her to elaborate, she did not. Feeling somewhat embarrassed now, I turned to go, my mind at once awhirl with other potential leads to the end of this issue. My hand had just brushed the curtain in the doorway when, without looking up, Trystera called, "But—"

I paused and looked at her hopefully, desperate for any information I could gather. Now she did bother to glance my way, lowering the glass pane into her lap as she did.

"Though I can't say I entirely trust you, slave, I will say I was relieved to hear you proved yourself when my lady's poor serpent was embroiled in this foul scheme. Well done."

This dry praise reminded me of certain very aloof members of Weltyr's temple—the sorts of priests who seldom had a friendly word to say to anyone, but whose occasional and faintly-levied praise rang truer and deeper than anyone else's constant warm wishes. Somehow taken aback by this comparison, I nodded to the vizier, then excused myself with the hefty tome in my hand.

On my way back to the lift, I was forced to reflect: Why was it I *really* pegged Trystera as guilty of conspiracy? Had the same situation unfurled in the Temple of Weltyr, I am not convinced I would have even known where to start. Here, my suspicions alighted upon a woman who had evidently been a loyal member of El'ryh's royal court for something in the neighborhood of six hundred years. Before my father, whoever he was, was born: before his grandfather's father was born, and even before that. This woman—why had I noted her above all others?

Perhaps because, of all the durrow, she least fit my mind's picture of a woman—what I had been coached to think a woman should be. Where I might have thought a man in her position professional, I took her as aloof and unfriendly. Where, in her reserved way, she did show concern, I took it with suspicion. Because Trystera did not fit my soft and shining vision of what a woman was, I was inclined to find her out-of-place among her own culture.

It was a quieting moment. I stepped into the lift and, owing to my deep thoughts and the book in my hands, almost didn't notice the berich forgemaster waiting for doors to close and the great box to continue its ascent.

"Ah!" I shifted the book and looked down into the bearded, gray-faced fellow's eyes, wondering if he had the least reason to remember me. "Friend, how are you?"

"Paladin," observed the berich, stroking his beard and greeting me with a nod. "Pleased to see you. Seems like you're settling in…finding your place in the palace." He added this with a twinkle of his dark eyes and a glance at the book in my hand.

"Something like that." While I hit the topmost button I had seen Valeria touch many times, the lift lurched into motion for the stop in between that was lit up with a bright yellow glow. "I just received a pass from the Materna to do a few favors for her. Is it the same with you?"

"My brand's my pass," said the berich, lifting his hand to show me the scarred palm I had been much too occupied to notice the first time we met. "The palace itself is my only true mistress—I spend most of my time traveling up and down in service of it."

"Is that so!"

The dwarf gestured with the rattling box of tools he bore at his side. "Problem-solving. Keeps a man from getting bored. They call me 'Nibel,' by the way."

"Rorke Burningsoul," I answered him, leaning away from the doors as we approached his floor of departure. "So I'd imagine you'll be assisting in some way or another with the preparation for the banquet?"

"Doubt that. I'm more a fix-it man. Fix this light, fix this window, fix this hinge. Unless the banquet requires something broken to be fixed, I can't imagine I'll see much of even its preparations."

"Just as well."

"Is it the anniversary of Valeria's birth already?"

"Ah, no—no, she's eager to send a message to the traitors responsible for trying so many times to take her life."

"Oh!" With a thoughtful sort of chuckle, the berich stroked his beard again. "She's certainly a brave woman. Most wouldn't be particularly eager to show their face in public after so many incidents. This bad business, it's been going on for years…frankly, were I her, I'd retire."

With a thought of my lady's ring, I admitted to Nibel, "I'm not sure that's an option for her—the way she speaks of Roserpine is so close to the way I speak of Weltyr that, without service to her goddess, I suspect her life would feel very empty."

"That's a pity…it would be easy enough to walk away from that ring and this throne and praise her goddess in the solitude of a happier life elsewhere, if you ask me. But what do I know? My only god's the forge. Safe travels to you always, Paladin."

The lift jerked to a stop and the doors slid open. Hefting up his box, the berich made his way into the hall, waved his scarred hand politely at the guards who nodded back, and was around the corner just as the doors shut again to leave me in solitude.

Soon enough, I found myself in my lady's chambers: the quiet almost frightened me after the ordeal of the night before, but upon setting down the catalogue I found her stretched out in the bed of her guest quarters and already dozing. Yet, while I undressed, she whispered, "Rorke."

My given name was a sound so rare upon her lips that it caught my attention immediately. Had I disturbed her? No—in fact it seemed she slept far more soundly than I anticipated.

A dream, then.

Another sound pierced the air—now not a word or a name but a desperate whimper. She produced a noise, a word catching in her throat as it tried to work its way up from the depths of her sleeping body. "Ah," she gasped, "ah, ah—Ror—Ror—ah—"

"Materna—" I hurried to her side to interrupt what seemed to be yet another nightmare, my hand fitting to the soft curve of her shoulder. The priestess winced in her sleep, jerking upright and raising an arm. Much to my surprise, a vase arranged upon a nearby stand burst in a little explosion of purple fireworks.

While my head whipped in its direction she awoke with a high cry.

"Oh—" Her bosom heaving in the loose-fitting confines of her silk gown, my lady recognized me and lay a hand upon her heart. "Oh, Rorke, oh—"

"It's all right," I told her, daring to lay a gentle hand upon her arm now that she was fully awake and the danger of her magic had passed. "It's all right, Valeria...I'm here."

She was so disturbed by the contents of her dream that she did not even protest at my calling her by her first name. Covering her eyes, then rubbing her brow, the priestess said only, "Thank you."

"I hope all your dreams about me aren't quite so upsetting, Madame."

"What? How did you know what I was dreaming about—was I talking in my sleep again?"

"Only softly. Only as much as you could through your sleeping body. You said my name...I thought you were speaking to me at first."

"I see." Hefting a sight, my lady lowered her hand, turned away from my touch, and attempted to lay back down. "Well, it's nothing. Just a dream. Good dark, Palad—"

"Wait, now"—I caught her hand this time, and she whipped her head first in its direction and then at me, visibly shocked by my audacity—"just a minute. Don't you suppose, if these dreams of yours are prophetic, that you'd ought to share them with me when they concern me in some way or another?"

With a dark laugh, the servant of Roserpine responded, "If you think that, Burningsoul, you clearly know nothing of the art and dangers of prophecy."

"Perhaps there's risk involved, yes, it's true. But I can't stand to see you thrash with terrors every dark and not know what they are…especially when it's my name you're whispering all through the hours. They may be your dreams to share or not share as you like, but if they're about me, then the decent thing is to tell me what you see. Not to torture me with not knowing."

"You certainly don't speak like a slave yet, do you, Burningsoul…"

Chuckling dryly, the Materna looked down at her hand in mine—at the ring glowing brightly there amid the darkness of her rooms. "I'm frightened of telling you the things I see in my sleep. I'm frightened that, if I do, they might come true…and that other, sweeter things might not."

"But sharing such sweet ideals is surely no different than a pair of lovers exchanging fond wishes for the future, Madame."

"We're lovers, are we?" Her smirk was faint and lovely as were all her expressions, a curl of white hair clinging to its edge. Glancing away again, she thought for a moment before saying, "Very well, Burningsoul…I'll tell you something of these dreams of mine—in exchange for a beating."

Scoffing slightly, then recalling the odd pleasure of the whipping I received at the hands of the durrow at Valeria's orgy, I stroked my jaw and suggested, "Surely even the worst whipping is a small price to pay to be able to set your mind at ease. Share your dreams with me, Materna, I beg you."

"In my dreams," she answered, pushing the blankets from her body and rising from the bed with the fabric of her gown gathered in one delicate hand, "the man with the sun tattooed upon his neck leads me to the surface. In my dreams, Rorke Burningsoul, you free me from this life. You show me the face of the sky."

She disappeared from the guest chamber without further word. I remained, somewhat stunned, upon the edge of the bed.

Well! What did all that portend, exactly? Sweet relief for me, to be certain. If such a vision was the least bit true, it was a great comfort to think that my bondage in El'ryh might have an end after all. Better still—to reach the end of that bondage and bring Valeria with me, my prize and my pride…my heart flooded with worshipful love at the possibilities. Being partners, peers together, as we might have a chance of being on the surface—it was a kind of dream.

But what stunned me was not the rising adoration I felt for my mistress in that moment. What shocked me was the way she phrased it. *You free me from this life.*

Already I had noted that Valeria was, in so many ways, as much a slave as any other—but now I had to wonder just how literally to take that parallel. Certainly I had perceived that she was a slave to her goddess as much as I was to Weltyr, but I had never considered that she might be unhappy within the confines of her role. Why shouldn't she be? The woman clearly longed for the surface; for the freedom to journey outside of her city and to explore the vast world about which she had heard little more than rumors.

She was gentler somehow than I thought she was—certainly gentler than the other durrow I had met in the city, who delighted in ownership of sapient beings and seemed to fully believe in their superiority over other races. Moreover, that sensitivity stirred in my heart a new pity: the pity we feel for those who have been, for one way or another, unable to fulfill their dreams within the course of their life.

Yes, by Weltyr. I would see to it that, one way or another, Valeria would experience the surface with me.

I had just resolved this desire of my own when my mistress emerged with a scourge in her hand—the same, I recognized, that I had used upon the elf and then endured myself. As I was already stripped down to my breeches, I began to slide from the edge of the bed to kneel against it, but she said, "No, Burningsoul—stand."

"I'll try to stay upright for as long as I can," I told her, adding in a teasing tone, "and if I last the whole time, will you tell me the contents of the dream that so frightened you tonight? Surely that was no happy vision of coming to the surface with me."

A shadow crossed her features and she said quite sternly, "I'll not speak on it. Not tonight. Perhaps not ever. I'm sorry."

At my surprise for her apology, she surprised me further by tossing down the whip and undressing. "I know it must be frustrating for you—I used to enrage my mother by refusing to tell her the dreams that woke me every dark. Did I do that?"

While the nightgown pulled free of her head, she gestured in the direction of the vase. I nodded, explaining, "You destroyed it on waking, as if something were attacking you."

"Well! Then I certainly deserve a beating for ruining such a lovely piece of art."

With a dry laugh—for her own statement or for the look on my face, I am still not sure—my lady knelt at her bedside and drew the long tendrils of her hair from her back.

"Go on, then. Give no quarter...how glad I am to have a loyal slave with a strong arm."

After glancing between the curve of her splendid back, the beautiful round seat of her backside balanced upon her heels, and her perfect shoulders proud even as she awaited the lash, I then studied the whip waiting to be used. "I can't help but wonder if this is some kind of test, or a trap...are you sure, Madame? Is this truly what you want?"

"As I told you, Burningosul...there are those who enjoy the fire of a good whipping. I never sleep more soundly than I do when I have been the recipient of a rare and happy beating. Treat me as though I were your slave; as though I were the spoil of some war, or a maid-servant whose misstep has displeased you most severely. Not that such a thing would be possible...you are too kind for your own good, Paladin."

That may have been so, but the richness of the desire in her voice inspired me to find within myself qualities I did not normally possess. After considering for a few seconds the fact that her words seemed truly meant and this was no test of obedience or loyalty on my part, I dared caress the voluminous mane of her hair to inspire a gasp.

My hand slipped down to the back of her neck; I gripped her by the nape and tilted back her head, warning, "If you are to play at being my slave, Valeria, be warned...I will fulfill my role as master in the game as thoroughly as a man can."

Her bosom heaved with anticipation, her dark eyelids twitching as her pale eyes searched my face. "The qualities of all men, when measured against my master, are second-best. Use me as't pleases, Paladin of Weltyr. Whip the heresy from me."

I repressed a laugh in favor of maintaining the stern affectation my expression had adopted; nonetheless, at the burning of her eager eyes into mine, I bent my head and roughly kissed her upon that ready mouth. Her moan resonating through my body and in my very lungs, Valeria accepted the plundering of my tongue and arched her back into the explorations of my hands over her shoulders, her bosom, her back. Finally, gently, I pushed her forward against the bed and assured her, "You overflow with such wickedness that I doubt even the lash could properly purge it from your body, but we must try everything, mustn't we?"

Her breath hitched with her slight smile, though she did not turn her face to show it to me and in fact folded her hands at the back of her head as though to keep herself still. How beautiful she was—like a statue of obsidian, one that animated to quiver with anticipation while I took the scourge in my hand.

"Tell me if I take it too far," I bade her, drawing back the implement and swinging forward with it to strike. The many leather tentacles slapped down against her flesh to provoke a gasp that was perhaps the sweetest I have ever heard—only to be outshone by the next, even sharper gasp. While she shifted to steady herself more adequately against the bed, I lowered my free hand to caress the first welt that had drawn itself from relief.

"I feel almost too cruel damaging such soft and perfect skin as yours, Valeria..."

"Please, Burningsoul. Please, I crave it as I crave your touch—ah! Oh, yes, please—"

My arm flew into motion again, the same muscles that made me so adept at Strife's use likewise providing a certain knack for applying the lash to a willing woman's back. Especially when, on the next strike, a moan drifted from her glistening lips. Ah, my heart! Though the elf-slave had quite obviously taken pleasure in the whipping I gave her before the audience of durrow, there was something so much more sensual and erotic—deliberate, perhaps—about Valeria's appreciation for the same. She shifted again, groaning at the fifth and sixth strikes, her pleasure still resonant in her voice as I lowered my free hand to tickle the raised stripes.

"Yes," she whispered, "yes, oh, Burningsoul, the sting-ing is so sweet—sweet as the stinging love you make me feel. Oh! By Roserpine, what am I saying? Harder, slave! Beat me harder—ah! Yes—"

I bit back a small smile at this slip of affection, this forced but accidental confession that escaped her lips and filled my heart with pure warmth. Saying nothing lest she take it back or in some other way deny her claim in retrospect, I went on with the beating. Each strike of the lashes produced a lower moan along with the natural hisses of pain, but soon enough those hisses faded completely. Only the pleasure of a desperate woman remained.

Her thighs rubbed together and her fingers curled in her hair. Seeing how obviously she ached with far more than the pain of the whipping, I sat upon the edge of the bed and drew her into my arms. With a mewl of semi-protest to have her beating stopped before she commanded, Valeria permitted me to embrace her for a tender kiss. She seemed only about to demand I go on when I turned her delicate body over my knees and angled her forward to expose the luscious round flesh of her bountiful haunch.

Understanding now, my mistress gasped with pleasurable anticipation. I took up the lash and applied it in brisk, sharp strikes along her thighs, her backside, and the hint of lips that appeared between. This she loved most of all, moaning from the first untoward contact of leather against love's valley. Bracing herself against me and the bed, she spread her legs as though to encourage me, and from then on I did nothing to prevent the thongs of the whip from occasionally extending their reach across her tempting labia. They glistened with her eagerness for the beating and soon I could not resist my desire to touch her, my free hand running from where it had rested upon her upper back to instead massage and fondle the stripes across her rear.

"Burningsoul," she said, the noise an eager gasp, "oh, Burninsoul—take me, Rorke, oh, by Roserpine, by Weltyr's single eye, take me now—I must have you."

My heart surging with desire for my mistress, I dropped the whip and obeyed.

11

TO TRAP A TRAITOR

PREPARATIONS FOR THE party were infinitely duller than I had even imagined. Unfortunately, as my lady's shadow, I was subjected to all of them. In matters of selecting food, wine, decorations and guests, I was forced to stand and stare into space and try to think of anything at all while Valeria—who, for her own part, barely seemed to tolerate the process of decision-making—made her ideal choices. Neither one of us was interested in anything but seeing the results of the banquet: in seeing whether or not our plan would work, and my lady's assassins would be tempted to action at a crowded public gathering.

It was my great relief that no assassins came for her in that week, nor contrived any means that either of us noticed to lay a subtle attack—but it was my far greater frustration that our only leads came up cold. After sending a number of guards to interrogate the wadjita responsible for giving shelter to Al-listux, we discovered the smithy abandoned. Its cache of precious weapons had only been partly removed, as if, in a great hurry, the artisan could only afford to take those pieces that were most dear…or most useful. The building was watched for the rest of the week, and no one made any move to enter or exit. So far as we were aware, Al-listux and his servant had disappeared.

While she dressed on the eve of the gathering, a distant look in her already permanently distant white eyes, I asked her, "Are you frightened, Madame? You have been quiet."

"Frightened for myself—no. Roserpine will see to it that I am protected. But, when it comes to you…"

Her lips pursed and she wandered off in thought, drawing her hair atop her head in a glorious white crown she fixed into place with a golden pin reminiscent of a dragonfly. "I can only pray that my goddess is not cruel enough to have given you to me only to take you from me straightaway again."

Love inspired a throb of my heart to hear her say such a thing. Over the past week, distant as she had been, Valeria had made little use of my extra services for her—and, in truth, I had been making ample use of my pass. Each bloom I had explored the various halls of the palace under guise of being encouraged by my mistress to acquaint myself with its halls. Wherever I went, I listened and watched for the least sign of subterfuge.

Nothing, not even a trace of untoward gossip, revealed itself readily to me, and the evening of the banquet arrived as if out of a puff of smoke. We were both frustrated, I sensed, but neither one of us wished to share these thoughts—as if speaking of our discouragement would produce the same ill effects on our future as the discussion of one of her prophetic dreams.

Regardless of the fact that I had not been put to extracurricular use at any more orgies or titillated by another thrilling show in the baths, however, something had changed in the aftermath of the assassination attempt. Though she had looked at me with fondness since my arrival, there had been an aloofness there, too—a wry skepticism, almost a kind of interest in hazing me to test my mettle.

Now, however, I had proved to her that I intended to fulfill my duties as her protector, regardless of how I had come to inhabit the role. Now there was a trust that I had not seen before. A gentleness, too. Rather than simply asking me to sleep beside her, she asked me to hold her as she slept.

When we were alone together in her chambers during waking hours, she showed me great affection, often coming to perch upon my knee and stare into the distance, thinking strange things that were the secrets of priestesses while her fingers curled through my hair. I wondered sometimes if I was not as much her savior and lover as I was a replacement for the snake who once served a similar purpose of comfort…but, of course, I knew that I was more to her than some mere pet, no matter what she had to say.

Before her dressing table, she hesitated between several necklaces displayed upon a stand. Seeing this, I reached past her and plucked up the one whose great purple gem burned less brilliantly than but nonetheless recalled the indigo one upon her finger. She glanced at me, laughing just slightly, then lowering her head a degree in deference to my gesture.

Draping the jewels across her clavicle and bending my head to fasten them at the soft nape of her neck, I assured her, "Whatever your goddess intends for me, great Weltyr protects his loyal servants. Though it is a pity to think our gods might be at odds in the heavens, I personally take comfort in the thought that I have the finest of advocates."

Smiling slightly into my reflection, Valeria caressed the necklace upon her sternum and said, "Aye, there is some comfort in that. A fine thing Weltyr is not half so cruel as Roserpine!"

"All gods are cruel to mortals, my lady…or they seem as such, for we small beings that have no comprehension of their wills and greater plans."

"Too true, Paladin…too true."

Sighing, Valeria rose from her dressing table and looked me up and down. Against all expectation, she plucked a thread from the collar of my tunic, then leaned upon her toes to tenderly kiss me. Though surprised, I yielded to the gentle caress of her lips, my eyes falling shut and my arms sliding around her soft, warm body.

"How glad I am that you have been brought into my life, Burningsoul."

So was I. Though slavery was far from a comfortable lot, and though I was constantly swallowing back frustration at the daily belittling that occurred every time I was ordered here and there by even those who were not my mistress, the confidence my presence instilled in Valeria gave me some of my own. Protecting her was most assuredly the purpose of this trial being forced upon me. By the end of that ill-fated banquet, any doubts I had of the matter would be erased for good.

I have never been a man who does well at parties. I detest smalltalk, and though I speak charitably to all strangers—knowing, of course, that they may be gods or angels in disguise—it is difficult to argue that my experience with Branwen and the rest of my traitorous party did not leave me particularly eager to make new friends who did not fall directly into my lap, as had Indra, Odile and, of course, Valeria.

You may imagine my relief, then, when I discovered among the crowded banquet hall those same two durrow females who were my saviors as much as my slavers. Alert as I was to all possible threats, I noticed them quickly among the far more aristocratic durrow who had been invited to the gala. The under-dressed pair of adventurers hovered around a table of displayed delicacies intended to be enjoyed prior to the meal, but I laughed to myself to observe Odile slipping grapes (an expensive rarity in the Nightlands, I was informed) and various cheeses into a bag of Indra's. The girls looked nervously around all the while, and in this inadequate scouting Indra's eyes fell upon me.

Her lips contorted in a gasp. She caught Odile's arm, gesturing eagerly toward me, then waving with delight.

I waved back, openly laughing beside my mistress who filled her throne and barely tolerated greeting each guest approaching to shake her hand. Sitting target that she was, I dared not leave her side or even distract myself overlong, especially since the point of the banquet was to prompt the conspirator into action. All the same, after a brief discussion, Indra and Odile hurried over to meet me—oblivious to or ignoring the more refined conversation being held by Valeria and some high-class durrow from the peak of El'ryh society.

"Burningsoul," cried Odile, genuinely overjoyed to throw her arms around my neck and feel again my embrace. Indra squealed to enjoy the same while her older companion went on. "It's great to see you! How are you, warrior-priest? You look healthier and happier than most slaves, I'd wager."

"You'd win that wager, then," I told her, trying to keep my volume modulated with respect to the mistress who was already barely able to maintain conversation for the sake of formality, let alone with a distraction now in her periphery.

Valeria and I really did have very much in common, and it seemed a general distaste for boring banter was one such trait. I sympathized with her, but was beyond relieved that I could avoid similar pains now that these two rogues had managed to find me.

"How have you two been," I asked before, with concerned thoughts of the wajita and her spirit-thief conspirator, adding, "keeping out of trouble, I hope."

"You clearly haven't known us long enough to realize we *are* trouble," said Odile proudly, grinning at me, then at the glamorous durrow holding court with my mistress. The aristocrat had glanced over with a look of oozing displeasure for the loud-mouthed adventurers, who ignored her aside from that mocking smile. Odile continued, "Thanks for convincing the Materna to invite us to this thing, though—it's wild!"

Indra nodded eagerly, enthusing with a mystified look around, "I've never been to anything like this before!"

"I'm glad you two are enjoying yourself," I assured them warmly, "but I didn't ask Valeria to do anything."

As the aristocrat abruptly slunk off, having ended the conversation with Valeria in a passive aggressive statement on Indra and Odile's volume, my mistress assured them, "I invited you both so that Burningsoul wouldn't fall asleep on his feet and fail me when I most needed him. Thank you for accepting my invitation."

"The pleasure is ours," insisted Odile, hurrying over to genuflect before the Materna and briefly kiss her offered ring. "What a beautiful scene it is! You've really pulled out all the stops, Materna."

This was true. Using that catalogue the vizier had thumped into my hands, Valeria had selected an artful array of banners, tablecloths, candlesticks and decorative flowers. A group of musicians filled the air with lively music, their merry flutes joined with lutes and bright percussion to lend a celebratory background to the throne room-turned-banquet hall. Off on the far side of the room, near the entry doors, durrow danced together arm-in-arm while others watched and clapped to egg them on. I, romantic that I was, dreamed vaguely of dancing with Valeria in some other time and place while she entertained a few moments of conversation with Indra and Odile.

"I must say," Valeria at last confessed to the two, reaching out and surprising me with an affectionate pat of the hand resting upon Strife's pommel, "I owe you two far more than I could hope to give...inviting you here was the least I could do. Burningsoul is the finest man I could have in my employ...to call him a 'slave' before the two of you would do a disservice to the willing heart with which he has taken up the duty of serving as my protector, and my companion."

"Isn't he a nice man," agreed Indra with approval, smiling over at me, then frowning slightly as I was forced to glance away to follow something that caught my eye. Regaining her mirth, she returned to conversation with my mistress while my concentration honed in on Trystera.

Although I was satisfied after my first solitary journey through the palace that Trystera did not mean ill will toward my mistress at that particular point in time, I was not satisfied that she was wholly innocent in matters concerning the conspiracy.

However…in fairness to Trystera, I was suspicious of everyone with whom I had contact. It even crossed my mind that Indra and Odile might prove at least tangentially related to the crimes, as they had a pre-existing relationship with the wadjita; however, the unfeigned aggression between Odile and the snake woman made me confident that the two had nothing to do with any subterfuge. And though they may have been regular enough at the Palace to earn the honored recognition of the Materna, that was almost a flaw in and of itself. After all: they were certainly not there often enough to go unnoticed in its halls. Their presence was exceptional, or at least interesting. Interesting was something an assassin could never afford to be.

It was more likely that the conspirator responsible for the death of my mistress's serpent, the attempt on her life, and any previous assaults before my arrival, would be someone who worked in the palace or was in and out of it with daily regularity. Someone so commonplace they were like a bug on a wall—invisible, unseen. And who better to fill that position than a vizier? The closest to the Materna, and the most blessed with connections throughout the castle. Even once I managed to distinguish logic from my kneejerk feelings on the dearth of femininity that made her stand out, I still could not help but think that there was something very suspicious about Trystera.

This was why I focused in on her, I think, as she made her way through the crowd—but why she attracted my attention in that moment only became evident when I took a longer look. She held in her hands not one goblet, but two.

Upon seeing my lady occupied with Indra and Odile, a look of displeasure tightened Trystera's permanently irritated features. Nonetheless, she slipped through revelers and soon emerged at the base of the Materna's throne.

Valeria looked up from her conversation. "What is it, Trystera?"

"A bit of wine for you, Madame," Trystera suggested with as close to cheerful a tone as I'd ever heard from her. "You've been sitting up there for hours now—you need to have something to drink, you'll lose your voice."

"Ah," said my lady, extending a languid hand without looking the vizier's way, "yes, thank you, Trystera…"

How ridiculous I would feel for this moment in retrospect! How it pains me to look back through the tunnel of time and feel my stomach twisting into knots of panic as Trystera mounted the stairs to the Materna's throne. How ridiculous now my fright seems as I tried to determine a graceful way to prevent my lady from drinking what could quite possibly have been poisoned wine. How I cringe and grind my teeth and awaken in the dead of night with a groan of embarrassment every time I remember taking what I hoped would seem like a casual step forward—ostensibly toward Indra and Odile—that instead resulted in my shoulder bumping roughly into Trystera's arms.

Both goblets of wine flew from her hands, red wine spraying across me while the gilded cups clattered upon the floor. While Indra, Odile, and a few guards gasped, high-strung Valeria made a noise that was closer to fright before she realized that her life was not at imminent risk—that it was only me, an oafish, clumsy human. Red wine splattered all across my tunic and stained Trystera's cloak, and while the women around me gasped I tried to come up with a quick, feasible explanation for why I had stepped forward at the time that I did.

Luckily, there was no need. Trystera, wide-eyed, gasped in a fury and looked down at herself. Her clothes were as drenched with red wine as mine. Stripping out of her spoiled cloak and down to her dry bustier, the vizier looked at me with absolute disdain. "You absolute idiot—if you weren't as soaked as I, I'd have you whipped right in front of this blasted banquet. I've half a mind to anyway."

Above the giggling of Indra and Odile, Valeria arched a brow. "*You* would have my slave whipped, Trystera?"

The tranquil expression my lady turned in my direction demonstrated perfect understanding of why I had done what I had. "You cannot stand here in clothes dripping wine, Burningsoul," she told me. "Is your pass ruined?"

I slid the scroll from my belt and rolled it open. The sigil still had one more day of use before it would dissolve in my hand, and though it was now spotted with a few drops of wine, the collision had left it no worse for the wear. "It's fine, Madame."

"Then hurry up and change your clothes. Be back here as soon as you can."

With a hard look of concern, I realized I had miscalculated. I might have saved the Materna from potentially poisoned wine, but I was now forced to leave her alone at this banquet overflowing with people. Seeing my concern, she caught the attention of a nearby guard and assured me, "I will be perfectly fine without your stewardship for a few minutes, Burningsoul."

"I'll get you some more wine," the vizier began, turning away with her cloak under her arm.

"That's not necessary, Trystera." While the right hand of the throne paused to throw a curious look over her shoulder, Valeria smiled thinly. She waved down at the shimmering gold gown clinging to her curves and revealing, as usual, a distracting amount of flesh. "I quite enjoy my dress the color that it is…and if my voice does decide to depart for the night, so much the better. Saves me a responsibility."

Though a look of even deeper annoyance pinched Trystera's features, she nodded to my mistress and stormed into the depths of the banquet. Though Indra and Odile looked poised to tease me for my apparent clumsiness, the Materna waved a hand to me. "Go on."

I nodded, said my good-byes to Indra and Odile, and then, pass in-hand, made my way through the party. The wine caused the fabric of my tunic to cling uncomfortably to my flesh, its resemblance to blood earned me more than a few stares while I slipped past the durrow guests— but, in as merry a mood as the revelers were in, not even a guard saw fit to stop me while I exited the throne room. The halls of the palace were littered with guests going to and fro, sometimes slipping from the party to head to someone's apartment.

Truly the atmosphere was different than I had ever experienced it—bright enough to match the glowing aesthetics of the Palace itself.

As much movement as there was, and as many people as there were coming in and out of the banquet hall, I was surprised to see the guard who usually stood watch outside my lady's chambers was in her usual anteroom post.

If she was at first surprised to see me, she soon glanced at my reddened torso and understood so well she laughed. I had not yet seen her so much as smile, I realized, and chuckled a bit with a glance down at my person.

"I didn't know the party was so wild," said the guard

with good humor. "Maybe I should have asked for the shift off after all."

"Just me and my clumsiness...are you alone here today?"

"Only until the banquet's end...Madame's empty chambers don't exactly need an excess of protection from the repairman."

"The repairman?"

"Yes," she said while leading me to the front door of my lady's chambers. "That little berich, the handyman—I can never remember his name."

"Nibel," I answered, impressed with my own ability to recall the name from the mists of my busy memory. "And while we're on the subject—this is embarrassing, Madame, as I see you all the time, but—"

"Fiora," she reminded me, nodding in my direction while she opened the door. "You'll have to forgive my professional distance...Madame does not have a history of longstanding slaves, so I don't really bother getting to know them. Although, after that business with the serpent, I have a feeling I'll see you around for quite awhile."

Holding the door for me, the guard nodded with respect as I waved back to her. "Sorry about the wine," she added with a chuckle.

"Don't worry...at least it wasn't mine."

The door shut behind me and, alone in my mistress's chambers, I did not even think about the guard's mention of the repairman. Sighing in relief, I removed my wet tunic and only when free of it heard the grinding of some metal tool. A few steps into the hallway adjacent the sitting room, I saw the cause:

Nibel, down on one knee, busily fixed the hinge of my lady's bedroom door.

At my footfall, his head whipped in my direction, hand frozen in motion with its dwarfish screwdriver.

"Ah," he said, "Burningsoul, isn't it?"

"That's right—it's good to see you again, Nibel."

"Likewise." His voice was faint with distraction as he turned back to his work, bending over the hinge again while saying, "Hope you're not trying to get in here just yet."

"Oh, no, just here for a change." I showed my wine-stained tunic and the berich looked at it somewhat disinterestedly. Perhaps there was envy there, I decided while vanishing into the unused chambers intended for me. It seemed the berich, like Fiora, was expected to work nearly round-the-clock. In other words, it didn't seem likely that the almost invisible man would be offered even the opportunity to have wine spilled on him, let alone to drink it or revel with the rest of the palace.

I shook my head, pitying him while I dried my chest and changed into a fresh tunic. What a shame that a man should be called upon to slave in my lady's chambers, even on a feast day!

A shame, too, that it was *here* he found himself. Somehow I felt almost responsible for his assignment—though they were not my apartments, I nonetheless spent as much time in them as my lady and felt a misplaced sense of ownership developing.

But, a funny thing. In all the time I'd spent there, Valeria had never complained to me of the door. Nor had I noticed the hinge whining or rusting or otherwise exhibiting any other kind of issue.

Stepping out again, now more quietly, I observed the berich produce an oddly-decorated pin for his hinge. He was about to slide it home into the embrace of the leafs when I announced my presence by saying, "You know—"

Nibel jumped slightly, cursing, almost dropping the pin that he held quite delicately in his hand.

"—who was it, exactly, responsible for mentioning to you that the Materna has a problem with her door?"

"Couldn't tell you who noticed it," answered the berich with a grunt as he went back to the task, moving a little quicker now. "I'm dispatched by the guards who work down below overseeing the forges. They say, I do. I don't ask in between."

"That may be the case, but I think there's some confusion. To my knowledge, that door has never given us problems. Perhaps you were meant to go somewhere else?"

Sliding the pin home in the new hinge, the berich said without looking, "If that's the case, I'll hear about it soon enough and rectify the situation."

Inspecting very quickly the completed task, the berich rose, took the toolbox in his little gray hand, and turned to head down the hall. "Worse things in the world than a new door hinge you don't need."

"I suppose that's true...ah! But wait, friend—"

Nibel tried to make his departure fast, but I rested a friendly hand upon his shoulder and smiled evenly at him. "Don't you think you'd ought to try the door to make sure the hinge is in order?"

"I'm not about to go opening doors uninvited into the Materna's chambers," he protested. "I'm just here to fix the problem."

"Why, sure—but you don't want to be called up here out of your way again, do you?"

"I go up and down that lift all day anyway, Paladin—let me go, now. I have other jobs to complete."

"But how can you, when this one isn't complete? Go on." I twisted him in the direction of my lady's chamber, then released him with a shove in the direction of the door. "Why don't you check to see if it's working now?"

Looking at me sidelong, the dwarf asked, "Why don't you?"

My hand rested upon Strife.

The dwarf exhaled low and glanced back toward the door again, shaking his head. "This is what happens when slaves spend too much time around durrow…they get the idea that they're better than the rest of us. You have no power to order me around."

"And I will apologize to you when you show me that the door works," I said, still far more comfortable with Strife's pommel against my hand. "But, at the moment, I can't help but wonder something rather concerning… and until I have it proved to me one way or another, it is, in fact, my responsibility to demand that you fulfill the task allegedly assigned to you."

"'Allegedly,'" repeated the berich, a faint sneer in his voice as he bent to place his toolbox down. "And what is this concerning notion you've begun to wonder?"

"That the conspirator within the Palace walls is neither a regular visitor nor a member of the Court, but a lowly slave just like myself."

"Oh, Burningsoul!"

Laughing low, the berich lingered by his toolbox for a second before straightening up again. "Don't insult me— you and I have nothing in common."

In a movement far faster and more startling than I'd given him credit for, Nibel whipped his screwdriver from the toolbox and lunged at me with the head poised straight for my gut. Strife was free of its scabbard before the Nightlands dwarf could fully close the distance. My blade slashed, the magical steel singing through the air to the berich's curse of pain.

The screwdriver fell from his hand.

As acidic blood splattered across the handle, the device corroded before my very eyes.

12

IN THEIR MIDST

THERE WAS NO time to fully absorb what I was seeing before Al-listux emerged from the body of the dwarf who had long ago been added, by one spirit-thief or another, to the collection of forms the hideous extensions of the alien hivemind assumed. While its cells changed so radically that the increase in size brought to mind the growing of a plant from the depths of the earth, I struck another blow with Strife, or tried. The demon caught the blade in its good hand, a hiss crawling from its hideous tentacles as its yellowed eyes stared dead into mine.

You would have done well to take my offer of friendship, Paladin, said the demon, shoving me back a few paces down the hall. *How great the rewards would have been! Now, the only reward I have to offer you is death.*

"Weltyr will decide when I've earned my rest," I assured the beast, raising Strife as its facial tentacles vibrated with a green energy. The plants on either side of the hall slowly swayed and waved, their motions faster as I took a step toward the beast. Swinging Strife in a broad arc was a struggle in the confines of even the wide hallway: I made do, striking forward with the blade as though it were a lance.

The branches of a nearby plant flung themselves out at me and caught Strife's blade in its grip. Jaw set, I attempted to tear the sword from its clutches to no avail. A tendril soon snapped out and gripped my wrist in an effort to prise me away from the sword.

You survived my broodmates only by virtue of your companions, warned the beast, *making a steady approach. You will not be so blessed a second time.*

Funny it should have said such a thing at such a moment. With the sword caught, my instincts turned immediately to the powerful prayers I had been taught as a boy. I called upon Weltyr, my lips moving fast in a silent chant that ran through my mind as effortlessly as a dream in sleep. Within that same mind, I visualized one of my Lord's runes—a vial component of our prayers, and more powerful when physically represented but still imbued with great divine energy when envisioned in the mind.

As I called upon my god to dispel the hateful magic of the spirit-thief, the vine wilted upon my wrist. Soon the branches of the plant loosened their grip on Strife. I managed to jerk the blade away, but by that time the spirit-thief had closed the distance between us and caught hold of my tunic. It dragged me close, its foul-smelling tentacles enclosing my face and wasting no time in attempting to fill my every facial orifice.

Since you love your mistress so, you'd might as well be the one to kill her. Here, Paladin—ah!

Gritting my teeth, I slashed Strife wildly through the air. I might have cried in victory to feel it catch upon demonic flesh if doing so would not have permitted the entry of those hateful probes into my mouth. While the pain of the spirit-thief echoed through my mind, I drew the sword back and hacked forward again, now slamming the blade all the deeper into the damned creature's wrist.

As its tentacles loosened its grip on my face, I snapped the bone of its wrist clean through and savored the slap of its slimy hand flopping to the floor. While I leapt back to avoid the spurt of acidic blood that followed, the hateful demon reeled away and braced itself with its good hand against the marble wall.

Burningsoul, you fool! Why would you put so much at stake to defend those who enslave you against your will? What could you possibly have to gain by consenting to a life of servitude?

"I wouldn't expect a monster like you to understand."

Strife at the ready, I charged forward—but the demon was readier, still. With a magic word in a language like the wet gasp of a drowning man, an animated sword appeared out of nowhere. The blade floated in the air before the demon as though held by an invisible soldier. It parried Strife and sent me bouncing away, backing toward the sitting room while I caught each strike of the magical weapon with my own. "Nor would I expect a monster to fight like a man…it still strikes me as pathetic that you would stoop to means such as this."

Another prayer sped past my lips while the demon, protected for the moment, followed me out to a space more suitable for battle. One of its tentacles curled as though in a hateful sneer.

How can you think your god will protect you from me, Burningsoul? He was the one who sent you here to die!

As if in answer to the disgraceful thing's question, I raised my blade. The subterranean room flooded with a bright explosion of daylight—as though the sun itself stood above my head. Even my eyes, having missed the sun for some weeks now, filled with tears and had to briefly shut: but the spirit-thief, with its sensitive eyes unmeant for the surface, howled with agony and stopped in place to throw its hand over its blinded face.

The magical sword that had kept on slicing managed to sweep across my arm and leave a trail of blood behind, but it was a small price to pay to incapacitate the sorcerer for even a few heartbeats. Incensed into action amid the flood of adrenaline the energy caused me, I struck the magical blade heavily from the air. It bounced across the floor, then disappeared as though in a kind of sudden implosion.

"Weltyr sent me here to defend an innocent life," I assured the demon, leveling Strife once again for another charge. "Whatever the durrow people have done, Valeria is not responsible for the sum total of their crimes."

Is a sovereign not the representative of its people?

With a wave of its good hand, a shining purple shield appeared before its body. Strife impacted upon this astral barrier, sending a wave of energy through its surface as it absorbed the blow. Gritting my teeth, I glanced at the hand lying limp on the floor and thought fast. Another prayer to Weltyr poured from my heart, but the snarling spirit-thief paid this one no mind.

Perhaps the problem lies with you, Burningosul—perhaps you feel that the races the durrow subjugate are truly lesser. Perhaps you believe we are worthy only of slavery; of extermination.

I ignored it, my lips still moving, this prayer far longer than the prior ones. Behind the spirit-thief, its hand twitched upon the floor.

Your god certainly seems unconcerned with all the death you brought to my people, it continued, a spell of its own slowly lighting its remaining fingertips. *How pathetic mortals are, relying on the generosity of invisible beings! What could such entities possibly care for one such as you, or the life of the Materna? This foolish obsession with such antiquated notions is what keeps all the species of this planet from reaching the peaks to which my people have struggled to bring you. Why please the gods when you can displace them?*

I ignored it and completed my prayer. As I did, the severed hand twisted upon its fingers. Weak without the tension of tendons attached to an arm, it nonetheless managed to drag itself forward along the floor. From the safety of his shield, the spirit-thief completed its spell sooner than I'd hoped: lightning shot from its fingers and into Strife's blade, burning my palms and racing up my very skeleton while I screamed in agony. Hideous laughter filled my mind only to be stopped abruptly when the hand caught hold of its cloak and, at a faster pace, scaled the spirit-thief's body.

My skin sizzling with the aroma of smoking meat, I realized I had been brought to my knees by the pain only when the lightning had passed.

Head throbbing, every muscle in me tight with the electricity and searing with burns, I had no choice but to chant a healing prayer while the demon's hand worked as a suitable distraction.

As Al-listux worked to yank the hand from its cloak before the appendage could reach its face, Weltyr's grace flooded my body with a relief far superior to that granted by any natural endorphin or healing plant.

It were as though light itself surged through my veins. My tensed muscles relaxing, the headache faded in an instant. While I clambered to my feet, the beast tossed the hand away. The animated fingers twitched while it landed beside the toolbox.

I'll give you a last chance to turn around and pretend you saw nothing, the spirit-thief told me, its tentacles already glowing with yet another spell. *Should you persist in this foolhardy effort, I can promise that you will not even live to regret it.*

"You're a powerful sorcerer, Al-listux—where were you when your brood was falling to my sword? They might have lasted a few minutes longer, had you been with them."

Hissing, the beast's mental echo rose in a chant I did my best to shut out—but in the end, there was little need. The animated hand, lacking any intelligence but for my will and Weltyr's, had dragged itself upright and pulled the freshly-greased pin from the lowest of those hinges. The explosion as the trap's mechanism was disturbed was tremendous, and I still fill with dread to think what would have happened had I not spilled Trystera's wine and been sent back to our chambers for a fresh change of clothes. The gods truly work in mysterious ways, and it was that same boon that permitted the trap to work for me rather than against me.

As the fireball flooded the hallway, Al-listux managed no more than a glance over its shoulder and a sharp cry of surprise before being knocked forward by the explosion and blasted into the sitting room. Even I was blown back, knocked completely off-balance while shards of marble and pieces of decimated plant rained down around me. Having slammed my just-healed head, I groaned and tried to sit up.

The spirit-thief, even injured, was upon me quickly. Its shield had absorbed the energy of the explosion and so it was, like me, left with only the damage of having fallen. Able to overcome this, (no doubt, thanks to whatever energy allowed it to fight this well with a freshly missing hand), the beast once more snapped its tendrils around my face and sent them slithering into my nose and ears. I cried out on instinct and a few managed to enter my mouth. The ache in my head increased twentyfold and, as I screamed in greater pain, a hideous vision unfolded before my eyes.

A great red organ, throbbing like a beating heart yet unlike anything of mortal anatomy, clung to the walls of some dark cavern; a symphony of voices screamed in agony and I knew somehow that they were the captured spirits of those the thieves had claimed in this same way; Hildolfr stooped over me the morning before the extermination of the spirit-thief brood, that most sympathetic of my three traitorous companions regarding me gently with his one good eye.

"Wake up, boy," he said in his gruff way, hand upon my shoulder while he shook me awake.

The hideous scream of the spirit-thief was what truly awakened me. Its tentacles, not having done their job to completion, swiftly withdrew from my face as the demon stumbled back from my body. Delirious, I lifted my head in time to see it clutched its previously wounded arm: a crossbow bolt protruded from the black cloak and, almost uncomprehending, I glanced toward the door where Fiora stood, ready for another shot.

"Burningsoul," she called, "can you kill it?"

Strife had been knocked from my hand by the blast—I reached for the handle, so close, yet not close enough. With an animal snarl, the spirit-thief pulled the bolt from its shoulder and hurried to a nearby window whose glass had been blown out by the explosion.

Don't think yourself safe, Paladin, the spirit-thief warned me, disgusting fleshy wings throbbing out from a pouch in the creature's back and protruding from the black cloak it wore. *You and the Materna are doomed—I'll see to that, myself.*

Before Fiora could lay another bolt in its back, the beast clambered from the window and took to the air as naturally as a bird. I stumbled up with the help of the guard who hurried over to assist me, and together we beat a fast path to the window. The spirit-thief, still dripping its corrosive blood, glided across the glittering city of El'ryh beneath the black stalactites that were its only sky. Soon it was too far away to be seen, and I released a breath I had not even realized myself to be holding.

"The coward," said Fiora, her lips curled in displeasure. Lowering the crossbow, the guard swept her gaze up and down my body. "How are you? It didn't get to you, did it?"

"No—by Weltyr's grace, I am still myself. Ah, Fiora! Thank you, thank you for your assistance."

"I'm only sorry I didn't hear something sooner...hard to miss that explosion, though."

The durrow elf regarded the ruined hallway and the rubble still occasionally dropping from the ceiling. "I suppose we should consider ourselves lucky that it wasn't worse. That berich—that was the spirit-thief?"

I nodded, my expression grim.

"Who knows how long it's been sneaking about in Nibel's guise, assuming its old form only to corrupt other members of the palace and use them for its own ill intent—by Weltyr, I'm so glad I happened back here when I did."

"Meanwhile, I feel like a fool for letting the blasted thing into the Materna's chambers in the first place."

"Don't," I told her, touching her arm and eliciting a quick glance but ultimate acceptance of the camaraderie earned not by station but by battle. "You couldn't have known—no one could have. It's why this demon has been so successful at remaining in the Palace for such a long time."

Nodding slightly, Fiora looked one more displeased time at the rubble around us. "Why don't we wait in the anteroom—I'll call for my superiors."

Soon, while I took a well-earned seat in one of the benches arranged for those waiting for a private audience with my mistress, the guard stood at a desk in the corner that was designed to check those visitors in. From this, she removed a strange black box that glowed as she took it in her hand. After a few seconds, it emitted a noise that I recognized to be another durrow's voice. More dwarven technology of some kind, I supposed. I had little interest in speculating on such things while my head was awash with such agony and the cool marble wall behind me proved such relief.

Soon enough, Fiora's call was answered. A pair of high-ranking guards, their status discernible by the sigils upon their helmets, arrived in the lift with tight-faced Trystera—and, to my relief, Valeria herself. The Materna set eyes on me and, seeing my state as I swayed to my feet, gasped softly to herself. Without the least care for the company surrounding us, she pushed through the guards, calling, "Rorke!"

The arms she wound around me were not just a relief, but the finest of rewards. I glanced only once at the stern vizier before daring to wrap my arms around my mistress in turn, savoring her embrace and the soft flesh of her back before she leaned away to take my face in her delicate hands. "Oh, sweet Burningsoul—what's happened?"

"I'm afraid we're going to have to move you to temporary quarters until your chambers can be repaired, Madame," answered Fiora, who very kindly did not so much as bat an eye at the perhaps inappropriately intimate embrace of the mistress and her slave. "The hallway has taken substantial damage, as you will see."

"I can't stand to," answered Valeria, releasing me to speak face-to-face with her entourage and the guard who saved my life. "I won't see it. Call on me when it has been fixed, no sooner. What trap was it?"

"A loaded hinge," I told her, "fixed with some kind of spell—placed there by the conspirator, Nibel."

On hearing this, the vizier looked at me more sharply. "The berich?"

I nodded. As that same mistrustful servant of the Materna looked at the woman who had come to my aid, Fiora confirmed for me. "Aye, the berich dwarf. It's all my fault. We see him about so often that I didn't look closely at his assignment papers."

"Even if you had," I dared interrupt, "I'd wager they would have seemed in perfect order. It was no berich, Madame."

I looked seriously into the face of my mistress, knowing she would understand the significance when I told her, "A spirit-thief had been wearing his form about the Palace to do foul business undetected. Al-listux—a powerful sorcerer. Its magic permitted it to survive just long enough for it to escape. I'm as blessed by Weltyr that I kept my life as I am that I caught the demon in the first place."

"A blasted spirit-thief," the vizier repeated, glancing

toward the shut door of my lady's chambers. "No wonder...no wonder all this has been going on for so long."

"It tried to turn me to do its will—no doubt the assassins responsible for the attempts upon Valeria's life were similarly corrupted. If not for Fiora, I myself might have put my lady in danger."

"A good thing you were on duty," said the vizier, nodding at the guard, then reluctantly looking me in the eye. "And a good thing, I suppose, that you so clumsily spilled my wine."

While I withheld the somewhat embarrassing truth—that I had been thinking at the time she was the conspirator, or at least somehow related to the matter—Trystera turned her attention to the guards. "Remove my slave from my quarters and find a guest apartment for us on the fourth floor. The Materna will require more suitable housing than their small spaces."

With a bow, one of the guards left to obey. Meanwhile, the vizier continued to Valeria, "It is my strong suggestion that we suspend your duties for the present moment, until the matter of hunting down and slaying this spirit-thief has been seen to."

"Permit me," I began, but the vizier cut me off with a scoff.

"We have plenty enough guards for that, Burningsoul. Lucky as you were to make headway against this—thing, this task is better left to those slayers who are trained in the execution of spirit-thieves."

I bit my tongue, annoyed, unable to explain that I only found myself in a situation such as this to begin with because I had, mostly on my own, claimed the lives of the rest of Al-listux's less powerful brood. To my surprise, however, my lady leapt to agree with me.

"Burningsoul is more than capable of finishing the wounded spirit-thief," said Valeria, "and I for one would like to see the creature's death with my own eyes."

Balking, Trystera asked, "You mean *you* wish to be involved in the hunting of this thing, Materna?"

"It would help me sleep at dark if I could observe firsthand its final moments. Surely you can appreciate that."

"Then we'll bring you its head," said the vizier tersely. "What an outrageous thing to say! For the security of the city and your own personal safety, I must insist that you remain in the Palace—in my chambers for as long as possible, until we're able to confirm its death."

"Would you make the Materna of your city, the servant of Roserpine upon Urde, a prisoner in her own Palace?"

Though the vizier looked stricken by this—almost fearful that she had overstepped a boundary, I thought—her features soon firmed again.

"I have served as vizier to more Maternas than you," she reminded Valeria. "And there are times when my decisions have been better-weighed and more well-informed than even the most loyal of the Dark Queen's servants. I will not permit anything to happen to you, and will not see you put yourself in danger. As the spirit-thief intimately knows the ways of our Palace and could take the form of anyone at all, I insist that you remain in my quarters—and remind you that the Palace guards do not answer to you, or even Roserpine. They answer to me."

Arms crossed, Valeria glowered with great displeasure at her second-in-command. The vizier turned to the other guard who had arrived with them and demanded, "Bring my lady to my chambers and see to it that she's comfortable."

Nodding, the guard gestured toward the lift, saying,

"Right this way," while Trystera approached Fiora and commanded, "Show me the damage."

As Fiora bowed and led the vizier into the chambers to demonstrate the extent of the rubble left by the explosion, the higher-ranking guard led us to the lift. While she hit the button to summon it back up, Valeria gritted her teeth.

"A prisoner in my goddess's own Palace," she said, fingers sinking tightly into her crossed arms. "Trapped in my servant's chambers, unable to perform my duties—are we to bow to the mockery and assaults of all terrorists? This is unacceptable."

"Perhaps it would be wise for you to lay low awhile, Madame," I advised her, trying to keep both tone and wording diplomatic. Though she looked sharply at me, her arms became somewhat less tense as I went gently on. "Such acts of violence are often the catalyst for others. It would be too easy for the spirit-thief to corrupt someone from the city of El'ryh and send them into the Palace, ostensibly for some form of arbitration or advice. And... to be fair..." I chuckled in a humorless way, unable to help my smirk. "While I am sure I could fend off another attack if required, a few blooms of rest would be most appreciated."

Nostrils flaring with her sigh, Valeria fully relaxed her arms and took my hand in hers. "Are you all right, Burningsoul?"

"By virtue of Weltyr, I will live—and sleep very, very well when at last I can have a bit of rest."

"My treasure! My poor protector. How I hate the thought of anything happening to you—of what could have happened. How much worse it could have been!"

She looked pained, though by the possibility of my demise or by the fact that she could not kiss me in that second, I was not sure. The lift doors opened and we all stepped inside while I assured her warmly, "Perhaps it could have been worse, yes...but it wasn't. I stand before you, praise my god and yours."

Exhaling low, Valeria leaned her head against my arm. Before the guard could touch the rune that indicated the 51st floor where Trystera's apartment lay, however, my mistress commanded, "Wait—before we are to be brought to the vizier's quarters, take us to the baths."

"But Trystera—"

"Trystera does not wear the ring of Roserpine," said the Materna tersely, lifting her fist to show the guard the indigo ring that I swore glowed brighter with her anger. "I will go quietly to Trystera's chambers when the time comes, and stay there as though I am a slave of the very Palace I oversee—but before that, I and my own slave are both in sore need of the comfort of the baths. Accompany us if you would feel safer; better still, lead us there and call on Fiora to chaperone us back."

With a hefty sigh and a long look at the ring, the guard lowered her head, turned back to the panel, and struck the more familiar rune that would lower the lift to the floor where the baths were. Valeria sighed in relief and said in a gentler tone, "I appreciate your flexibility. Please, don't worry—I will see to it that Trystera does not punish you for obeying my command."

The guard remained visibly wary, but made no further arguments and looked quite relieved to see the baths from a distance. The humid air was a relief to my aching senses as we entered the warm chamber, and it was so soothing that it became my entire focus—so much so that it took me a few seconds longer than it should have to register the amount of sighing, moaning, and name-crying going on around us.

It would seem that, in light of the uproarious amount of fun all the banquet-goers were having, those who had slipped away to the baths had transformed the spa into the sight of an orgy outrageous enough to put my mistress's to shame.

At the very least, durrow caressed one another in groups of threes, fours, and mores while we made our way to the private chamber set aside for my lady. I tried not to stare…but it was quite difficult, and the whole scene was so distracting that I realized only belatedly we had not been greeted by any slaves. There were so many durrow in the baths that they were all occupied with the inundation of guests, and so, to my relief, Valeria and I were left alone in the Materna's warm rock pool.

As the door shut behind us, Valeria threw her arms around my neck with a noise like a sob.

"Rorke," she cried, holding me all the tighter as I embraced her, "oh, Rorke! My sweet hero—I am so sorry you were forced to risk your life for me again—"

"Oh, Madame, please—it's my purpose in this place. My one and only duty. Seeing to your defense is an honor I would not exchange for any other."

"But—oh—"

She pressed her weeping face to my neck, her eyes overflowing with tears that inspired a pang of adoration. While I drew her face back to wipe those lovely tears from her soft cheeks, she gazed up at me from beneath a furrowed brow.

"When I heard something had happened, I was so afraid—and now, to know that it was a spirit-thief—I ought to have relayed to you the truth of my dream. Oh! I dreamt a terrible thing, your death at the hands of just such a hateful beast. Now, knowing what occurred here, I'm terrified."

Overwhelmed by this information, relieved to think I had avoided such a thing, I kissed her brow and swore to her, "I would never let such a thing happen—never permit such a demon to take me from you."

"If it did—if Weltyr or Oppenhir claimed your life before I could tell you how I love you, how *deeply* I love you—I wouldn't be able to live anymore, Rorke!" Her sobbing peaked in an emotional wail that moved me twice as much as her admission of love. Valeria buried her face in my chest amid her hiccups of narrowly-avoided grief and continued, "Oh, Rorke! I don't know how I lived without you to begin with—I never want to do it again. Never want to awaken again if I can't look upon your face as I do."

"Valeria—you mustn't say such things. How much longer elves live than humans! As deeply as I love you, my mistress"—her breath hitched to hear me say such a thing, and the very utterance proved a sweet relief to my own burdened heart—"I would not be able to look Weltyr in his face if I thought that your own vitality wilted because I had lost mine."

Sobbing still, perhaps now in relief to be loved in return as much as to find me still alive in the wake of the battle, Valeria shook her head against me and managed after a moment to say, "We must not speak of such things now, Burningsoul—oh, Rorke. No: let us leave such grim conversations for the future, the distant future, when all this has passed us and you have been my companion for many more years."

"As you wish," I told her, kissing the tip of a lovely, dark ear and managing somewhat to ease her weeping through caresses of her back and shoulders. "Come now, Madame…perhaps you need to unwind even more than I do."

My hand had been raising to the clasp of her dress, but at her cry of, "Wait," I hesitated.

After briskly wiping her tears away, the Materna of the durrow gazed into my face. "Permit me to serve you as your slave, Burningsoul. Let me bathe you, let me see to your wounds and this aching body that would have so willingly sacrificed itself to maintain my own much too long life."

"Just long enough," I corrected her, pushing a lock of hair that had been stuck to her cheek back in place among its fellows. "Long enough to meet me, and fill my life with such unexpected joy. I would be honored were you to tend my wounds, Valeria."

Her pained lips managing to find their way to the barest hint of a smile, Valeria's eyes swept over me before focusing upon my belt. She removed this, reverently placing it aside along with Strife. In fact, to my greater love—and an odd trill, I admit—she stroked the scabbard and planted a tender kiss upon the pommel as though to thank it for its service in defending both her and me. Then, turning back to look me in the eye, my mistress reached behind her neck and unclasped her dress. The fabric pooled at her gold sandals, which she soon enough also removed. Then, naked before me but for her many jewels, Valeria stepped forward to undress me.

Each graze of her hand reminded me of the soreness of my muscles, the terrible tension provoked by the demon's electrical shock even after I was blessed by the healing power of Weltyr. The mere removal of the tunic from my head was a relief second to none, and I closed my eyes with a hefty sigh only to open them again when Valera trailed her fingertips down my chest and stomach. Upon her knees, she slid away my breeches and smiled at the natural result of those gentle touches of hers.

While her hand ran over my straining member, she rose deftly to her feet and took me by my hands. Together, we entered the pool, and as she eased me down into the baths I sighed with hefty relief to shut my eyes in the warmth of the water.

Soon her hands were upon me, the lathers and oils that she applied second in their comfort to the touch of her hands. We barely spoke; I was too exhausted for it, and Valeria, clearly too shaken. Those caressing hands traversed every respectable inch of my body, and by the time she had finished, those most unrespectable nine inches throbbed with desire for her attention. Valeria slid into the water than and, gazing with adoration into my face, she stroked and pulled my present ache. I tenderly held her face and drew her close for my kiss, drinking love and gratitude from her mouth like the finest of wines. Soon, enamored with the tension that was so sensitive to her touch, Valeria climbed into my lap and impaled herself upon me.

How wet she was! And not with the waters of the baths. I groaned and held her in my arms, the pearlescent pools of hers eyes the source of my singular focus. Much to my amazement, these great white orbs filled with tears that soon spilled over. I kissed her, held her, drew her out of the baths with me and made love to her upon the cushions of a nearby bench.

By the time we were finished, it seemed that the banquet-goers were none the wiser to the events that had occurred so many floors above them. Their revels continued uninterrupted, and my mistress and I emerged from the baths to find, as she had commanded, Fiora. The patiently waiting guard stood at attention, asking, "Greetings again, Madame. I have been assigned to accompany you to the vizier's quarters."

Her face twisted by a look of displeasure that she simply couldn't help, Valeria weakly nodded and permitted the guard to lead us to the lift. Her hand rested upon the central gem of her necklace, fingers worrying the setting of the stone and those of a few others. Only as we neared the lifts did I register how many more guards there were on this floor than on the average one: a full detail had been added to the existing staff, and I wagered a guess that many more had been placed upstairs, around the vizier's chambers.

Valeria, also, took notice. While the lift doors shut, Fiora reached for the panel of ruins, intent on activating one. My mistress caught her hand and gazed into her eyes.

"Fiora," she said, "bring us to the Palace entrance."

Surprised, Fiora said, "But my orders were to take you directly to Trystera's apartment for your own security, Madame."

"Trystera thinks she knows what is in my best interest," replied Valeria, doing an admirable job of keeping the terser notes from her calm voice, "but I am not a child. I am perfectly capable of making my own decisions, and of knowing when I am safe. Until that thing is captured, I am unsafe no matter where I am. I would see it killed myself. By my own hand, if need be. Until then, I will not be able to rest."

With a concerned look, first into my lady's face and then at the gem of Roserpine's ring, Fiora said with a faintly pleading tone, "Madame, the other palace guards are already aware of what has happened. You saw them all as we were coming to the lift."

"All the more reason you should help us leave now. Fiora. If the guards are already well-informed enough to be on the alert, think how much better-able they'll be to

241

identify and stop any attempt of mine to leave the Palace. If we leave now, it would be the last thing they expected."

"But—they'll see you. You can't just walk out the front gates! Even servants' exits are suspect."

"Give me your armor, then," said Valeria, no hint of jest in her expression or voice. "It'll prove a bit big for me, from the looks of it, but—"

Balking, Fiora said, "I can't give you my *armor, Materna! I'll be dismissed from service!*"

"Tell them I commanded you to do it and left you with no other choice. It was the will of Roserpine. Who are any of us to deny her desires, especially as they concern our fates and duties?"

With a miserable looked down at herself, Fiora sighed heftily. Finding no recourse, the durrow slid her helmet up over her head. Braided hair tumbled down around her shoulders while she passed the crested helm over, her displeasure to do so audible in her voice. "Please, Materna—if I am dismissed—"

"You won't be." Trying on the helmet and finding it workable size, Valeria passed it over to me and waited for her guard to remove the golden breastplate that resembled, in all ways, those of the other guards. Beneath she wore a tunic bedecked with a family crest, a phoenix sigil embossed in golds and reds upon the pale fabric. I tried to take it as a positive sign—a sign of my leaving the Nightlands, like that sacred bird rising from its own remains.

Meanwhile, Valeria continued, "If anyone takes exception to how you've helped us, tell them it is my command that they await my return and discuss it with me then. You are to be commended for your service and your assistance, Fiora…both here, and in saving Rorke's life."

With a quick glance my way, the guard shook her head and bent to remove her greaves. "I only hope that in doing this, I haven't endangered my own."

Soon enough, the lift let me out on the main floor. I remembered the disorienting trip taken by myself, Indra and Odile on the way to the throne room that first time; now, still disoriented as I was, I followed armored Valeria and considered the matter of navigating the Nightlands. Not just for the sake of finding the spirit-thief Al-listux, but for leaving the subterranean lands altogether, I would need the assistance of someone who could navigate this place.

A fine thing Indra and Odile saw fit to tell me the district where they lived.

In the end, praise Weltyr, we made it through the gates with relatively little fuss. The guards did glance at us briefly, perhaps struggling to recognize their comrade beneath Fiora's helmet, but we were stopped only to ask our business in the city.

"This slave has information on a potential lead concerning the latest attack on the Materna," answered Valeria, her firm voice's faint anxiety audible only to me. "He has agreed to return with me to the location of a prior incident in order to gather more evidence."

"Well, don't let him wander off—that's the Materna's slave, right? She'd be upset to lose him."

"Yes," agreed Valeria, leading me past the guardians of the palace entrance, "she would, indeed."

It seemed we both held our breaths until far enough from the palace that our gasps of free air could not be heard by those same guards who had let us through. My head swam with possibility. Oh, Weltyr! I knew the task was not over, but the hardest part of it all seemed to me to be the matter of our leaving the Palace. With that over, exiting El'ryh would be more of the same... so long as we could leave quickly enough. Who knew how soon it would become apparent that my lady was not where she was expected to be, and that her slave had also disappeared? If word traveled as fast through El'ryh as it did in the Palace, it was only a matter of time before we would be unable to leave the city at all.

We had to hurry, then—and as sore as I still was from my skirmish with Al-listux, the urgency that struck me seemed to promote a new flood of energy through my bones.

"What will we do now?" Valeria was clearly pondering the same issues I was, albeit with less success. Voice lowered, she asked, "Where do you suppose that beast flew off?"

"It seemed to be headed in the same direction as the city entrance Odile and Indra and I used when we arrived here together—perhaps, since the smithy was compromised, it has returned to the original home of its brood to mend its wounds."

"Do you know the way?"

"No, but Indra and Odile do. They said they live south of the auction quarter, and that most around there know them well enough that they could direct me."

"Then we'd ought to hurry and get them involved in the operation. The longer we delay, the more difficult it will be to leave the city. This way."

Taking a sharp left, my mistress led me down an alley between a few shops that, owing to their proximity to the Palace, were clearly quite glamorous inside and out. Likewise, the farther we got from the palace, the more run-down areas became. Only as we edged out of these slums and into the area that Odile had referred to as the "meat market" did the quality of the buildings once more raise, though at the outskirts there were still some very untrustworthy-looking establishments.

Not to say the auction quarter itself was a particularly safe and comfortable place—especially for me. In fact, I was shocked. Human beings stood in windows, slaves owned by brothels to be used by those visitors who had no means or interest in owning a slave of their own. Buildings were mounted with signs advertising the sale of human and surface elf children as young as five, evidently bred to be quality workers of this or that trade by their parents' durrow owners.

Most terribly, the central square of the district was arranged with a sorry sight indeed. Stocks lined the district's northern side, each containing a miserable slave who had in some way sinned against his mistress—but not so much that he had earned himself a hanging, as had the man whose body still swayed on display at the gallows. I averted my eyes with a quiet prayer to Weltyr, and even my mistress was visibly taken aback. After assessing the corpse with wide eyes and a slightly open mouth, she turned to me and said, "I have heard the auction square to be a grim place at dark—I have only been here in the bloom, and only passing through."

"There is no such thing as happy slavery," I told her, unsmiling. The guard noticed us and I gestured toward her, drawing Valeria's attention that way. Straightening her shoulders, clearing her throat, my lady led us forward and hailed the guard with an unpracticed salute.

"Hello, sister—you wouldn't happen to know Indra of Nocturna and Odile Darkstar's home, would you?"

"Just that way, a left at the end of the block and somewhat down the street from where the shops leave off for houses. Have they finally made trouble enough to call for Palace intercession?"

While I registered the nuances distinguishing Valeria's borrowed armor from the armor of the guard before us, my lady shook her head. "This slave and I are coordinating efforts to gather evidence in the plot against the Materna. We believe Indra and Odile may have valuable information based on previous conversations with them, and I need to go over some details again."

Valeria's lies were so fluid even I was almost convinced—certainly, very impressed. The guard didn't think twice, although she did ask with a grim expression, "Was there another move against her?"

Glancing my way as if to telegraph her displeasure at having begun the viral spread of gossip through the city herself, my mistress did her best to stay focused on the guard. "There was, unfortunately. As you can see, the danger is so severe that I permitted the slave to bring his weapon along."

With a grim shake of her head, the guard said, "It's disgusting, this terrorism. I've not met her myself, but I've heard the Materna is a good and gentle woman. Certainly preferable to any who ruled the city in my mother's time. Why make this one a target of deadly attempts?"

"Perhaps it's for that very reason—that her enemies see her as too soft to inspire any kind of counter-attack against her detractors." Turning to lead me away, Valeria added with a newer, far darker tone than I had yet heard her use, "But I think they will find themselves surprised, sooner or later."

ESCAPE FROM EL'RYH

WHAT HORRIBLE THOUGHTS plagued my mistress as we made our way through the city? Paranoia no doubt settled heavily upon her mind. Many people milled about even in that late hour, and we got a stare from more than one group of hoodlums lingering at a corner or drinking on a bench. The area was far from good, or safe, but Valeria held no compunctions about asking for details on which squat hovel belonged to Indra and Odile. Soon enough, we found ourselves upon a concrete stoop, the metal of Valeria's borrowed gauntlets ringing sharply against the peeling paint of the door.

It took another repetition before, looking irritated, Odile threw open the door—and recognized me after a few seconds, much to her shock. Perhaps it was that context that brought on the greater shock. Upon noting the disguised Materna, Odile genuflected in astonishment.

"Your highness! What in Roserpine's chaos could bring you here, of all places? At this hour, in this section of the city?"

"We need your help, Odile—please, keep quiet."

While Odile stepped aside, (and, curious to see the visitor, Indra popped her head into the room from an adjoining one only to express similar shock), Valeria and I stepped into the squat cabin's foyer. Valeria removed the helmet that somewhat obscured her face and sighed with relief, passing it to me to hold while she looked seriously between the two rogues.

"You two know the Nightlands as well as any adventurers in El'ryh," said Valeria to the both of them.

"Better," bragged Odile, grinning with pride at the Materna's praise. "Why, I could find my way through it blindfolded—with Indra on my back!"

"Hopefully it won't come to anyone carrying someone else. We need you to guide us back to the den of the spirit-thieves."

The cocky grin fell from Odile's face, replaced by an open-mouthed frown of visible dread. "Uh! Back *there?*"

"The spirit-thief Al-listux made an attempt on my lady's life tonight," I told them, daring to interject in a conversation only because of my friendly relationship with our present hostesses. While the two exchanged a glance, I went on, "I and the guard called Fiora were able to chase the creature off, but Valeria and I strongly suspect it is camping in the remains of its original broodsite. It would be beyond helpful if you could guide us back—a heroic task, one of patriotism and compassion. We have nowhere else to turn...and, very soon, the palace will be looking for us."

Odile said with a scoff, "I didn't know spirit-thieves had names."

"This one introduced itself when it tried to seduce me against my lady's cause—that time you brought me to serve the wadjita."

Odile looked as though she had difficulty understanding this piece of information for a few seconds, but Indra's dark face managed to pale a tone or two.

"I always thought there was something strange about her," said the gentler durrow, looking at her companion with distress. "Was she a traitor, Rorke? Did she know that the beast was staying with her?"

"It appeared to me in its true form, unfettered by any disguise...she knew."

"And she has since vacated her shop," added Valeria tersely, looking between the two durrow. "The thing she serves knew it was better if they flee. I would wager a guess that where we find it, we will also find its protector...or its pet, more like."

Groaning, Odile ran her hand over her forehead and looked up at the ceiling. "Now I just feel guilty—like all this time I've been abetting this conspiracy against the Materna's life."

"You haven't intentionally," Valeria said, her voice as tranquil and matter-of-fact as the one she used in the throne room. "But, regardless of your intention, you are right to be concerned. It would be very easy for my vizier, mistress of the courts as much as the royal guard, to claim that you were willfully embroiled in the scheme and responsible for the escalating attempts on my life."

All the more annoyed to hear that, the elder of the two durrow looked at me as though to tell me to talk some sense into my mistress, the woman whom many in the city seemed to revere as a goddess. In response to her look, I spread my hands helplessly. Odile rolled her bright eyes and said, "I understand there's a risk here, but the fact of the matter is that we didn't do anything. Unless you're admitting your own courts are rigged against the people who have to defend themselves in it, I don't see why we should be punished just because we brought Burningsoul to Kyrie as part of a fair, previously-arranged deal that had nothing to do with your assassins."

Offering a glance toward her hand—as though contemplating her ring beneath the finger guards—Valeria removed her gauntlets. As observed, the guard's armor was too big for her, and it allowed an excess of space within. She had therefore not worried about removing her bangles, her necklace, or the earrings that swayed within the veil of her hair.

Wordlessly striding to a nearby table, she began one at a time to divest herself of every piece of jewelry she had on her. Everything but that ring. When she at last set the hefty necklace I had picked for her atop the pile, Odile's eyes glowed golden with Oppenhir's thirst. She looked questioningly at the Materna, who waved to the precious plunder and said, "I will give all this to you, plus promise you more riches than this, if you will take us to the spirit-thieves' den and assist us in the slaying of the sorcerer, Al-listux."

Exhaling low as Indra came to her side to investigate the priceless jewels with her, Odile shared a glance with her friend and said, "Sorcerer, huh…"

"Wounded," I assured them. "Very badly wounded—missing a hand."

Odile's lower lip ground into her teeth. She lifted a lesser ring from the pile and examined its brilliant diamond in their home's candlelight while Indra asked, "Does he have any other spirit-thieves still with him?"

"We don't know." As I confessed this, Odile set the ring back down, still gazing at the pile of gleaming money. "He's powerful enough without help, in truth—all the more reason why the two of you would be a great boon to us, if only you would consent to help."

"If only we would consent to risk our lives, more like…" Snorting, closing her eyes, Odile sighed up at the ceiling and then looked at her feet—consulting the gods of heaven and underworld alike as to a graceful way out. Seeing there was not, the elder adventurer shook her head and said, "Fine. We'll do it."

At my noise of joy, she ignored me and continued, "It's not every bloom the Materna herself comes to visit, after all…certainly not every bloom that she asks you for help. Roserpine would fill my bed with serpents and spiders if I turned you down, Madame."

"The Dark Lady is sure to reward you for carrying out such a selfless risk." Once she had spoken these words out loud, Valeria's face seemed to change. The tension in it dissipated just the slightest bit. It made me realize that since I had known her she had been forever distant, her lovely features tinged with fear—dark acceptance that she might at any moment meet her fate at the tip of a poisoned dart or dagger in the back. That haughtiness I had seen in her? Fear was what it truly was. Separation from the world, in anticipation of her death.

But now all that began to lift. Much as my face had surely changed when we stepped together outside the Palace walls, her tense brow soothed and the strain of her jaw began to vanish. "Roserpine willing," she said softly, "when all this is over, I'll be able to live in peace again, and so will the city I love."

It had not yet occurred to me how impacted El'ryh was by the Materna's constant close calls—but as we, a small party of four, soon made the long journey up the coiling ramp out of the city, I wondered how much of the vaguely antagonistic culture I sensed on my arrival had to do with the grim possibility that any boom the citizens might awaken to some of the worst news imaginable. Skythorn had, in my time, received its share of terrorist assaults, and though they did not occur often, they rattled the entire citizenry. For these attacks to have continued for a time so long (as many as four years before my arrival, I had been told once by Valeria), El'ryh had been existing under a cloud of great oppression.

"We should have bought a cart," lamented Odile as we approached the gates of the city. "Or left tomorrow at bloom's first light...what a time to set out on a journey!"

"It couldn't wait," Valeria answered. "The longer we wait, the more likely I am to be found out and prevented from leaving at all."

I feared that might still have been a problem. As we approached the guards, it became apparent that the dark staff was less friendly than those who worked during bloom. Neither Indra nor Odile knew the one who finally called us up from the line, and she looked sternly between the four of us before focusing in on Valeria in her guard costume. "Name?"

"Fiore Cobalt," answered the Materna. "I am accompanying Indra and Odile here, along with their slave, on a mission from the Materna."

The guard did arch a thick brow at that, looking between us again and saying, "These two, sent by the Materna? On what?"

"A scouting mission, with the intention of hunting down the latest assassin who made an attempt upon our lady's life."

The guard looked all the harder at Valeria upon hearing this. "Is that so? Then why isn't an entire detail of guards and professional scouts, being sent out to look?

Why send the rabble? I've half a mind to suspect you lot are responsible for any incident tonight, coming across as suspicious as you do."

"What, exactly, makes us suspicious?"

"Aside from how bizarre it would be for the Materna—or anyone from the Palace, for that matter—to employ the help of freelancers to chase down an assassin, you know as well as I do that you ought to have written orders clarifying the nature of your task. So, where are they?"

With an annoyed glance at me—perhaps because now she understood a little better my restriction without one of the Palace's treasured passes—Valeria said, "Ah, I have it here, just a moment," and removed her gauntlet as though to take a scroll from her sleeve.

Instead, she let the guard see the ring.

The impatient woman almost didn't notice it at first, on the verge of tapping her foot as she was. When she did see it, however, her eyes grew wide. That gaze snapped from the glowing indigo gem to Valeria's face and took in more clearly the aristocratic bearings of her features. The soldiers opened her mouth, appalled at herself, but Valeria quickly said with respect to the other guards still checking people in and out of the city, "No need to say anything."

"Of course," said the flustered guard, still too shocked to fully formulate her thoughts. "Of course—this looks to be in order, uh, fine, that's just fine. Go on then."

"Have a good night," said Valeria, nodding to the guard while Indra and Odile passed the woman smugly by. I stepped over the gate after them, another cool wave of bliss sweeping across me to think that I had just perhaps permanently escaped El'ryh—but only on its other side did I realize Valeria had not followed me.

I turned to find her looking at the earth; glancing back

over her shoulder at the city. Her confession, that she had never before been out of the city, struck me in the heart somehow. What a powerful moment this must have been for her—powerful, and frightening.

At last, her expression growing firm with purpose, she stepped outside of El'ryh and closed the short distance between us.

"I love you," I whispered to her gently, moved by her growth—her true power. Her eyes flickered toward me; her head lowered. With respect to our companions and the guards nearby, she said nothing, but her hand did brush mine on her way past me.

And then, we walked. Indra held the magical lantern ahead of us, its golden light allegedly the reason why our journey had been so peaceful the first time. Despite this, Odile insisted on taking up the rear so as to keep the Materna from traveling with her back uncovered. We marched in this column formation unbroken, forced occasionally to press against the side of a narrow cavern to permit the passage of a latecomer into the city gates. By the time we emerged into the more open network of caves and tunnels that made passage possible throughout the Nightlands, however, we saw no other travelers, and Valeria had slowed significantly beneath the weight of her armor and the indolent lifestyle that left her unaccustomed to military marches. Three hours turned into four into five. Eventually she began to slow us down, and proceeding along our journey was bound to do more harm than good without giving her rest.

"Perhaps we'd ought to stop for the dark," I suggested when we approached the source of a dripping I had noticed for some time. In the distance, a natural fountain gushed from the wall and into a small subterranean creek. It curled off through a distant tunnel to disappear into the stones, and the sight and sound were so refreshing to all of us that it was quickly agreed we had ought to spend the night and prepare for a well-rested altercation with the spirit-thief. Valeria drank greedily from the cold crystal tap, gasping to lift her head away and wipe her damp lips against the back of her hand. Indra and Odile preferred the wineskins brought with them, saving their swigs until our small camp was sorted out.

The women had brought only two bedrolls, having only two to their name; however, blankets had been packed to serve as impromptu extensions. After a quick meal of travel rations, mostly consisting of salted lizard meat and those thick hardtack biscuits meant to last on the trail, we organized ourselves into pairs. With Indra and Odile in one bedroll and Valeria with me in the other, we all reclined upon the ground and struggled for the least wink of sleep.

At least, Valeria and I struggled. Indra and Odile both fell to girlish snoring in an instant, their arms wrapped around one another in an almost sisterly manner, Indra already twitching with the promise of future fidgeting sure to annoy her friend. Valeria looked over at them before whispering to me, "How can they feel so comfortable? I'm afraid to fall asleep, lest some hideous beast come out of the dark."

"That lantern of theirs is enchanted," I told her. "Enough to keep us safe from any boorish monster that may happen by."

"And spirit-thieves?"

"That, I don't know…but you have me. I'm as good as any magic lantern, or better."

"I suppose," said Valeria, laughing lightly. Abruptly squirming beneath the covers quite a bit herself, she soon slid her golden dress up over her head and set it carefully aside. "Hold me, Burningsoul," she begged, turning to rest her backside against my lap when I shifted over to do so.

The shape of her body! There has never been anything more natural to me than caressing the slopes of Valeria's body. I only realized I was doing so when she shuddered, goosebumps rising along her flesh while my fingertips trailed over her ribs and around the plane of her stomach. Her sighs were sweet as a ripe berry while I teased her, my mouth brushing the ridge of her ear. With a glance at the sleeping guides, she soon looked back at me in invitation. Her legs parted beneath the blanket.

My caresses lowered. Her mouth opened with a gasp of pleasure as my touch traversed areas that seemed more sensitive upon Valeria than upon any other woman. As I toyed between her silken thighs, my free hand slid beneath her to caress her breast. I rolled a dusky nipple between my fingers and she arched back against me, whimpering while I covertly fondled her beside our sleeping companions.

Her heart raced beneath my hand. Those slender fingers I loved so terribly trailed back over me, dancing down my thigh and between us. Soon they found my desire for her, renewed since our intimacy in the baths, and while they wrapped around this column the breath was stolen from my lungs. My tongue lashed the long ridge of her beautiful ear and, while she worked her hand, I caressed between her legs and felt her tension increase in my arms almost constantly.

I was on the verge of almost begging her to do something about it for the sake of my sanity—to permit me the favor of quiet, tightly-bound coitus, like two snakes coiled into one—when I realized that Indra and Odile were no longer snoring. I glanced up from quietly panting Valeria to see our companions watched, embracing, their hands moving beneath the blankets in a clearly sensual exploration.

"Maybe we ought to put the bedrolls together," advised Odile, producing a slight jump of surprise from Valeria, then an eager lifting of her head at the thought. "We'll stay much warmer if we're all together."

"That seems like a pleasant suggestion," agreed the Materna, breathless while I had particular success stimulating a certain nerve of hers. Smiling, Odile kissed Indra upon her sighing lips, then drew her upright to gain her help in moving the bedroll.

It had been my previous observation that Valeria was a splendid lover, enthusiastic and responsive in all ways that counted when she was in my arms—but as responsive as she was when we were alone, she was even moreso when we performed in front of someone else. Whether slaves, courtiers or the other members of our small traveling party, the simple act of being seen astride my cock left her not just wetter, but more awash in the actual receipt of pleasure than at any other time.

The moans that wracked her body were soul-deep. Seeing my tongue plunge into Odile's mouth as she bent for a kiss, or my fingers explore Indra's body to coax an orgasm out of her, only seemed to increase Valeria's joy. Each time, her body tightened around mine in a vise grip while she worked up and down my length.

For my own part, I had already seen Indra and Odile exchange many a fine-to-observe kiss or caress, but as both turned their attentions upon my mistress, I thrilled to think I had never seen a thing so beautiful in all my life. While she rode me, the two adventurers kissed her ears and tweaked her nipples, sometimes letting their caresses slide down to toy with the gem crowning her holy valley. She moaned while they tickled that sensitive nub, her body flooding all the more, her mouth gasping open for passionate kisses from both.

All the while I explored her curves, gripped her hips and rear, caressed her back: soon her pace grew wild and she exploded with delight, my name echoing on her lips until she fell from me and demanded, "Oh, yes, yes— Now let me watch them have their turns, oh, Burningsoul… but save your seed for me."

And so the pattern continued, me laying Indra down in the bedroll to take her from atop while Odile, incensed by the sight of Valeria's masturbation to the scene, lowered her head to kiss and suckle my lady's feminine valley. During the course of these operations, Indra and the Materna exchanged kiss on kiss, and I ached to burst but reminded myself I could not.

The sheer desire within me to obey Valeria's every command made it doable, though not necessarily easy. It was more difficult still when at last it was Odile's turn— especially because she wanted it so roughly, presenting herself upon her hands and knees and forever demanding, "Oh, more! Sweet Roserpine, more, more, take me like the beast you are, human—oh, yes! That's it, hard, hard, just like that—"

When Odile was wracked by an orgasm, her hair in disarray and her bosom rapidly rising and falling with her panting, Indra held her and slowly caressed between her splayed, wet legs while they watched me take my mistress a second time.

Valeria was wetter than ever—lewder, too, now offering herself to me upon her back, her legs splayed as she reached down and spread herself with the tips of her fingers. The quivering pink flesh within appeared more inviting than I had ever seen it.

BLOOM & DARK

My manhood leapt in my hand as I aligned to the sweet cavern. While I plunged into her, she groaned with delight and glanced back with a shudder to see the two pairs of watchful eyes upon us. It was not long before my lady and I shared a powerful climax: one that rattled through the both of us and seemed to inspire one in Odile.

Then, beneath the weight of this pleasure, we collapsed in a heap. Odile and Indra fell asleep instantly, far more heavily than they had before, and I was certainly on the brink of exhaustion myself.

Valeria, though, was not so fast to sleep. Her warm, soft cheek rested upon my chest and her eyes, though heavily-lidded, still fixed into the distance. I enfolded her in my arms and softly asked, "Are you afraid?"

"Afraid—yes. Yes, I suppose I am."

"I know you've never left El'ryh before. I'm proud of you for wanting to—if you can hear me say such a thing and not feel patronized for it to come from a man so much younger than you."

Laughing, the Materna glanced up at me and kissed the patch of hair on my chest. "You mean it purely, Rorke. Kindly. I know your intent, and it's sweet to me. You're right…I've never left El'ryh before."

Her lips pursed as her cheek lowered upon my chest again. "I ought not to say this," she whispered, "since I only recently chided you for wishing to know too much of my visions of the future…but I am not sure I will find myself back in El'ryh. At least—not for quite some time."

My heart leapt. I wished to ask her more, but she shut her eyes and nuzzled her face against my heart. "Sleep well, Burningsoul, my hero."

The kiss I pressed to her brow was as passionate as anything I had delivered her during our wild romp with

Indra and Odile. I dared not ask her too much, lest I distress her by making her contemplate her own thoughts too readily. Instead, I lay my head back and shut my eyes.

I should venture a guess that each one of us slept so well it was a miracle we awoke at all upon the arrival of the misshapen.

IN THE EYE OF THE

THE MALE DURROW had spider legs.

Nothing about the sentence made sense, but it was the first my brain constructed when I stirred from the depths of sleep at the scuttle of something across the cavern of our camp. From the waist up, the creature upon which I gazed was obviously the male counterpart of the durrow beside me: svelte, leanly muscled and long-limbed; befit, like all elves, with an almost feminine beauty. But his lower half, the sight of which chilled my blood, was in the form of a tremendous spider, as though he were some hideous arachnoid centaur of the Nightlands.

Alert at once, I pushed sleeping Valeria down in my place while springing up with my hand outstretched for Strife. On my sharp motion, Indra and Odile also leapt from deep sleep to the defense, their bodies trained by years of traveling to posses muscle memory that was downright dangerous. While they readied themselves for action, nude though we all were, the misshapen threw up its hands and begged, "Please, spare me! I'm no threat to you, I swear it by Hamsunt's sacred name."

Somewhat surprised to hear this creature invoke the god of poetry, crossroads and signs—and mischief—I asked, "Then what cause have you to lurk around our campsite?"

"I saw the glow of the lantern and thought it was my duty to come and warn whoever owned it—there's been a spirit-thief about, the constant dangers of my feral kin aside."

Relaxing somewhat, I nodded at the lantern and observed, "You can come into its light."

While the misshapen looked at me in confusion, not understanding the meaning of this observation, I glanced at Indra and Odile while slowly easing Strife back down. "Excuse our reactions," I said while they, too, lowered their arms, not completely relinquishing them but neither poised to attack at a second's notice. I added then, glancing at myself, "And our state of undress."

Just slightly, the misshapen laughed and looked down at its black spider abdomen. "Only if you will excuse mine, travelers. I am very sorry to have frightened you—I wasn't sure if it was right to wake you, being what I am, but it was unjust for me to let you go about your business when I know what lurks out there in the caverns this dark."

"You said there was a spirit-thief about?"

The misshapen nodded, glancing up the very same route we had intended to take to the spirit-thief den. "I saw it limp past, missing an arm."

"We're on the hunt for that one," I told the misshapen, earning a lifting of its eyebrows as though to indicate surprise. "I was with the party that slew the den of spirit-thieves, but evidently I missed at least one."

"Oh! You?" Hand upon his heart, the misshapen's eight legs scuttled forward a few steps. I tried not to let my skin crawl—tried instead to respect the dignity of all life. In the name of Weltyr, I focused on this stranger's compassionate heart while he went on, "If that was really you, we owe you much. My kin would not acknowledge it to you were they under threat of death, but I know more gratitude than they. Thank you. Our lives have already improved immensely in the past two weeks."

"By the All-Father, my heart overflows with joy to hear such a thing." Memories of the battle with the spirit-thieves flooded my mind—moreover, memories of my near-death and the subsequent resurrection. In so doing I pictured the hateful temple where the demons dwelled and asked this misshapen spider-durrow, "Say, friend—I'd wager you know the Nightlands even better than the durrow who pass through these tunnels from town to town."

While Odile muffled a little snort of jealous derision, the flattered misshapen smiled. "Yes, friend, I know it well indeed!"

"Then perhaps you might be able to tell us—are there alternative means of entry to the den of the spirit-thieves? Odile and Indra and I know of only one. Ah, and what is your name, might I ask?"

"Adonisius," answered the creature with a bow, its spindly front legs bending at the joints to permit the motion. "And there is, I think, a rear entrance to the spirit-thieves' den, but it is rather treacherous for even something like myself."

"I fear no danger," I told him, the brashness of my youth still hot in those days and stoked by my escape from bondage and the city of El'ryh. "Only tell us what it is, and we'll see it accomplished by one means or another."

Stroking his jaw, the clean-shaven misshapen looked over his shoulder and suggested, "I'm not entirely sure this is a danger even the bravest mortal adventurers could conquer without magical assistance."

"And what's that?"

When Adonisius did not look back at me and remained staring over his shoulder, I realized this was not an affectation of habit, but a directed gaze.

He stared into the water by which we had encamped.

"By Weltyr's beard," I said, stroking the stubble of my own from the night before. "Of course."

"The rear of the temple has long-since flooded," explained the misshapen. "You're very clever to wonder about a way to sneak in, rather than walk straight through the main entry...but the truth is that I most often see the spirit-thieves come in and out by way of the water system. At least, I see them by these areas often."

"Then we're lucky the rest were exterminated," I found myself saying, faltering only when I recognized the word I had used.

I absorbed it for a few seconds before going on, wondering about the power and meaning of my language. "We could have been killed in the night, otherwise... might I ask, brother"—the misshapen looked pleased to hear himself addressed this way and looked at me expectantly—"how is it that you've come to be so friendly?"

"I was just going to ask," interjected Odile, her expression hard even as she and Indra took the opportunity of this conversational lull to throw on their clothes. "How is it that you're so knowledgeable, so forthcoming with this information? Perhaps you're just that spirit-thief we're hunting in disguise."

"No," insisted Valeria, still undressed beneath the beddings but propped upon her elbows to watch the scene unfold. "Were that the case, he would still be missing a hand."

The friendly misshapen glanced down at his hands and waved them together.

"Perhaps it's illusory magic of some kind," suggested Indra.

Onee more, Valeria shook her head. "Roserpine has long-since taught me feel the magic that lurks about a being—the feeling of an electrical storm contained in a room. I need but say a prayer in my heart, not even out loud, and the houses of enchantment upon an entity reveal themselves. There is nothing here."

"I really am sorry to have startled you," the misshapen said earnestly. "My way of making money is by helping return the lost to where they meant to be. For a little fee or even promises of future favors I act as guide—and it would not be good for business were I as hardened as my kinfolk."

"I suppose that's true," grumbled Odile uncertainly, taking up her dagger and re-sheathing it with a significant look at Adonisius.

I studied the waterway beside our camp more carefully, wondering about that point around the bend at which the water flowed into the rocks. "Do you suppose there's a way to drain the temple's flooded areas enough for us to safely swim there?"

"I think it must be quite a long ways," advised the misshapen, studying the water again.

"I have no real way of knowing, of course, but these

waterways run all through the Nightlands. Stopping up but one would be quite a project."

"I see."

Indra, who I was beginning to suspect had something of a sorceress's interest, inquired of Valeria and myself, "Do either of you know a spell or a prayer that might let us breathe underwater?"

"No," said Valeria with a shake of her head. "Such things are not my lady's purview."

"Nor Weltyr's," I agreed, frowning in the direction of the waters we needed traverse.

After thinking on it, Adonisius said reluctantly, "I do know of a certain mushroom—a strange and misshapen sort of orange blossom once pointed out to me by a knowledgeable traveler. He explained they granted one the power to breathe underwater...this must have been so, for they were all picked ages ago. The only patch I know of is guarded by...a thing."

"'A thing?'" I laughed at his obscurity, inquiring further, "What sort of thing, man? A dragon? A manticore?"

"Nothing of the sort. It is—a creature covered in eyes." The half-spider being shuddered, folding his arms over his chest against the thought.

"It does remind me in some ways of the spirit-thieves, in that some of these eyes are mounted upon stalks like hideous tentacles and it may assume forms other than its own. But rather than taking the forms of those it has seen, all this unnameable beholder of mortal minds need do is look into the heart of the man who stands before it.

"At once, without any sort of transformation, the thing is replaced by a person with a special place in the love or hatred of its visitor. Many who have seen it claim they never saw its real form at all. I saw it once. I was curious, so I brought a mirror with me one bloom when I went to ask its wisdom. I regret ever looking."

Fending off a chill while the women exchanged a silent glance, I asked, "This is the only patch of these fungi that you know of?"

"Yes," he said, "and I know the whole of the Nightlands, but especially this region."

While Odile rolled her eyes, I began to dress. "Please, bring us to it."

"Are you sure this is really wise?" Odile set her hands on her hips and arched a brow, going on to insist, "Perhaps the best way in really *is* through the front door. It'd be faster, anyway."

"And one of us would end up killed for certain. Let's try our luck with this 'thing' of Adonisius's. I will address it, and you three remain behind to listen. Come to my aid only if necessary."

Indra frowned. "What do we have to pay the guide with, though?"

Glancing down at her wrists, my lady found her cache of jewelry gone. Then, however, Valeria's eyes drifted toward the suit of armor. It had brought us this far, but was far too heavy a burden for the priestess. "Would you be interested in determining if any of this armor fits you, sir?"

The spindled legs of the misshapen scuttled toward the borrowed suit of armor Valeria had arranged on the ground before bed. "Oh, why—some of it might, yes. Let's see—"

How convenient the similarity between male and female elves proved to be in that moment! The breastplate was too shapely, but the helmet fit Adonisius perhaps better than it had Valeria. Looking quite overjoyed, he enthused about it most of the way to the creature he had so ominously described. Valeria turned down putting on the rest of the armor and so Indra and Odile split it between the two of them, with Indra taking the grieves and Odile accepting the breastplate. Throughout this march, my lady fared much better—though I certainly noticed a fearful rigidity to her posture as we approached the thing's cavern by midbloom.

"Here we are," said Adonoisius, his voice a murmur. "If it's all the same, I'll stay out here. When two or more enter at once, its powers are confused, and you risk seeing its true shape. I have no interest in experiencing such a thing again."

"All the more reason for me to enter alone," I said, nodding. Valeria looked at me with profound concern; I swept up her hand and kissed her knuckles. "Worry not, my lady. We'll have the fungus that will bear us to the death of your nemesis in no time."

Looking no more relaxed for that, Valeria gently caressed my face and then stepped away. I nodded at Indra and Odile, who knew their parts and watched me stride into the creature's cave with one hand upon the pommel of Strife.

Even by the standards of the Nightlands, this cave seemed very dark. I gradually realized as I moved deeper into its moist environment that this was because there were no blooming fungi to give the place a hint of light.

Perhaps I ought to have brought Odile's light, but after meeting the misshapen called Adonisius I suspected the magic in it functioned based not on species but on a certain threshold of intelligence. To bring such a thing would only insult the creature, and I did not want to do that. From what the misshapen said, this thing was very intelligent, and I intended to reason with it for only four of the orange mushrooms.

But when I at last came to the cave's termination

and found a man sitting in the dark, I was somehow too taken aback to ask what I had intended. Yes, I knew what Adonisius had told me: but it was still quite a shock somehow, and I fell back upon my heel.

The man, whose features I could not quite distinguish even with my darkness-adjusted eyes, asked me with a stroke of his beard, "You look surprised, boy."

"Well—preparation is one thing, but—"

"Seeing is believing," said this creature in a man's flesh. Some manner of rattling occurred in the darkness and, just as my mind placed the unexpected voice to its name, this being that had stolen Hildolfr's form from my mind lit a pipe with the old man's misappropriated hands. The adventurer, whose eyepatched face was briefly illuminated by the silver lighting device of old dwarvish design, puffed idly on his pipe.

"How are you, Rorke?"

I shook off the illusion as best I could, though it was so well-conceived that I still struggled to believe it was not Hildolfr—the most painful of my betrayers—seated on a boulder before me. I cleared my throat.

"If you would excuse me, sir, I have no interest in playing such games. Nor in fighting. I have only come for four of your mushrooms, to permit myself and my companions to breathe underwater for a time."

"All business!" Hildolfr's laugh was so familiar that my heart ached to hear it emulated. The entity puffed on his pipe, continuing, "I like that…but what I don't like is people coming to raid my garden. You know why there are so few of these mushrooms out there in the wild now, don't you?"

"Yes, sire," I assured him, bowing. "But it is an emergency. My lady's life has been threatened by a—"

"I know all that," answered the thing coolly. "You think

I can reach into your mind and pull out old Hildolfr here, but I can't see what you've been through?"

"I apologize. I did not mean to be presumptuous."

"Ah, that's all right. I know you want to respect me. I appreciate that. Wise of you, too. Everybody who comes to kill me ends up dead...and those who want to see my true form are making a mistake."

"So I've heard. I would not dare attempt either one of those ill-advised actions. My only desire is to ask what I might trade or do in order to earn a few mushrooms from your garden, about which I would never tell anyone. If you see into me so well, then surely you see that."

"I do," said the stolen old man, cryptically adding after a second, "sort of."

Before I could ask him what he meant, he cleared his throat and shifted around on the rock to face me properly.

"I'll tell you what," said the creature, lowering the pipe. "Let's make a deal. I love to see the process of a human at thought. It thrills me...especially an intelligent human. Answer three of my questions to let me see you think. If you answer them correctly and reason through them well, I'll give you what you came here for."

"And if I don't?"

"Then I'll take your lady's ring," said the beast in Hildolfr's skin. "So?"

"You must see I am confident that you would be unable to do that. Certainly not with my consent."

"Then you'd better answer my questions correctly, huh."

Curiously, the thing seemed to become more like the individuals whose personas it adopted, unlike the spirit-thieves for whom a stolen form was but a puppet. That, or the creature before me already had a personality resembling Hildolfr's.

"Very well," I said, folding my hands. "Go on with your questions."

Lifting the pipe again, the being asked, "What are you?"

My mind leapt to work at once and I swore I saw the creature's smile even in the dark.

What was I? My instinct was to call myself a paladin, or a servant of Weltyr. Yet neither of these seemed right, or even fully true. The life of the paladin was a pursuit—and 'pursuit' was a word to be taken with special significance, as many points to it as there were to the sun on my neck. We were meant to be humble and understand that our faith was a matter of practice; that our highest and best self was always somewhere off in the distance. That we were, next to Weltyr, at once mighty and nothing at all.

"I am an animal," I said after thinking at last of the magic lantern used by Indra and Odile, and of our conversation when first I learned the function of its light.

Its smile remained in place, even and somehow knowing. "Interesting answer. Who are you?"

That, I did not know, and faltered on the asking. Rorke Burningsoul was what I was named at the Temple—but who I truly was had always been the foremost mystery of my existence. I had only one Father I could name, and answered, "I am a son of Weltyr."

"Very good," said the creature. "Your thoughts are extremely interesting to me. One last question for you, Rorke Burningsoul, Son of Weltyr: Who is watching you think, right this very moment?"

Once more, I faltered. I stared the creature down. It was not telling me to guess its name, I was sure. Beyond that, I felt lost. What could it mean? Who was watching *me* think? Who was I? A son of Weltyr—an ape-man blessed beyond all reason with consciousness. With the gifts of Weltyr's two great birds, Thought and Memory. Those feathered saints flitted around in my head, seeking for the means by which to help me in my predicament. I glanced away, my thoughts no doubt a fascinating cascade of reason for the creature before me to observe.

In the end, the only answer I could give was, "Weltyr."

I expected the creature to say something—to mark me either right or wrong.

Instead, I glanced back to the point where this duplication of Hildolfr sat. To my wonder, it had disappeared entirely.

With a glance around—and a certainty that it had only retired to some other dimension of reality so as to oversee my harvest of its garden—I got on my hands and knees to avoid ruining so much as one of the precious fungi. After a few paces, my fingers brushed the cool, moist flesh of a ruffled mushroom: my heart soaring, I plucked up that one plus three more and made my slow way back through the dark.

As I emerged from the cave, all three durrow cried out with pleasure. Valeria in particular almost sang my name, dashing forward with an astonished laugh for the mushrooms in my clutches. Beaming with approval into my face, she fit her hands to my cheekbones and kissed me. "Well done, my beloved! I heard not the least sound of struggle."

"There was none. The being gave them freely, in exchange for the asking of some questions."

"What a relief," said Adonisius, straightening the helmet and waving a hand. "I've heard it said the creature turns men to ash."

"You didn't tell us *that*," Odile complained in a tone of supreme annoyance as the misshapen led us back the way we'd come.

It was only a matter of a few hours before we once more found ourselves by that crystal river, but it felt to me like an eternity—no doubt, everyone else took it much the same. I thought the whole time only of how powerful the spirit-thief had proven in combat at the Palace. Were there more than one spirit-thief, we might have been in trouble.

Frankly, even if he had only the wadjita by his side, the challenge and danger would both be significantly increased. We therefore spent the way there speaking softly: developing a general plan to send Indra and Odile forth in a scout capacity, for me to use their advice with their back-up in battle, and for Valeria to stay behind and involve her magic only if necessary.

"How long do these mushrooms last?"

I asked this of the misshapen before we parted ways, the pleasantries he exchanged with the elves much more light-hearted on both sides now that the ladies knew he was not a traitor.

Looking thoughtfully at the one in my hand, he suggested, "I've heard it said they last variably depending on the size of the person, but that six hours is the average. I can't imagine it will be that much swimming, though. The spirit-thieves' den is south from here, so if you can avoid getting disoriented and focus on heading that way"—he gestured in the mentioned direction—"you should find yourselves there soon enough."

"It's almost an hour to the front door of the den from here by land," Odile answered, at least now on relative speaking terms with the misshapen.

He nodded in response. "Yes, that's about right. I would expect it to be about as much underwater—more or less, depending exactly on whether the current is with or against you."

Praise Weltyr, we would find it to be with us. One at a time, we ate our mushrooms, then looked queasily at one another to feel a strange effect in the depths off our throats. While the mouth salivated, the windpipe opened and gill slits emerged on the inside of the windpipe. The queer experience stung only a few seconds, then passed by quickly and left us able to take in water just the same as we did air.

Then, all together, we dove into the waters of the subterranean creek. Owing to the weight of their armor and their packs, Indra and Odile had to leave these things behind—hidden among a patch of boulders at a juncture of the cavern tunnels. Free of these burdens but for a pair of necessary pouches at their hips, they swam gaily as mermaids. Each laughed in astonishment to look around beneath the water with the unhurried leisure of a tourist admiring the neat streets of Skythorn. Even I confess I had a bit of fun experimenting with flips and various swimming strokes.

Only Valeria seemed too driven to enjoy the novelty of water-breathing. For her it was a means to an end—the end of ridding herself of the entity so eager and willing to bring her death that it had risked its own life to live among us in the Palace. I fully understood why the task was at such a high stake for her, and so, seeing her grim expression, I let Indra and Odile have the fun. I reached out and squeezed Valeria's hand beneath the waters where we swam, then urged forward to make our way through the Nightlands river as directed by our guide.

Though our lungs may have been temporarily equipped to process the water through which we navigated, our mortal bodies remained subject to hypothermia—and our weapons, to rust. Blessed as it was by Weltyr, Strife would be unharmed by such corrosion, but I felt concern for Indra and Odile. Hopefully they would sell off some of Valeria's jewelry to buy better weapons when they returned to El'ryh.

Would I ever know if they did? I was not sure. Then again…I was not sure of anything that would happen once we had taken the life of Al-listux. I tried to stay focused as we swam with the current to the flooded temple of the spirit-thieves, but my mind constantly wandered to other concerns.

Mostly, that concern was singular: Valeria.

Now I understood a little better the dilemma previously described to me, about slaves earning freedom through the love of mistresses they could not leave. Though we had not long been together I couldn't help but find the idea of abandoning her to be reprehensible. After what she had told me of her dreams, and after her heartfelt confession of love, it would have been a betrayal of romance itself were I to leave her standing in the temple of the spirit-thieves where I had once been saved from certain death.

Yet…how could I ask a queen to leave her people? How abhorrently selfish would it be were I to ask her to abdicate her throne and fulfill her dream of seeing the surface with me? There were many other, far more pressing matters, but these issues set themselves heavily upon my mind and lurked more heavily still in the background when, at last, the environment around changed.

The riverbed through which we swam was a strange, dark surface, deeply cracked and flanked on either side with similarly marred panels of gray concrete. These cracks were not the host of plants or vents as one might find in the ocean, but rather provided evidence of the water's impact on a surface that seemed to have once been deliberately paved—at least, that was the impression the caverns through which these waters ran gave off. At times it even seemed the walls and ceiling were crafted with some form of brick, but my eyes were weak in those dark waters and I could not always make sense of what I saw or thought as a result of the sure hypothermia into which my body descended while we swam to the temple.

In fact, I was beginning to worry that the well-meaning misshapen had sent us to our doom—but then, like the glow of gold in the waters of that helpful river, light shown down ahead of us. Odile made a noise that seemed to be one of excitement as much as relief: sure enough, the four of us broke the surface there to realize we had discovered a set of stairs.

One at a time, we happy travelers hurried from the water. My elfin friends at once perched upon the stone steps, shivering, praising Roserpine, calling from distant regions of spacetime the blue heat of their wisp fires. Three lapping flames merged into one that, owing to its magic, required no wood to settle safely upon the stones between us. We huddled together, shuddering in each other's arms and gathering as much strength from the fire as we could.

"What fun that was," enthused Indra, meriting both an eyeroll and a sharp shushing from Odile.

"Quiet, you! You want us to be detected before we've even scouted this place out? Anyway, who could find such a thing fun! If elves had been made to swim, Roserpine would have given us fins."

"Some elves were made to swim," I advised, remembering with fondness the lovely naiad maid who served my lady in the baths. Now Odile looked sourly at *me*, her generally cross mood having grown all the more irritable for nearly freezing to death in the unlit Nightland waters.

"That may be so, but durrow aren't among them. All right—" Having reached the limit of her annoyance with us, it would seem, Odile stood and smoothed her tangled hair from her stern face. "Indra? Come along, let's see what we can find. Burningsoul, come running if you hear us imperiled."

Drawing her dagger, Odile led the way up the algae-coated stone steps and into the depths of the temple. Close behind, Indra waved to us, pressed her finger to her lips, and disappeared behind her friend as they rounded a curve.

Alone with me, Valeria began again to tremble. I took her hands in mine, kissing her fingers and murmuring softly to her, "Soon enough it will all be over, Madame— Al-listux will be dead and you, free of these many attempts on your life."

"And then?"

I looked up from her hands to find those splendid opaline eyes staring deeply into me, attempting to divine my thoughts either metaphorically or literally. Hands still around hers, I confessed with a glance to the waters lapping the stones beneath us that, "I was just wondering the same thing."

She took my meaning. Her next words were soft with conflicted pain. "How am I to free from service the slave I've been shown in dreams all my life?"

"By remembering the slave is also a man, perhaps, and that men do best when granted liberty."

She snorted slightly, following my gaze into the sloshing black abyss. "I suppose so. I've heard it said that Skythorn is a place where all men and women, all races and creeds, are considered free and equal."

"In concept, yes. Not always in practice, but we do our best." My rubbing of her hands slowing slightly, I dared tell her, "You should let me show it to you."

The indigo ring of Roserpine glowed beneath my caress. Valeria looked sorrowful even without having to see it, her head lowering.

"Nothing would please me more, Rorke," she told me softly. "To see the stars I've glimpsed in dreams…to see the rising of the sun. To see you—oh, Rorke."

Tears dropped down her cheeks and stirred my heart to action. I enfolded her in my arms and drew her head to my heart. She wept there, her shoulders trembling while she whispered, "How can I be parted from you?"

"You don't need to be," I told her. "Whatever you choose, I'll remain with you."

"I cannot ask you to continue to choose slavery for my sake, Rorke."

She had not used my first name so much in all the time I'd known her. My lips brushed the top of her head.

"Then don't," was all I said.

To that, my lady had no response. We sat quietly in one another's embrace, watching the crackling blue flames, each of our bodies tense with anticipation for what was to come—for either our scouts to return with news, or to be beset upon by the tentacled demons of that unholy temple.

At last, we were startled by the almost completely silent appearance of Indra. The two of them were truly the finest rogues I'd ever known, and I marveled at that aptitude for silent motion even while the breathless woman urged us upright.

"We've found them," she whispered, glancing over her shoulder as if afraid she'd been followed. "You'd ought to come look for yourselves first—I've never seen anything like this."

"Like what?"

"I'm not sure," she answered, those three simple words awash with bafflement. "Some sort of altar, Odile thinks…but I don't know. You'd better take a look."

Exchanging a glance, Valeria and I set off after Indra, our steps a great deal less silent than hers. Thankfully, as we reached the floor to which the spiral staircase led, we discovered a moss green carpet that cut the stone floor in half and led throughout the rooms. This helpfully muted our strides.

All the chambers through which we passed were dimly-lit—but even my poor human eyes could recognize in faded tapestries and painted frescoes the tentacled faces of the demonic spirit-thieves, their pulsating hivemind, their hideous god that resembled them in innumerable ways but was said to sleep beneath the ocean and therefore was depicted in their heretical artworks with green, algae-covered flesh. I shuddered, averting my gaze from the awful depictions, and let Indra lead the way until we found Odile alert before a half-shut door. As soon as we set eyes upon it, Indra pulled us to the side and bade us move all the quieter, all the slower.

Soon enough, I perceived why. Kyrie evidently spoke to her master, who projected responses into her mind. Without the spirit-thief's half of the conversation, the meaning of it all was difficult to divine—but it left more space for a strange tap-tap-tapping sound that emanated from the room. While Odile waved us over, Kyrie could be heard asking, "What of the lantern we sold to Odile? If they don't come to us here, we may never get it back."

The durrow all exchanged looks and continued listening closely. I peered around the edge of the door to see what it was that had so baffled Indra…and I must admit, I fared no better in discerning what the object was.

As best as I could tell, Al-listux stood, back to us, worshiping before a strange glowing box. Given the shape, I understood why Indra had perceived it to be a kind of altar—but the general cubic form was where the resemblance ended, for never had I seen an altar of dull beige substance, nor one that glowed so brightly from what seemed only one side. As to what produced the tapping, I could not be sure…but it seemed to me after a few seconds' study that, while Al-listux's good hand moved, the tapping filling the air. When the creature's movement paused, so did the tapping.

"Master won't like that," Kyrie said in response to the creature's statement, whatever it was. Her tail thrashing, the wadjita sighed at the scimitar sheathed at her waist and added, "At any rate, he was such a fine lover. One does rather hate the thought of removing a man so appealing from the world."

Having had a moment to grow accustomed to the bizarre box, my eyes were at last able to perceive other contents of the room. Namely, what looked to be a great doorway of stone and metal, a frame twice the height and breadth of a normal one. It stood in the center of the room, providing no entrance or exit to anywhere. Valeria exchanged some form of sign language with the rogues while I struggled to make sense of everything I saw. As softly as she could, Indra loaded her crossbow.

Having been ruined by the waters through which we swam—and, perhaps, some time of under-use—the string snapped with an unfortunate twang.

Both our enemies' heads whipped in my direction.

I drew Strife without delay.

15

SACRIFICE

THE WADJITA DREW her scimitar, but did not immediately advance. Perhaps that was because Allistux, still with that one hand upon the platform before the glowing box, did not advance either. It only stood in study of me.

Back again, Burningsoul, the creature observed, the tendrils of its words writhing through my mind. *Back again, to the site of your murders.*

"I kill only when it is in the name and will of Weltyr. Were your broodmates not responsible for the theft and heretical misuse of a sacred artifact, I would not have had to vanquish the lot of them."

Then you ought to be hunting down those so-called friends of yours, rather than wasting time with me. The demon turned its back on me to tap along that strange flange of the box again. From the corner of my eye, Indra—beneath the savage glower of Odile—bit her lip and, quietly as possible, restrung her crossbow from a replacement pulled from the (thankfully, water-proof) pouch attached to her hip. Al-listux, meanwhile, continued, *My people's rivalry with the durrow should not concern you.*

"Should'nt it?"

I stepped out from behind the door, glancing at Kyrie as she lifted her blade to show me she was ready. While the women operated behind the door, I took one step into the room. "If the spirit-thieves claim the Nightlands, it will only be a matter of time before you crave all of Urde. You say you wish equality and the abolition of slavery here beneath the ground, but it is evident to me that is only because you consider all sentient beings slaves to your unnatural wills."

'Unnatural!'

Hideously, Al-listux laughed—not just with mind, but with body. Its tentacles shivered and, with a gooey wet noise like the repeated popping of some aquatic organ, the spirit-thief showed whatever mirth it could.

'Unnatural,' it repeated, shaking its bulbous head and resuming its tapping. *You have no idea, Paladin…it is your durrow friends who are unnatural. The elves and dwarves and orcs of your world, these things would never have come to be in the first place were it not for my people. Even you, Burningsoul, are unnatural. You have me and my kind to thank for the love of your life…for your own life, and your so-called 'natural' will.*

"So you would equate yourselves to gods? At least you're doing it out loud for once, I suppose."

We are gods, insisted the sacrilegious demon. *We are, all of us, descended from the Dreamer's flesh—and you, from its mind. As the body controls the dream, it is our duty to shepherd the flesh of Urde to its destiny.*

"And what destiny is that?"

Transcendence, it answered, producing one more hefty tap from the flange it touched.

The building quaked beneath my feet and a strange smell filled the air—the scent of a thunderstorm. I recalled Valeria's description of the presence of magic and realized only belatedly that this was what I experienced now. The notion occurred to me a second before a bright blue strand of light bolted from the top to the bottom of the empty doorframe at the center of the room: a beam of magical energy so thin at first that I was not sure I correctly perceived the sight. Only when it began to bob out on either side did I realize I was looking at some form of portal, slow-growing but no doubt meant to serve the demon as a method of escape. I braced myself, Strife gleaming before me.

"So you would rather flee again than lose another battle with me, demon? I won't permit such cowardly behavior a second time. Have at you! I'll die before I see you return once more to threaten Valeria's life."

*Yes, agreed the demon, a*s I charged and its servant made the response. *You will.*

Our steel rang through the air from the first point of contact, the wadjita's strength surprising behind the gleaming scimitar. Strife had, on more than one occasion, broken the blades of lesser weapons at first contact; but the sword crafted by Kyrie was of no weak design. It sang with every parry, bouncing off to slice again through the air, and amid her hasty blows I was soon reduced to the defensive position. From the corner of my eye I maintained perpetual awareness of the growing portal, its every ebb out to the sides a little greater than the last. We were on a time limit: I had to slay Al-listux before his means of escape was traversable.

Luckily, I had some assistance in the matter. The wadjita elicited a cry of surprise from me with a particularly strong series of blows that occurred in rapid succession. Though I managed to parry and dodge most of them, my muscles rang like a church bell. Hearing my call, the trigger of a crossbow saved me as it had the first time I skirmished with the hateful sorcerer: Indra and Odile charged into the room, where Al-listux's tentacles glowed faint purple with a spell.

"You take the spirit-thief," called Odile, raising her dagger to sink it into Kyrie's tail. As the wadjita hissed sharply, Indra loaded her crossbow with another bolt and lifted it to fire.

"We'll get Kyrie out of the way for you."

"Weltyr keep you both," I said, turning to find the spirit-thief had once more thrown up a magical barrier against my physical attacks. Gritting my teeth, I pressed the flat of my blade to my forehead and prayed for strength from my god—prayed for the might by means of which I could slay this demon and put an end to its heretical designs.

The evocation provoked a faint white glow to the edges of my sword as my watchful Lord responded kindly, blessing Strife with divine favor to strengthen the blade.

Thus resolved, I charged forth and slashed into the spirit-thief's glowing shield. Each contact provoked a sizzle before Strife bounced off. Similarly, the force of my blows did nothing to damage the demon, but did push it back step on step behind the shield that went with it.

My magic is powerful beyond your comprehension, Paladin. You are a fool to throw your life away for this! All you had to do was fetch me the ring upon your mistress's finger—had you but done this, you and she would have been permitted to live as it pleased you.

I told it between glances of Strife off the surface of its shield, "That ring means too much to her—I would never let you have it. I would never betray Valeria. And she could not live if she betrayed her people. She has infinitely more honor in her heart than you do in yours, spirit-thief."

Honor is an arbitrary notion of fairness, only necessary to keep mortals obedient and cooperative with one another. My kind have no need of honor: only power.

"And that's why you'll never acquire what you seek," I assured it, grip tightening around the handle of my blade as the trembling of its tentacles and the light of its magic renewed. Hoping that, if nothing else, the destruction of the glowing box would halt the growth of the portal on the other side of the room, I took a calculated risk and turned my back to Al-listux.

Strife's blade cut through the air and shattered the glowing side of the box. All its light died at once, that bright face of bluish light proven nothing but glass.

The portal did not halt its development, but Al-listux produced a terrible hiss that seemed as though it ought to have come from the wadjita who gradually struggled more and more to fend off the dexterous attacks of the rogues.

You fool, the spirit-thief condemned me, its tentacles curling up around the awful hole of its dripping, fanged mouth. *You fool! You cannot imagine how long it took me to restore that device to working order—you cannot fathom how rare, how invaluable, the artifact you just destroyed truly is.*

Before I could so much as mock it with another slice through the gleaming glass that had revealed an interior of blue and black and red veins of some kind, bolts of bright crimson light arced from the demon's tentacles and closed in on me like a set of missiles. I hefted Strife and successfully countered two such shots, but four more made it through, each impacting upon my body and searing my flesh with a rattle of pain that seized my muscles much as had the lightning strike at the Palace.

Valeria's cry drew the demon's attention as, watching the battle from the doorway, she shouted, "Rorke!"

So you brought her with you, the demon remarked while I gathered my strength, making its way to her at once. *What an idiotic thing to do! But convenient for me, to be certain...*

Before it could take even a third step toward Valeria, I sprang at the beast and brought Strife against its shoulder with every ounce of my remaining strength. That magical shield rotated without its owner even turning to face me, but I sensed it was less sturdy than it had been for my first few blows.

Bolstered, I threw my all into destroying the magical barrier with strike on strike of my broadsword. Each contact, Strife rattled to worsen the headache that had begun when the magical missiles took their toll on me. No matter: I fought through it, satisfied as the irritated spirit-thief stopped to face me. Another spell gathered on its tentacles, but Valeria extended her hand and the creature was flung away as if it had been gored by an invisible animal.

"Master," cried Kyrie, turning toward him and receiving an opportune dagger in the chest. With a noise of shock, she touched the wound and collapsed. While her heart pumped blood from her supine body, the spirit-thief righted itself to snarl as its shield faded into oblivion.

If you wish, I'll kill all four of you rather than just your cult leader.

Those twisting tendrils renewed their summoning. Soon an enchanted blade once more danced between myself and the hideous being. I gritted my teeth and slashed against the mystical opponent with all my might, but that might had been significantly reduced as a consequence of my injuries. While Indra hurried to hold Valeria back from the fray and protect her from assault, Odile dashed to my side to attempt, by weaving beneath the slicing of the blade, to bury her dagger in the spirit-thief.

A blast of light halted her in the deed, and as it cleared from both our sets of wincing eyes we shared a look of dark displeasure. Two spirit-thieves, now: each the same size and shape, each moving perfect unison. Each befit with its own dangerously magical blade.

"It's only a magic trick," called Indra while my lady raised her ringed hand and prayed. I lifted my blade and did not look at Odile as I spoke to her.

"One of us has to be right," I said.

In my periphery, she nodded. She raised her blade, her other leathered hand in a fist, both arms in a defensive cross. The swords kept moving all the while and I launched into the defense, meeting strike on strike to make the perhaps illusory blade glance off of Strife. Then the unseen opponent would charge forth again, on and on, Al-listux or his double advancing all the while.

With certain magics, such things as the illusory nature of a faerie object were difficult to tell. I had heard it said even permanent cloning was possible when a skilled sorcerer or wizard was the one up to the business. With such magical doppelgängers and all other convincing images, I was always taught that it is best to consider them real until they prove themselves otherwise.

Or until someone else proves them otherwise. While nimble Odile dodged and ducked her share of swipes from the magical sword, never getting quite close enough to put a knife into her visible opponent to see if it disappeared, Valeria prayed on and on.

Just as my opponent's blasted sword was poised to stab past Strife, her prayer raised to an elvish cry. The light that revealed the figure before me to be a sham was sudden and bright, a more vivid cousin of that gloomy indigo stone upon her finger.

When it faded, so did the false Al-listux before me.

I lifted my sword with renewed urgency. Odile was forced to parry with her dagger, which flew away. Behind it the portal ebbed to the edges of its frame and caught there like soapy water in a loop: as if one might blow through the great portal and send it floating off, a bubble.

While my disarmed friend darted away, I met the magical sword of my hideous opponent amid a second wind. Al-listux watched calmly from behind the blade, its words patronizing in the patience they exhibited within my mind.

You're extremely powerful, Paladin. I hate to think I find myself your enemy. I could teach you very much.

"There's nothing I want to know from you," I managed to grunt between the final two slashes I was forced to lay against my magical opponent.

At last the enchanted blade broke to pieces beneath Strife's force, those shards vanishing like wine left out in the sun.

"Nothing except your word that you will leave Valeria alone, but you only just told me you find honor a valueless notion…and, at any rate, you have tried too many times to kill her for me to let you live now."

I swept Strife at the spirit-thief and gritted my teeth when the nimble thing dodged away. If I could only sink my blade into its flesh! I knew it would be physically weak. All of them were, or had been when I and my traitorous party members from before interrupted their ceremonies. After a certain point, the most dangerous thing about spirit-thieves was their blood…but until then, they were extremely dangerous in all other ways, and I recognized one of the most dangerous things about them at work. Al-listux braced upon one heel and lifted taloned hands to its throbbing cephalopod head.

"Get through the door," I shouted to my friends, repeating the command more urgently at the glowing of the demon's eyes. I charged, attempting to interrupt its psionic stunning with the help of Strife.

Too late: a shock wave rippled through the room from the center of the spirit-thief's mind, and it rolled through me as though I were merely the medium for that violent wave. My bones were rattled like my sword, and in my head I swore my brain rippled like the ocean. A great sickness overcame me: had I not been so stunned, I might have vomited. Instead I stumbled forward, Strife falling from my hand.

The beast had collected Odile's dagger.

I staggered, unable to maintain my balance amid the bright shock of pain any more than I was able to keep a hold on my sword.

"Rorke," screamed Valeria, already defying my demand to stay away. In fact, she pushed back through the door in time to see me stabbed.

My gasp was sharp, but the sting of my lungs was so severe I delayed in taking another breath. The thing drew out the blade and stabbed me again, this time in the stomach. I lurched uneasily into the dagger, then back from it.

While it drew back the blade one more time, Valeria, expression desperate, skidded to a halt near enough for the beast to see clearly the ring she slipped from her finger.

"Is this what you want? This?"

The sorcerer stared her down, perhaps weighing what sort of trick this was. But it was, sadly, no trick. To my astonishment, (and the gasps of Indra and Odile), the Materna of El'ryh hurled Roserpine's ring across the floor and off to the direction of the portal before I could wheeze the word, "Don't."

The band rolled, skipping across the masonry, while the squid-demon's greedy eye followed it.

Al-listux quite literally dropped the dagger to hurry after the prize. Valeria knelt to embrace me, tears filling her eyes. Her hand smoothed my brow, then lifted my tunic to see the wound beneath. Her expression transfigured in even sharper fear to see the blood flowing from my lung.

"Valiant Burningsoul," my lady whispered, pressing her hand to my side wound. "Oh, my friend! My champion."

"Ring," I managed with struggle. "The ring, Valeria."

"The love of Roserpine is not worth half as much as your love," she answered earnestly, looking up only when Al-listux filled our minds with speech.

I never thought the Materna of El'ryh would show so much sense, the spirit-thief mockingly commended while straightening up with the ring between its slimy fingertips. Admiring the gem in the light, the beast then studied the two of us. *I think I'll leave you here to die,* it told me, *turning away.*

BLOOM & DARK

Indra called out and took a step forward, lifting her crossbow too late. The demon touched the portal and the bluish bubble light shifted. A brilliant gold-orange glow manifested from within, quickly resolving to the image of some great chamber. Braziers burned; a window let in the beauty of my long-missed night sky.

An old man stared back—not at the spirit-thief who passed into his domain, but at me.

My vision failed; I wondered if perhaps I was going mad. Yet, I recognized the man. This gray-bearded fellow in a dark cloak, his face appeared to me as might the face of an old friend—one whom we meet after years of estrangement and find, to our shock, still recognizable in spite of perhaps decades' worth of change. It was in this way that I recognized the man on the other side of Al-listux's portal before I lost my tenuous grip on consciousness.

I was looking at myself.

16

A NEW PARTY

HILDOLFR GUTTED A trout beside the stream, then flung the organs into our fire.

"For Weltyr," he said.

I looked around, somehow disoriented to realize we were alone. "Where are Branwen and Grimalkin?"

"Wandered off," said my one-eyed friend, deftly slicing off the fins and commencing to scale it with his hunting knife. "Don't worry too much about them. Worry about yourself."

"I can't help but worry for my friends. I love Branwen— and even Grimalkin does have his charms."

Speaking of love reminded me, with a pang of guilt for having forgotten her, of Valeria. I straightened up where I sat in the grass, looking around again and asking,

"Why, where is she? Valeria? Indra and Odile, too. My friends—"

"They're around," he said. "And you must do all that you can to help them. Especially Valeria."

"I would never fail her."

"It's easy to get distracted in this world," the ranger assured me. "It's easy to give into the temptation to be comfortable, and stop the pursuits that are most important. Just remember: it may seem like this is about Valeria…but this is really about you."

As I puzzled over his words, the whinny of a horse drew my attention. My heart warmed at the thought of seeing Hildolfr's steed, a white mare left in the care of an innkeeper before we made our way to the Nightlands. I looked, expecting to see it—to stroke its mane and pat its powerful neck.

The eight-legged stallion that reared there instead was so startling that I awoke at once.

"He's back," said Odile, her voice overflowing with relief as she set an empty bottle aside. Delirious, disoriented, I looked between the faces of the women bending over me and belatedly remembered Al-listux.

"The ring," I said with a gasp, sitting up only to be pushed back upon the floor of the temple.

"Al-listux is gone," said Valeria softly, running her soothing fingers across my forehead and into my hair. "Oh! Burningsoul—and you're here. My love…thank Roserpine, oh, praise your god and mine!"

"He's gone? But your ring—"

Now I did sit up, ignoring the elfin hands attempting to push me back down. They had spoken the truth: the frame of that vast portal was empty. Just to set eyes upon it brought to mind the vision that I had caught within. My blood chilled with the memory and I looked between the women before settling on Valeria. "Did you see anything inside?"

"A man," said Valeria. Odile and Indra nodded in agreement while my lady went on, "But aside from that, no landmarks I could identify."

"That was what I perceived as well," said Odile, who slipped the empty potion bottle back into the pack at her hip. "The portal showed its destination for but a few seconds before shutting behind the spirit-thief."

"By Weltyr, what are we to do? Why did you throw your ring away, Valeria? It hold all El'ryh's power. Without it—"

"I would throw away all my magical abilities twenty times over if it meant saving you once." The Materna of El'ryh took up my hand and caressed my knuckles before, with a sad gasp, she fit her hands to my face and buried a kiss deep in my mouth.

"It's the least I could do," she said as we parted, "to repay the kindness you've already showed in protecting me."

"I only wish the cost were not so high."

"It's nothing. I am still Roserpine's servant, now more than ever. Surely—surely my people will understand."

Indra and Odile exchanged a look that said they were even less sure than the woman whose tone faltered to say such a thing. Looking driven, my lady stood upright and said, "Let's make our way back to the city and explain what's happened. We'll come up with a solution of some kind, I'm sure."

Her optimism was moving, but the general atmosphere was one of hopelessness. In the new silence of the temple, with Kyrie's dead body not far from us and the vibrating of the portal having disappeared entirely, a strange anxiety took hold. Perhaps that was only my perception—the anxiety accompanying the question of how I would get out of returning to El'ryh, and in such a way that Valeria's heart would not be broken.

You must do all that you can to help them—especially Valeria.

My vision of Hildolfr—surely one that only arose in my mind because of my earlier encounter with the thing that took his form—seemed to speak in me again, so clearly I heard it a second time.

Hand running over my face and into my hair, I thought also of my vision of the horse.

Such clear and significant dream-signs were the purview of Weltyr and handed directly from him, but I did not know in detail what these things meant just then. I only knew that I had been firmly instructed to remain with Valeria. To help her. There was an implication there that I might have to sacrifice something desirable or distracting if need be; at least, I perceived the message as such.

And if my freedom was what needed sacrificing, well…after the willing heart with which she threw away her own ring of power, how could I refuse to cooperate in their return to the city? If nothing else, Valeria would need someone to defend her physically should things go really awry.

"Then we'd ought to get going," I told the women, pushing myself upright despite their protests. "I'm fine, truly—but the sooner we make it back to El'ryh, the better our chances of being able to set out and find the ring again, or to come up with some means of summoning it back, or…I don't know." My head still ached and I swayed somewhat, earning a touch on the arm from my mistress. "I'm fine," I swore to her. "Just a little dizzy."

"Are you sure you're—"

A commotion from a room away drew our urgent attention.

"Here's another room," called a woman, her firm voice emanating from the source of the clamorous sound.

I looked at my traveling companions and without hesitating hurried to the ruined altar with its broad table and thick, strangely textured black vines trailing off into another black box as though growing out of it.

While I crouched behind this mess of tendrils, the women found other hiding spots—the tapestries shielded Indra and Odile, and my mistress ducked behind a few over-sized plants that had victoriously overwhelmed their pots and now seemed for all the world a natural growth. No sooner had we taken these positions than a scouting party of durrow burst into the room while talking among themselves, scanning the area only briefly before their attention was stolen by the dead wadjita on the floor.

"They might have been here after all," said one, hurrying over to check the body. "That, or the spirit-thief killed her."

"And went where?"

"Deeper, perhaps. There are only so many places it can go—come on. Let's see what it's done to the Materna before we kill it."

"I still think it was that slave of hers—working with the spirit-thief, dropping poison in our lady's ear. Isn't this the wadjita always trading with Darkstar and the Nocturna girl?"

"They must have been involved."

"No wonder they were all seen leaving the city together. So they've brainwashed the Materna...we'll have to hope they haven't taken her ring along with her mind."

The durrow hurried on in the name of clearing the area, no doubt planning for a more thorough sweep when they confirmed they were not in imminent danger. As they exited through the doors that would gradually lead them to the flooded rear of the structure, I and my friends peered at one another from our hiding spaces.

When the guards were a room away, we quietly reconvened by the primary exit of the room.

"They're blaming *us* for this," Odile hissed.

Indra, looking shocked, gazed in obvious sorrow toward the departed team of guards. "But I would never do a thing so sinister," she protested.

"Nor I," I agreed.

Distressed, Valeria looked between the three of us, then over at the inoperable portal. "If theirs is really the general perception, we can't go back now—not empty-handed, at any rate. They'll think the ring was sold off, or that I was forced to give it up. And…"

Her lower lip disappeared between her teeth to worry there for a few seconds. She neglected finishing her thought, but we all knew what she was thinking anyway. Without that ring, she had no power—in fact, without that ring, no one had power in the city of El'ryh. This might have been literal as much as it was metaphorical, for I suspected that ring was the source of Valeria's greatest magical abilities.

Without it, her powers as priestess were surely limited to the same level as most other devout practitioners of Roserpine's faith.

"I cannot return to El'ryh without the ring," she summarized, looking between us. "If I do, I will surely be a prisoner or worse for my failure to protect the artifact. I am grateful it was there as a sacrifice in my time of need, but I must find a way to get it back."

"I'll help you," I swore to her, taking up her hand. She looked at me earnestly, almost pained by affection while I squeezed her fingers in mine.

"How could I ask you to do such a thing, Burningsoul? After you've already put yourself in danger for me so many times."

"Why, it's nothing, of course. Aren't I your slave? Order me, and I'll do as pleases you."

Her lips turned up in a wry sort of smile, a soft laugh raising from her. "You are no slave to me, Rorke. I cannot own a man whom I love so deeply—nor one who has proven so loyal and good."

Scoffing, Odile looked at Indra before asking, "You mean to say you're freeing him?"

"He has freed himself through noble deeds. But"—Valeria pressed a hand to my heart, gazing hopefully into my face—"were he to choose by his own will to help me find the ring, he would be master of my heart and I, as good to him as any slave."

As thrilling as it was to be so called by Valeria, I could not help but smile tenderly and draw her into my arms. "You are worth far more to me than a slave, Valeria. It will be my joy to help you retrieve Roserpine's ring. You owe me nothing…but if you would still give me your love when we retrieve it, it would be the sweetest reward a man could receive."

Her mouth yielded with great joy to the depth of my kiss, our lips mingling as one while Indra cooed and Odile rolled her eyes. While we separated, still embracing and gazing into one another's eyes, the more jaded of the rogues said, "Well…we'd might as well come with you."

Looking relieved to hear such a thing, Valeria swore to them, "It would be a boon to us, a great help—you'll both be paid lavishly when all is said and done."

"It's not like we can go back to El'ryh right now," Odile said sourly, her glance darting in the direction the guards had gone. "So we'd might as well get this sorted out and clear our names. Oppenhir crush your scaled soul, Kyrie! Blast it, running us out of El'ryh...well, come on! Let's not stand around watching you two make goopy eyes at each other for so long that the guards come back."

While Odile marched off toward the front entrance of the temple, muttering to herself all the way, Indra smiled more kindly at us and enthused, "How exciting! I've never done anything like this before...Odile and I travel quite a bit to scavenge as we do, but I get the feeling we'll be going awfully far out of our way for this."

"I get that sense as well," I agreed, adding that, "I noticed that a window was set into the wall of the place where Al-listux fled. It overlooked the night sky."

Valeria's body tightened in anticipatory hope in my arms; Indra gasped with delight. "Oh, the surface! I've always wanted to see the surface...I hear it's a very strange place, full of all kinds of odd creatures and plants."

"And sky," whispered Valeria.

I brushed my lips over her brow. "Yes, Valeria. The sky."

A tapping sound filled the room. We glanced up to see Odile waiting, the toe of her boot drumming in impatient rhythm on the ground. Together, the three of us laughed, then went to go meet her.

The journey back through the temple and around to where was started was tedious, but simple. We spent the whole way on high alert in case we should hear, from one direction or another, the footfalls of another group of guards, but Weltyr saw us through to the hidden cache of supplies the women had made up before we dove into the waters. After once more gearing themselves and taking up the lantern, my friends looked around.

"I don't even know where to start," Odile said, sighing heftily for effect as though in an effort to keep us aware of what an inconvenience all this was to her. "Any ideas?"

I meant to suggest that we might try the surface, where we could ask around for a wizard who knew something of scrying—but my blood ran cold.

A woman's scream cut through the air like a new knife in my side, echoing terror through the tunnels of the Nightlands.

"Oh, great," said Odile as, without a thought, I dashed off in the direction of the noise. "See what happens, Materna? You free a man from slavery, and suddenly he thinks he's in charge…"

While the durrow hurried after me, I drew Strife and sprinted in pursuit of the sound. My magically healed wounds still ached, but I cared less for them than I did for whatever danger lurked at the end of the tunnel the second scream convinced me to follow. On I went, plunging through the bloom and dark, glowing fungi lighting the way in groups here and there until a mass of them illuminated the shut door at the passage's end.

Another scream rose up, now accompanied by the word "Help!" in a voice I swore I recognized. With my right shoulder, this side having been unwounded in the fight, I threw my weight twice against the door before backing up a step to kick heftily above the knob. The wood cracked open around the lock and I shoved it wide, stumbling into the den of misshapen bandits whose spider legs skittered on the ground as they turned to see their interloper.

But, as the durrow caught up with me, I found I barely saw the enemies who made ready to fight. Rather, my gaze was caught and held by the beautiful woman wiggling in the tight bonds of her captors' webbing—her hips and bosom bursting from the white silk, her hands firmly bound behind her despite her efforts to break free. Golden hair poured around the peaks of slender elf ears…but even with these sensory instruments mostly hidden, I would have recognized Branwen in a second.

Blue eyes lifting to mine, her expression filled with shock, shame—and, I was glad to see, hope.

With an assessment at the five misshapen around her, I raised Strife.

Together, my companions and I charged into the fray.

ABOUT THE AUTHOR

Regina Watts is the penname of a woman who certainly is not also M. F. Sullivan, founder and flagship author of Painted Blind Publishing. From her cozy home a few universes away from this one, Watts transmits stories to Sullivan that are then transcribed and published. Her available titles range from transgressive erotica to psychedelic fiction to horror to romance. Be sure to check out her website, join her Patreon, or sign up for her mailing list at hrhdegenetrix.com!

ABOUT THE PUBLISHER

Painted Blind Publishing and its erotic imprint, Painted Blue Publishing, are the brainchild of author and devoted editor to Regina Watts, M. F. Sullivan. Founded in 2015 while Sullivan resided in Tucson, PBP is a house dedicated to bringing readers the finest in consciousness-expanding fiction. Be sure to check out the wide variety of essays available for free at paintedblindpublishing.com to learn more about the company, Watts, and Sullivan.

OTHER PAPERBACK WORKS
FROM PAINTED BLIND PUBLISHING

REGINA WATTS

INDUSTRIAL DIVINITY (2020)

WILD GIRL RUNNING (2020)

DOTTIE FOR YOU SEASON 1 (2021)

SEDUCED BY SABINE (TBD)

M. F. SULLIVAN

DELILAH, MY WOMAN (2015)

THE LIGHTNING STENOGRAPHY DEVICE (2017)

THE DISGRACED MARTYR TRILOGY (2019-2020)